GHOSTS OF THE MILL

ANNIE SHIELDS

CHAPTER 1

*L*ena made her way along the darkened hallway, noticing that the further she got away from the hum of conversation, the easier the band of tension around her head became. Quiet as a church mouse, she slipped through the veranda doors, pausing to take in greedy gulps of the frigid December air.

Snow clouds from earlier had cleared and the moon, in its crescent phase, cast a silvery glow across the gardens. Stars twinkled in the velvety sky with only the distant rush of water from the river Birch reached her. The path under the eaves was clear yet she stepped into the snow, relishing in the chill that reached her toes through her new boots. She stood at the edge of the stone balustrade, closing her eyes to allow the silence of the night to wrap around her.

She detested nights like this one. As the only daughter of mill owner Edwin Pemberton, Lena had been coached her whole life that she was the heiress to a grand empire. Countless soirees had drained her spirit. It wasn't that she was stupid, but she was aware that her societal circle was drawn to her because of her father's influence. For tonight's gathering, she'd adorned herself in a sumptuous gown of rich azure and had gone to painstaking lengths with her appearance because that's what was expected of her.

Indeed, she often felt that the glittering elite merely endured her company because she was a Pemberton.

Hawk's Mill was a prestigious employer in the region, and Edwin Pemberton's business acumen was the stuff of legends. It was no wonder that their mansion was always bustling with visitors.

A distant owl's call roused Lena from her thoughts. As she gazed into the nocturnal expanse, the lavish gardens lay draped in mystery. Hawks Mill perched alongside the banks of the river like a resting beast. Tonight, even the massive waterwheel was still. She would also be free of the non-stop rumbling sounds of looms and overhead shafts all day tomorrow, too. Christmas day was the only time of the year that the mill remained closed, apart from Sundays.

Across the moonlit landscape, she could see the faint glow of the worker's cottages. And on nights like this, as she often did, Lena contemplated their uncomplicated existences and yearned for a touch of their simplicity in her life.

When the hand slid around her narrow waist, Lena whirled, stifling the yelp that was trapped in her throat.

Thomas Cavendish loomed over her, chuckling, "There you are, my dear. I've been looking for you."

Lena laid a hand on her chest as if that alone could steady her racing heart. Even in the soft light that filtered through the glass behind him, Thomas looked devilishly handsome. "H-have you?"

"What are you doing out here?" He pressed.

At that moment, she considered telling him the truth. That watching him fawn over and flirt with Elizabeth Breckenridge all evening had been humiliating enough, without the pointed looks that drifted in her direction from the other women seated around the table. More than once, his mouth had been almost indecently close to Elizabeth's pretty ear.

A cunning light gleamed in Thomas' dark eyes. He took her hand and brought it up to meet his chin, eying her over the top. "What is it, my love?"

Lena longed to snatch her hand back.

Each time she'd broached the subject of calling off her engagement to Thomas with her father, he'd deftly sidestepped the issue. While the attentions of a striking and distinguished gentleman like Thomas Cavendish had initially flattered her, accepting his proposal of marriage had unveiled glimpses of a side of him that she found unsettling.

She forced her lips into a smile. "I just needed some fresh air, and it's such a beautiful night."

"Are you sure that's all?" He prodded, gliding his thumb over her hand which caused a ripple of apprehension to steal through her blood. "You seemed a little put out at the dinner table. I know there was a

3

lot of business talk, but some of your comments were inane at best."

Lena tugged her hand out of his and tucked it safely behind her. "Thank you, Thomas. I am interested in business and the mill. It would be nice for people to consider my input at times."

Thomas smirked. "As Edwin Pemberton's only daughter, your job has always been to look good on a man's arm. Our sons will be the ones who need to know and speak about business, not you.

"You should stick to what you're good at, my dear."

The words, familiar as they were, needled her deeply. But she knew all too well how quickly his mood could sour when challenged, so she bit back any retort.

"You ought to pay attention to Elizabeth. She's well versed in commerce and industry..." His mocking laughter filled her ears when her gaze fell away from his. "Come now," he moved closer to her. "You're not pouting over a harmless little flirtation with Elizabeth, are you?"

He would dismiss anything she said as poppycock just as he had in the past, so she shook her head. "It was stifling inside," she lied, "and the smoke from the fireplace was getting to me."

"I see," he murmured. He tilted his head, reaching out to run a finger down her cheek and along her jaw. It set off a chain reaction inside that made her meal boil nauseously in her belly. "I have told you in the past about how I have to keep the daughters of the wealthy landowners happy for the sake of my father's bank. You know I only have eyes for you, my dear. But I can't have you fly into a fit of jealousy each time I speak to another woman."

"I realise that, Thomas," she replied as evenly as she could, edging back, unwilling to set off his fearsome temper again. "I just hope it won't happen after we're married. How would it look to others when I'm your wife?"

His eyes flashed ominously. "It will look like my wife trusts me implicitly."

Fear dripped along her spine as he closed the gap between them. She moved to pass him by, intending on going back to the safety of being amongst people when he lunged for her, driving her backwards until the snow-topped balustrade pressed against her lower back. He seized her, closing off her protests by swiftly crushing her mouth with his. Lena struggled futilely, no match for him. He held her easily, tightening his arms around her to deepen the kiss.

She turned her face this way and that until he grabbed her by the hair to still her movements.

Cruel light flashed in his face. "Why are you fighting this? We're to be wed in a few short months and I plan on making the most of your nubile beauty whilst it lasts." He took her mouth once more, rearing back with a pained hiss. He swiped a hand across his mouth, glaring furiously at her when it came away bloody. "You little harlot!" He ground out, freezing when the door rattled before opening behind them.

"Miss?" Gwen, her maid, spoke tentatively. The young girl's eyes wavered between the pair: Thomas savagely cursing and Lena's unkempt appearance. Her gaze dropped to the ground. "Your father, miss. He says I'm to fetch you right away, miss," she bobbed a short curtsy. "Pardon, miss."

Thomas was the first to recover. "My fiancée will come in when I say she can," he snapped, adding, "And when I become master here, you'll be the first to go." Gwen darted back through the door and Thomas rounded on Lena. "You can't put me off forever," he spat. He shook out his handkerchief and dabbed his mouth, fresh fury bubbling in his eyes when he spotted the blood red against the white cloth. "I will make you pay for that, Lena."

He slammed back through the veranda door, vanishing from sight. She wilted weakly against the stones, holding back her tears. She whimpered when the door opened once more but it was Gwen's face that appeared in the moonlight.

Sensing Lena's distress, Gwen reached out to comfort her. "Can I get you anything?"

Lena's insides quivered. Gwen was the closest thing she'd ever had to a friend, even though her father paid her a wage to spend so much time with her. Straightening up, Lena set her shoulders back. "I'll be fine, Gwen. Thank you for coming out."

"I saw the two of you through the window. I wasn't sure if I should…"

Lena offered her a wobbly smile. "Thank the heavens that you did. I am grateful to you. And I'm sorry if that frightened you."

Gwen snorted. "Cook would say that he needs her

good pan wrapping around his head. Him being a gentleman and all."

Lena patted her hair, dismayed to feel that her coiffed style was in tatters. "We'd better get upstairs and make the best of a bad job."

"It shan't take long," Gwen said gently.

"Did my father say what he wanted?"

"No. He had Mr Brown ask me to look for you," Gwen pulled open the door for Lena.

Lena paused in the doorway. "For what it's worth, your job here is secure. It's Christmas day tomorrow which means my father will be at home all day."

"Miss?"

Lena nodded determinedly. "That means he won't be able to use work or visitors as an excuse for not speaking with me. I'm calling off my engagement to that execrable man."

Gwen's slack face was almost enough to make her laugh.

While many regarded Thomas Cavendish as the county's most eligible bachelor, his actions were far from refined or chivalrous. This evening was the last straw. Regardless of her father's endorsement of such a favourable match or any repercussions, she was resolved to be rid of Thomas Cavendish as soon as possible.

CHAPTER 2

"*Y*ou do it."

"I don't want to. You should do it."

"But why?"

"Because… because you're the eldest."

Libby Baker cracked her eyes a little as the whisperings continued.

The dormitory room was still shrouded in darkness, a little of the pale moonlight filtering through the broken windowpanes. Libby moved her eyes towards the foot of her bed where she could just about make out the shape of two young girls, engrossed in a low-pitched argument. The air was bitterly cold, and she knew from experience that the wooden floors would feel like ice underfoot. And the girls' feet would be bare – no one dared to wear clogs on this floor until Mrs Reid, the house warden, called them from their beds.

"Enough," she murmured, her voice croaky from her slumber. Years of sleeping in a room filled with others just like her meant that she could sleep on a sixpence, but today was Christmas day, so she had been looking forward to a rare lie-in. She pushed herself up onto an elbow, the thin ratty blanket sliding off her as she did. She blinked through the gloom. "Polly? What are you doing out of your bed? If Mrs Reid catches you, you'll know about it."

Libby was the eldest of the apprenticed girls. As such, many of the girls looked to her for help and advice. She scrubbed the sleep from her eyes, frowning at the pair when neither of them made a move.

Polly, a sixteen-year-old lass from Liverpool with mud-brown hair and a quick temper, shoved her associate closer to Libby's bed. "Do it."

Libby dragged her hair off her face as she recognised the new girl, Thea, through the gloom. "What is it?"

Even in the low light, Thea was a pretty girl. She'd been orphaned when her parents had succumbed to typhoid and had been plucked out of the workhouse and brought here to Hawks Mill to replace Mary Nuttall after she'd died. Libby wasn't sure if a cotton mill was much different to the workhouse, though she'd be indentured here after her parents had died when she was six. A cotton mill was all she'd ever known.

Thea was a quick worker but a quiet girl. Libby offered her a reassuring smile and beckoned her closer. "You woke me up so it must be important."

Thea glanced back at Polly who nodded at her

9

encouragingly. A few of the others had begun to stir, and Thea looked about the room. Twenty wooden cots lined up against the white walls that ran with moisture; snow piled up at the window ledges. Libby's eyes adjusted to the gloom. Every box-shaped bed was filled with a straw mattress and two girls, each of whom was apprenticed to the Pembertons until they reached one and twenty years of age. Libby had less than a year to wait before she would start being paid money as well as bed and board for her ten-hour days. She couldn't wait for the time when she wasn't locked into this narrow room at bedtime. She had dreams of escaping, of falling in love and moving to the city, far away from the clickety-clack of the looms.

Polly sighed impatiently and moved closer to Libby so that she could keep her voice low. "She's... she has a... problem." Her eyes grew wider, the whites appearing around her irises. "You know, the same one that Peggy had?"

Libby's gaze shifted to Thea, who was casting nervous glances around at the other girls. It made sense; some of the workers earned extra rations by reporting things they heard back to the mill staff. Libby didn't know which – if any – of the girls in here would tattle on a girl being in the family way to Mrs Reid. A pregnancy meant that the mill would lose another worker, and that's all they cared about.

In the darkness, the girl's silhouette appeared normal, and Libby was unable to spot any discernible evidence of the *problem* under her smock.

"You're certain?" She whispered.

Thea nodded slowly; misery etched into her face when she finally met Libby's eyes.

Libby reached out to take the girl's icy hand in her own. "Oh, Thea," her voice echoing the deep sympathy she felt.

Thea had worked at Pemberton's mill for only a matter of months but with her sparkling blue eyes, blonde hair and upturned nose, she painted a pretty picture, even in the dark grey smocks and filthy aprons that each girl wore. She was different to most of the girls here because she could read and write. She'd heard from the others that Thea had once lived in a nice house in Manchester and the family had had a maid to fetch things from the kitchen at mealtimes.

She was bound to draw attention in a place like Hawks Mill.

The girl sniffed and Libby tugged her hand until Thea was sitting in the cot with her. Polly crouched down, offering a caring back rub. "Can you help her, Libby? I said you would know what to do."

Libby drew in a breath sharply, letting it out in a hiss as anger flared. "This bloody place," she patted Thea's hand as her mind raced. "I suppose you can't go to the father?"

Thea reared back; eyes wide in horror. "N-no! Please, I can't – I didn't mean for it to happen. I didn't ask! You have to believe me–"

"Shh," Polly tried to calm her. "She believes you, don't you, Libby?"

Libby bit her lip, thoughts racing. The girl's reaction spoke volumes. Had the father been one of the apprentice boys, young Thea would no doubt be thinking about getting permission to marry him. At least, that's what had happened in the past. But Thea's distress came from shame, and Libby knew that the man responsible would be one of the men who worked in a trusted position at the mill instead.

Women workers outnumbered the men in the mill because they were paid less. However, the number of children working at Hawks Mill surpassed both men and women combined. It wouldn't do any good trying to guess who the father was either. The mill required mechanics and joiners, overlookers, and turners to run efficiently.

Libby tamped down on her emotions, trying to settle the girl. "I do, Thea. I believe you. You're not the first and, God forbid, I doubt very much you'll be the last in this place. Please, sit down. Let me think a minute."

"What's the noise about?" A disgruntled voice called out from the other corner.

Libby felt Thea jolt and put an arm around her. "Go back to sleep, Daisy. It's fine."

"Please, Libby, I'm so afraid," Thea looked up, tears glistening in her eyes. "What is going to happen to me? I won't be able to hide it much longer."

"They'll beat her if they see she's slacking in her work. Mr Dower needs but a minute to use his whip on us or dunk us headfirst in the water barrel to wake us up," Polly muttered.

"He only does that to the little ones," Libby said, eying Thea worriedly. The girl looked terrified.

"They get away with it, all of it," Polly added bitterly. "No one ever questions the men, do they? Not even when the inspectors come for a look around here. Mr Pemberton and Mr Dower, they just have us sitting in a line on the benches with a clean face, telling us to smile like we're happy. Remember, when those men from London were here, when Peggy was too scared to speak out about what had happened to her? She was so worried that they would–"

"Quiet, Polly," Libby injected enough warning into her voice to shut the other girl up, although she knew all too well how handy Mr Dower could be if he thought one of his apprentices wasn't working hard enough. She'd seen bones broken, eyes blackened and heads bleed from the beatings from the overlookers across her tenure here. "You're scaring her more, and that ain't good for the bairn now, is it?"

"Sorry," Polly grumbled, "just saying how I see it."

Libby offered Thea a smile. "Mrs Reid is usually gentler with the girls who are... in the family way, so you don't need to pay much mind to that end. The sad fact is that, despite us being separated from the boys, and not having much to do with the men, well, babies are still... made here."

She felt the weight of responsibility settle on her shoulders as the young girls looked to her to help them.

In the silence, huddled together, Libby remembered all the other pregnant girls that had been sent away. No questions asked – just shipped off, and another girl from the workhouse was brought in to replace her.

Beyond the sighs and the slumber, the wind whistled through the gaps in the window frame. She knew that if she looked through the window, she would see the familiar lines of the mill with its tall chimney spout that stretched into the sky beyond the treetops. She would see the grand manor house, the warehouse and the dyehouse, and the barns, and behind those, the mill worker cottages. It would fall to her as the oldest apprentice girl to find a way to get to those cottages.

Thea touched her stomach, uncertainty rippling through her voice, "I'm scared."

Libby patted Thea's hand, a determined light in her eye. "Try not to worry."

"How can I not worry? My baby will be born a bastard."

Polly snorted. "Then your baby will be in fine company in this room."

Thea's lips flickered with the hint of a smile and Libby chuckled wryly. "You're not alone, Thea."

"I'm not?"

"No," Polly plopped down on Libby's bed and laid her head against Thea's shoulder. "You have us. And us Hawks girls stick together."

CHAPTER 3

$\mathcal{C}$hristmas morning dawned with a fresh snowfall, fluffy flakes dancing past the grand windows of Hawks Manor. The living room had been festively decorated by the staff, with garlands of holly and ivy draped elegantly over the dark oak bannisters and the marble mantelpiece, with shiny red berries peeping through the greenery. A spike of mistletoe hung over the fireplace, and the fire snapped in the hearth, casting a warm glow over the room.

A majestic tree stood proudly in the grand foyer, its thick branches burgeoning with delicate glass baubles and a golden star at its peak. Around the base of the tree lay bountiful, meticulously wrapped parcels, each finished with a pretty bow.

Beyond the door of the parlour, Lena could make out the chatter of the staff as they moved around the adjoining rooms. They were in high spirits today because Christmas meant extra time off to spend with loved ones or simply relaxing with a small glass of sherry. The faint clink of silverware and porcelain suggested that preparations were already underway for dinner. For as long as she could remember, Christmas day had been a time of magic for Lena. Her father would spend the evening reading to her. It was the only time of year that she could ever recall her father always being at home.

Lena sat on the plush mustard-coloured chaise longue in the corner of the room. She was elegantly dressed in her favourite deep red dress. She toyed with the lace handkerchief, nervously waiting. She had readied herself for the day, firming her decision to have a difficult conversation with her father. Yet, instead of the pleasant breakfast and cheerful mood she'd expected of her father, she'd dined alone.

The door swept across the plush carpet, and Lena sat up expectantly, though it was their butler, Mr Brown who appeared in the doorway. He ran Hawks Manor House in an orderly fashion. In his view, everything had its place and had to be done in a proper manner.

He was a tall, heavyset man with silver at his temples and a keen eye for detail. As he approached Lena, his gaze swept the room. "Pardon me," he began, "should we expect Master Cavendish to join us today? Cook is asking about the seating arrangements."

Lena's face clouded over at the mention of her fiancé. "Rest assured, Mr Cavendish will *not* be dining with us today, Mr Brown."

Memories of the humiliation from the previous evening made her teeth clench. Once she'd returned to the salon last night, Thomas had been aloof. He'd goaded her further by escorting Miss Breckenridge to the carriage that waited for her on the driveway. The rough treatment and heated words they'd exchanged brought a fresh wave of anger through her body. Lena seethed at the memory. No matter how handsome or well-regarded Thomas was, his behaviour was utterly deplorable.

The butler's brow quirked slightly at her clipped reply, although his expression remained neutral. "Very well, Miss Pemberton."

The large grandfather clock in the hall chimed the hour. Lena sprung to her feet with renewed purpose, intending to seek out her father. She had spent half the night worrying about the conversation she needed to have with him, and she was driving herself mad planning how to approach it. But as she reached for the door handle, Edwin Pemberton staggered into the room.

Lena gasped. Her father, usually a robust and imposing man, looked dreadful. His pallor was grey, and he peered at her through bloodshot eyes.

"Father!" She rushed forward, slipping an arm through his. "Are you quite alright?"

Irritated, Edwin Pemberton waved her concerns away. "Leave me be, child, I'm fine."

Lena frowned as her father made his way towards the drinks cabinet. She exchanged worried glances with the butler. "Father," she whispered. "It's not even midday."

Edwin reached for the bottle of port, ignoring his daughter's words.

"Did young Samuel fetch you your tray, sir?" Mr Brown inquired.

Edwin didn't spare them a glance. "I'm not hungry."

"We have your favourite," Lena tried again.

Her father set the bottle down with a click. "It's Christmas," he retorted tightly. "I think after the work I've done this year; I deserve a bloody drink." He snatched up the glass and raised it in a mock salute to them both. "A little port never did anybody any harm. My father swore by it to keep away minor ailments."

Edwin tossed back the ruby liquid, grimacing as he swallowed, and promptly poured himself a second drink.

Mr Brown, his expression full of reproach, discreetly left the room.

Lena's frown deepened. Her father could often be curt with her, but he was never discourteous. It was very unlike him to seek solace in drink, especially so early in the day. Edwin caught the judgement in her gaze and replied defensively, "What is it now, Lena?"

She hesitated, knowing that her father wasn't in the right frame of mind for such a deep conversation as the one she'd planned. However, with everything going on and knowing how busy her father's schedule was beyond days like today, she knew that now would be her only opportunity.

Tentatively, she took a step towards him, her

hands pressed together. "There is a matter of great importance that I wish to discuss with you."

Her father stared at her, his expression one of annoyance. "Out with it then," he gestured with the glass impatiently.

Lena flinched and wondered what was ailing her father. He was never quite this brusque with her.

"Well?"

She took a deep breath and said, "I've given it much thought. This issue has been on my mind for quite some time and reached a point of no return last night. I've come to a decision about my engagement to Thomas."

Her father glared, the only sound was the crackling of the fire and the muted conversation of staff as they set up the dining room.

She rushed on. "I can't marry him. I am going to end my engagement."

"Absolutely not!" Edwin roared, slamming his glass on the top of the drinks cabinet with a finality that exploded through the room. "Out of the question."

Lena's eyes widened in disbelief, and she involuntarily took a step backwards. She had hoped for more understanding from him, some semblance of sympathy. She wanted to share with him the depth of Thomas's despicable actions, but Edwin's stern gaze dried up her words.

"Is this because of Elizabeth Breckenridge?" His question sounded accusing. Edwin poured another glass, huffing impatiently when she hesitated. She shook her head, her throat tight with emotion. Edwin exhaled deeply, shaking his head. "Men will be men," he murmured, almost to himself rather than to his daughter. "That's just the way of the world, Lena."

His gaze locked with hers, challenging her to comment on his indulgence as he lifted the next glass.

"Please, Papa," she said, her voice catching over the word she so rarely used these days. "I cannot commit to a life with such a heinous creature."

For a moment, Edwin's demeanour softened, and she saw a glimmer of her beloved father under this harsh exterior. He rubbed the bridge of his nose as if trying to ward off a headache. "Perhaps this is my fault. I've shielded you from the harsh tribulations of life. Thomas is a fine gentleman yet, some men, have certain expectations and... desires. You should know that it's not for you to comment on any... activities he should indulge in. Thomas loves you. Last night's festivities just got a little too frivolous. He'll soon come around."

She couldn't contain her indignation. "Even when I'm his wife? Am I meant to simply turn a blind eye to such infidelities?"

Edwin's mouth bent downwards. He placed the glass down and crossed the floor. Up close, she saw fatigue and worry in his pale face. He reached out to gently cup her cheek, his touch cold and trembling. Her eyes stung at the tenderness she saw in his eyes as he traced her face. "My beautiful daughter. Some days, you're so much like your mother it hurts me."

Lena's heart skipped a beat. It was rare for her father to speak of her late mother. Anticipation mingled with hope inside as she yearned for more insights into the woman she never knew.

"She too faced trials, challenges," Edwin continued, his voice heavy with emotion. "But she knew when to turn the other cheek, and when to accept and move forward. Just as you must."

"I don't love him," Lena whispered desperately, begging her father to understand.

"You will learn to," Edwin replied, his tone resigned.

Lena felt a surge of defiance. "No, I won't do it," she asserted, her hands balling into fists. "He's deplorable and uncouth!"

Edwin's gaze hardened once more. "Life isn't always about love, Lena. Sometimes it's about duty and responsibility. About doing the right thing. Like you must right now. One day, you will understand. But for now, your marriage to Thomas Cavendish stands."

Lena's heart ached, torn between love for her father and the growing realisation that for the first time in her life, she was going to defy him. Her chin came up. "I have rights. Times are changing. I no longer have to marry who you say."

Edwin's face hardened, and Lena saw not her doting father but the formidable steely businessman who had taken her grandfather's dreams and sculpted them into a legacy.

"Sometimes in life, we are faced with decisions we'd rather not make. Choices that we don't like. We must do things we despise," he declared coldly. "This is one of those times, Lena."

She tried to protest, but he cut her off. "Thomas Cavendish will be an invaluable ally in the coming years. The world is shifting beneath our feet, faster than you could possibly understand. Alliances like these will be our saving grace. You have a job to do. A responsibility to the people who rely on the mill."

Lena's lips parted in disbelief. She wanted to shout, to protest, but the weight of his words held her in place.

"It's not about love or whimsical desires," Edwin continued with a determination that made Lena's heart sink. "Your role is to stand by your husband's side, to bolster and aid him, not become an incessant thorn in his path. You *will* marry him."

Anything further was cut off when a fit of coughing suddenly overtook him. Lena watched with growing alarm as he struggled to catch his breath, his face turning a shade of crimson. Concern overrode her earlier resentment, and she stepped forward, trying to offer help.

He'd been in fine form last night, hadn't he? Perhaps he hadn't.

Perhaps her attention had been on Thomas and Elizabeth, her mind occupied with them both instead.

Edwin quickly swatted her away, a mix of pride and discomfort evident on his face. "I have much work to do," he rasped, his breathing laboured.

"But Father... it's Christmas Day!"

With a terse nod, he turned away. "Merry Christmas," he tossed over his shoulder, the sentiment sounding hollow and insincere.

Lena was left alone in the grand room, the warmth of the roaring fire and the twinkling Christmas decorations contrasting starkly with the desolate feeling sinking inside. Bound by impending duty and her father's unyielding expectations, she faced a future with a man she couldn't bear, let alone love.

As the snow continued to fall on the world outside, the festive atmosphere, which had once brought her so much joy, now felt like a bitter reminder of the inevitable choices she was being forced to make.

CHAPTER 4

The village church was filled to bursting, brimming with local folk gathered for the Christmas Day service. The vicar stood at the pulpit, his sermon about peace and love resonating at this wondrous time of year. Candles flickered in their sconces, illuminating the ancient stone walls. The villagers, donned in their finest, were seated on pews adorned with festive greenery. Beneath the intonations of the vicar was a murmur of restlessness—children fidgeting and adults trying to keep warm in the unheated church, their breath visible as they warmed their hands.

Libby was seated towards the back with the other apprentices. Her gaze surreptitiously travelled over the congregation. Women in bonnets trimmed with ribbon sat alongside men in frock coats and top hats, their faces reddened from the chilly walk through the village. The wealthier parishioners were easily distinguishable, their vibrant attire standing out against the sombre browns and greys of the mill workers, and servants, clad modestly in their Sunday best. As Libby's eyes moved over the sea of faces, she appraised each person with intent.

From blacksmiths to weavers, mechanics to accountants, her scrutiny continued until she found one familiar face who might be able to help her with the problem that Polly and Thea had brought to her last night.

By the time the apprentices shuffled out of the church, their lower status marked by being made to wait until the last to leave, Libby's choice had already departed, no doubt having rushed home to prepare a festive meal for her husband. A coil of dismay tightened within her. She couldn't afford to wait; it had to be today—there were several more days until Sunday, their next day off. She wanted to be able to ease Thea's worries as soon as she could. Breaking away from the group, she placed Polly in charge of seeing the other orphans back to the Apprentices' house and asked her to tell Mrs Reid that she wouldn't be long. In all the years she'd lived at Hawks Mill, the routine on Christmas day had always been the same; prayers and a humble meal of a thin slice of meat and two potatoes, followed by a bowl of plum pudding. In the afternoon, they were allowed a brief period of leisure. There were no presents to be shared, nor a roaring fire to sit by and roast chestnuts on.

Tucking the edges of her shawl tighter around her throat, Libby set out along one of the cobblestone paths. Overnight, fresh snowfall had softened the landscape's contours. Drifts of powdery white nestled against buildings and covered the lanes, while dark hedgerows stood in stark contrast against the snowy blanket. The occasional robin provided a splash of red as the rough call of crows broke the stillness.

Built by the old Mr Pemberton in the days when he wanted to provide lodgings for his workers so that they could be closer to the mill, the workers' cottages were a neat, red-bricked row of houses tucked behind the churchyard. In recent years, as demand for mill workers grew, Edwin Pemberton had crammed more and more families into each dwelling. Houses built for one family now housed three of four, each stuffed into one room sharing a kitchen. Despite the houses being overcrowded, because work was scarce, workers accepted the lodgings like this as part of their pay.

Angus Ferguson and his wife lived in the cellar of one such cottage. Libby knocked, pasting a hopeful smile on her face. The black door swung open, revealing Bess Ferguson's surprised face as steamed warmth from inside billowed out around her. Bess had worked at the mill for many years and was now a skilled loom worker.

Her ruddy face was pink, and her customary stern look was absent. She appeared softer almost, and Libby wondered if the day would ever come when she was preparing a Christmas day meal for a husband in her house of her own. "Libby! Merry Christmas. What brings you by?"

"Merry Christmas to you, Bess," Libby replied. "May I come in?"

Bess hesitated, looking back over her shoulder, reluctance creasing her brow. "Angus is away sleepin' right now," she explained, her soft Scottish burr rolling off her tongue.

Angus was a labourer at the mill, employed to do the menial work that required a strong arm. He was big and cumbersome and had a vicious tongue that had gotten him a fine or two. Libby suspected that Angus had done what many of the mill workers did when they didn't have to work; he was recovering after spending his earnings in the Black Bull last night.

Bess folded her arms in silent inquiry.

Driven by the urgency of the situation, Libby asked, "Do you remember Peggy Daniels and the trouble she had?"

"Aye," Bess stepped out a little, pulling the door tighter to her. Libby was relieved that the other woman seemed to understand. "What of it?"

"We have the same issue but with a different girl this time."

"Who?"

"Thea."

"The new wee girl, aye?"

"Yes, I believe she came to be in this manner just as Peggy did. She's half-crazed with fear."

Bess's face shifted, empathy and concern in her kind expression. "I see," she murmured gently, "a terrible shame. Why are you telling me this?"

27

Libby offered her a sympathetic smile. "I've heard talk around the mill, about how you and Angus have been trying for a little one of your own but haven't yet been blessed with such luck."

Bess's mouth compressed, and she swallowed hard. "Aye, that's true."

Libby hurried on, "Thea's all alone. She won't be able to care for the child. Mrs Reid will surely cast her out. Peggy's baby was raised by the Cottle's. The child is thriving, and Mary is raising the girl as her own."

Bess' head shake accompanied the resigned sigh. "Aye, but that was different. Peggy hid it well and upped and died even before the wee bairn was oot! Even Mrs Reid wasn't so mean in spirit as to send a bairn to the workhouse!"

"Bess!" Angus's voice boomed behind her, startling both women. "Why are you leaving the door open, woman?"

The door was yanked wider, and Angus's considerable bulk filled the space, his face, framed by a ring of wispy orange hair, was as red as the bricks of the cottage.

Bleary eyes fixed on Libby, and it was clear why he had been absent from the church. "What is it, girl?"

Bess began to explain in hushed tones, but Libby could see the resoluteness in his face before Bess even began.

"I'll no have any Blackwood's bastards under my roof!" he declared.

"But Angus—" Bess's attempt was feeble against his thunderous resolve.

"No, Bess. That's my final word. Shut the door; you're letting the bloody heat out!" Angus nudged Bess back into the kitchen and slammed the door in Libby's face.

Libby stared at the door, debating knocking again, though quickly retreated when Angus' raised voice reached her. She hurried out onto the narrow lane, her boots crunching through the snow.

Regret ate at her.

The last thing she'd wanted to do was to cause problems for Bess. She pulled her shawl tighter against the biting cold, standing to one side in the lane when she heard a carriage make its way along the snow-covered road behind her. The driver didn't acknowledge her, perched atop the polished black cab with gilded trimmings, stirring the delicate mist of the frosty air as it raced by.

She followed in its wake, the wheels muted by the layer of snow and watched as it turned in the lane and made its way to the front of Hawks Manor.

Curiosity slowed her footsteps; it was well-known that Edwin Pemberton and his daughter enjoyed spending Christmas Day alone, not welcoming any visitors until the mill reopened on Boxing Day.

So, who could be visiting them today?

Through the black wrought iron fencing, she noticed more activity than usual at the manor. The cab door swung open, and a figure emerged, cloaked in finery to ward off the chill of the day. It wasn't the young and impossibly handsome Cavendish who glanced her way, though.

It was the local doctor, Dr Fitch.

Libby lowered her gaze as the butler opened the front door to welcome him inside. She hurried back along the lane and up the short hill towards the apprentices' house, hoping that the doctor's visit was for a social call and not for something more dire.

CHAPTER 5

*T*he click of the door handle pulled Lena's attention back into the bedroom. The door opened inwards with a faint tinkle of chinaware that wobbled on the tray Gwen carried. Lena offered the young maid a faint smile.

"Thank you, Gwen," Lena said as she elbowed off the wall next to the long bedroom window.

Gwen quickly averted her gaze from where Edwin Pemberton lay prone under the bed covers. Her father's pale, ghostly face was ghastly enough, without the dreadful rattling that accompanied his breathing.

"Cook asked me to fetch this up to you, Miss," Gwen murmured, setting the tray on the side. "Said I'm to make sure you eat today."

Lena didn't have the heart to tell the maid that she wasn't hungry, thanking her for the effort instead. She'd discovered her father slumped over his desk on Christmas day when he'd not responded to the dinner bell. Seeing him so helpless had scared her spitless. She'd summoned the doctor who tended to her father. However, despite reassurances from Doctor Fitch that the fever would pass, her father wasn't getting any better. Not even her prayers had abated it.

Christmas had come and gone, and the incessant growling rumble from the machinery inside the mill had resumed, telling Lena that life went on despite the head of the company having failing health. The wintry sun burnished the land beyond the window, turning the lanes and pathways to dirty mush.

Edwin mumbled incoherently. Embarrassed that one of his household staff should see him in a vulnerable state, Lena quickly rushed across the room, snatching up the damp rag off the side and laying it over his clammy brow. She murmured and it seemed to ease his labouring anguish.

Gwen sent her an odd smile. "Can I get you anything else, miss?"

"Thank you, no. That will be all, Gwen."

"You'll be sure to eat something? Cook and the rest of us, well, we are all praying that Mr Pemberton gets better."

"I should say he needs all the prayers he can at this moment." Lena brushed her father's hair back, his face smoothing at her cool touch. The maid let herself out. Lena wasn't sure how much of what Gwen said was lip service. Her father was a good employer, and they were probably worried about what would happen to their jobs if her father didn't pull through this.

"You must get better, papa," she said softly. "I know

nothing about running a business. You always told me that it was a man's job." His eyelids fluttered. Hope flared inside. "Papa?"

But the juddering groan that pained him squeezed his eyes shut tight.

Tray forgotten, she took a seat next to the bed and held his hand. His papery skin was hot to the touch, and she closed her eyes, her mouth moving soundlessly as she whispered another prayer. She worried that the argument they'd had on Christmas day had driven his body beyond recovery, and she prayed for forgiveness for adding to his troubles.

The gentle rap on the door snapped her eyes open, and she popped to her feet as the door swished open once more. This time, it was the butler who hovered in the doorway, concern in his eyes as he took in her father's motionless form. "Pardon me, Miss Lena," Mr Brown said quietly. "Mr John Sparrow is downstairs, he wishes to speak with you."

Lena turned her attention back to her father. "Tell him to go back to work. I am in no mood to deal with Mr Sparrow or anything to do with the mill today."

"He isn't alone, Miss. And they are both quite insistent that they speak with your father. I've tried explaining the situation, but I rather think it would sound more appropriate coming from a member of the family."

"Who is the other man? Mr Cavendish?"

She'd written to Thomas to let him know that her father was sick but hadn't heard back from him.

"Sadly, no, miss. I believe you've met the other gentleman, a Mr David Ward."

Irritation flashed through her. And she let him know she was annoyed with her sigh. "Can you have someone sit with my father then, please? I don't want him to be alone if he wakes.

"I shall sit here with him myself," Mr Brown said, as she stomped past him.

John Sparrow was the mill manager. As such, he was responsible for running the entire operation from roof to cellar. To Lena, it seemed he enjoyed the notoriety and having the millworkers touch their caps as he passed them by. Lena swept into the drawing room, both men looking up as she walked in.

John Sparrow was a haughty man, with a permanent scowl, as if he'd eaten something sour. He was tall and heavy set, no doubt, having worked his way up through the echelons to reach the mill manager. Other than when he'd been seated around the dining table in the manor house, her interactions with him had been minimal though she knew that his father relied heavily on his skill set. The other man was older, more pious-looking, judging by the way he peered down his long, narrow nose at Lena. She had a vague recollection of meeting him and of also being discounted by him in the past.

"Good afternoon, gentleman." She'd spent the last five days nursing her father and hadn't taken much care of her appearance. The men exchanged a look that spoke volumes. Whilst manners dictated that she be courteous to them, she wasn't much inclined to offer them hospitality.

At least the mill manager attempted a smile. "We were expecting your father, miss."

"I've travelled from London this morning," David Ward spat, without hesitation. Displeasure radiated off him, from his shiny hair down to his expensive, shiny shoes.

Lena prickled at the adversarial tone. "As Mr Brown has undoubtedly informed you," her tone dripped with disdain, "my father is indisposed right now."

Mr Ward snorted indelicately. "Likely story, I'm sure. You tell him I want to speak to him right this instant."

Lena's eyes narrowed, her irritation ticking over into anger at his boldness. She drew herself up. "My father is gravely ill," she enunciated with deliberate emphasis, "and I would appreciate it if you moderated yourself, Mr Ward. Such discourtesy would not be displayed if he were standing here with us." She waited a beat before slowly repeating, "He is indisposed."

"Ill?"

The little flare of victory at his shocked expression was doused by the knowledge that it was, in fact, the truth. "That's right, sir. He has been bedridden for several days. Now, should you have any issues regarding the mill, I'm certain Mr Sparrow here can accommodate your needs. He is the mill manager, after all. Now, gentleman," she indicated the door, "if that will be all?"

Ward scoffed, nostrils flaring. "Isn't that just like a Pemberton, expecting me to deal with an *employee* when the matter is most urgent?"

Mr Sparrow's downturned expression reddened, and just as quickly, Lena's brows climbed her fore-head. "What is the problem that cannot wait?"

"I'm not discussing business with you, a *woman*!"

"I am certain I shall inherit one day, sir," she stated, though she quietly hoped that day was far off just yet. "At such time you will have to deal with me. So please explain how different that is to now?"

"Women cannot understand business," he muttered. "And when the day comes, I shall simply deal with your husband, won't I?"

"Miss Pemberton is engaged to Thomas Cavendish," Sparrow supplied, and Mr Ward's brows moved appreciatively. Of course, neither of them knew that she was still planning to break her engagement.

Mr Ward turned an expectant look to the ceiling. "Is Mr Cavendish home?"

"Mr Cavendish doesn't deal with the mill. Mr Sparrow and my father do."

"This is most frustrating," Mr Ward pursed his mouth, his gaze going to the window.

Lena's jaw tightened as the silence dragged on. "It appears that our conversation is at an end, sir." She strode across the floor and pulled on the gold rope to summon one of the footmen.

"I'm not leaving here until your cowardly father shows his face!"

Lena rounded on him, eyes flaring with temper. "You will leave this house at once, sir. And as soon as my father regains his health, I shall ensure he deals with whatever nuisance you bring to his door.

"Until then, you are not welcome here."

James, the senior footman, materialised in the doorway. Lena sent him a grateful smile.

"James, if you would be so kind as to escort Mr Ward to the front door and furnish him with his coat. He is leaving immediately. Mr Sparrow, you can close the door on your way out."

John Sparrow opened his mouth as if to argue with her, but she cut off any response with a withering look. Each man reluctantly left the room, and the footman followed them out. She waited until the front door closed before she collapsed onto the sofa, a little shaky.

"Miss?"

Lena looked up, rubbing her mouth. "Have they gone?"

"Yes, miss. None too happy, mind."

Some of the tumult that boiled inside eased. "Thank you for your assistance, James. I shall see to it that my father knows who to rely on in this house."

"Very well, Miss. Thank you," James said, his back straightening a little more. "Will that be all?"

"Some tea, I think," she nodded. "If you'd be so kind as to have it sent up to my father's chambers."

James left, and she climbed the stairs on trembling legs.

She needed her father to get better. Mr Ward was right: she did not know the mill business well enough to be able to answer any of his questions.

She wasn't nearly ready to deal with business, or life, on her own.

CHAPTER 6

The Blow Room was in the belly of the mill, the floor where the cotton arrived in bales of raw material. It was then split and broken up by hand and fed into a series of machines used to clean and comb the fibres, spinning them into the finest yarn. Above this was the Mule Room. It was hot and humid, and fine cotton fibres spun in the air so that the room was shrouded in a permanent gloom. At the end of the day, her eyes were sore and her throat itchy from the flakes of cotton that floated, coating their clothing, and filling their lungs. The dreaded cotton lung had claimed many lives, but Libby had to work or end up in the workhouse.

The last machine in the cotton process was the mule, a giant machine that stretched the length of the room, each carriage holding more than five hundred threads. The machines moved in a choreographed dance, the carriage rolling away from the fixed frame along iron rails, unfurling the roving before spinning it onto bobbins with a stretch and a twist, allowing a few precious seconds for the scavengers to dart beneath the beast to retrieve the cast-off scraps of cotton waste before the carriage rumbled back into position. For six days a week, the machines hissed and clattered, each mule producing miles of fine cotton thread ready for the weavers on the floors above.

Libby was a mule spinner, responsible for several machines at once, piecing together broken threads and adjusting tensions to ensure the finest quality of yarn was made. Each spinner was like a maestro, conducting a relentless symphony, nimble fingers ensuring that the endless streams of cotton filled the spools evenly.

A mistake could mean her wages cup was empty at the end of the week or worse, that one of the children, scrambling into the underbelly of the beast, was injured. It was a dance of diligence that she performed with grace honed by years of repetition.

Arthur Dower, the room's overseer, marched and patrolled the aisles, his hands clasped behind his back as he scanned for a missed beat in the workers' rhythm. He had quick hands and a quicker temper, running the busiest room in the mill with intimidation and tyranny.

"We'll not have idle hands here!"

"Mind your spindles!"

"Keep your mind on your work, not on the clock!"

"Time is threads: threads are coin!"

He barked out these mantras, etching his words

into the minds of the children who worked tirelessly on these beasts, from sunup until sundown.

Libby watched carefully as Pip, one of the scavengers, his face smeared with dirty oil from the cans he used to grease the wheels, grabbed at the precious fluff that littered the floor. A warning sprang to her lips, but like a ballet he had performed many times, he nipped out just as the carriage began its reverberating journey back. Pip's grin was swift and confident as he caught her stern eye, and Libby couldn't help but return the smile. She had yet to see one of her mules injure a child, but she also vividly remembered the day when Maud was dragged into the teeth of one of the belts that rumbled across the ceiling by her hair, taking off her scalp and eventually taking her life.

Libby's concentration shattered when a shadow fell across her machine. Mr Blackwood, the foreman, lingered at the start of her row. A chill crept along her spine. The foreman was responsible for the workforce, and he wielded that authority like a harpoon on a whaling boat. His neat black suit and top hat looked out of place amongst the shades of brown and grey smocks. His eyes, cold and calculating, scanned the room before settling on Thea. He moved behind her, his attention on the pretty girl. Libby could've sworn she saw Thea's face grow redder in the humid atmosphere as the foreman leaned over her. The intensity of his stare unlocked a memory in Libby's mind that rushed in with a vengeance. She remembered how he'd once cornered her in the privy and the touch of his hands as they slid under her skirts.

She'd never spoken of it, the threat he'd held over her head was too much to risk. Instead, she'd prayed until his attention had moved on.

Shame and fury mingled.

Thea tucked her chin to her head, fear written all over her face.

I'll no have any of Blackwood's bastards under my roof.

Angus Ferguson's muttered words only reinforced what she'd already guessed – many of the young girls under Blackwood's watch ended up like Peggy, like Thea.

There but for the grace of God... she could have endured the same fate. She longed to stand up to the brute – to shout about the wolf in sheep's clothing who held their fate in his hands with such casual disdain. But who would listen to an orphan like her?

"Watch it, Libby!" Polly snapped at her. "Dower will have your head if you lose any more lines!"

Libby speedily attended to the threads that had broken. When she looked across the room once more, Blackwood was moving again back towards her. Thea had her head down, and Libby wondered if the girl was even aware of the tears that glistened on her cheeks.

The overseer's voice cut through the din, "Everything in order, Mr Blackwood?"

Blackwood's gaze flicked towards Dower. "Just making my rounds," he said.

"Very good, sir," Arthur grinned. "I like to keep everything running smoothly for Mr Pemberton, sir."

Blackwood's gaze slid back towards Thea. "That's

what I like to hear, Mr Dower. Keep making sure that everyone is doing what they should be."

"Of course, sir. No shirkers under my watch, Mr Blackwood."

The deferential tone lasted for as long as it took for the foreman to wander out of the room before the oily manners of the overseer vanished, and he began his mantras once more.

"Time is threads: threads are coin!"

The floor rumbled with the weight of the carriage, the air hummed with industry as scutchers and carders, can tenters and scavengers slogged until the supper bell went. It sickened her that it was well-known amongst the workers what Mr Blackwood did in the mill, but nothing ever changed. She paused the carriage with the clutch lever to disengage the belts, loading more spindles, all the while her mind drifting to thoughts of her escape from this place.

Could she walk away from Thea, from Polly, all the other girls that would come after her? Wouldn't that make her just as culpable as the men who turned a blind eye to the fact that Blackwood and the rest of the overseers used the orphans for their own selfish deeds?

Then again, what difference could someone like her ever hope to make?

CHAPTER 7

*T*he clanking of the fire grate startled Lena awake. She sat up with a snap and a sudden intake of air, wiping away the line of drool that had pooled on the coverlet of her father's bed.

Gwen gave her an apologetic smile. "Pardon, Miss. I tried to be as quiet as possible."

Uncaring about the state of her appearance, Lena looked at her father. His breathing was still shallow and rapid, with a dreadful rattle that had served as a lullaby as she'd dropped into an exhausted slumber. The lamps that Gwen must've lit around the room now illuminated the bed chamber, casting a soft glow in the space. The room had taken on a chill, but Lena hadn't noticed until Gwen's attention to stoking the fire began to ease some of the stiffness in her muscles as warmth spread through the room.

"The doctor left that for Mr Pemberton," Gwen nodded at the brown glass bottle on the sideboard.

Lena's brows shot up. "When was he here?"

"He left not that long ago, miss. He said you were to eat, and to sleep in your own bed tonight. You were too tired to stir, even when he was tending to poor Mr Pemberton," she told Lena. "You were dead to the world, that's for certain."

None of the elixirs the doctor had brought and administered to her father so far seemed to make much difference; she wasn't sure if this one would work, either. Her once vibrant and overbearing father had now been rendered almost skeletal.

She dragged her hands down her face to revive herself and then picked up the spoon. It clattered against his teeth as she tipped the medicine slowly into his mouth. She sighed as it dribbled back out.

She held back the bitter sting of tears, silently pleading with her father.

"Here, miss," Gwen nudged her back. "My ma was a bugger for taking her potions." Gwen expertly spooned the tincture in, and her father swallowed – a brief interval before that dreadful breathing rattle resumed.

"Thank you," Lena mumbled, "and for the fire, Gwen. I'm grateful for the heat in the room now that his fever has broken."

Gwen wiped her hands on her apron as she straightened up. "You haven't touched your tray, Miss."

"You'll have to forgive me and send my apologies to the cook; I have no appetite."

"You'll be no good to man or beast if you yourself get poorly, Miss," Gwen chided gently.

45

A smile ghosted over Lena's lips. "You sound as if you're talking to a child."

"I don't mean to," Gwen took a tentative step forward. "We're all worried sick about you and your father. And you're running yourself into the ground, being a good daughter. Mr Pemberton... he knows you're here with him. Why don't you let me run a bath for you, and maybe take an hour off? One of us will stay in here and fetch you if there is any change?"

Lena hesitated. She had spent the past three weeks watching her father wither away under the doctor's care, each new medicine making no difference to his condition. Deep down in the recesses of her heart, she knew that it would take nothing short of a miracle to bring him back from the brink of death yet hope still burned inside. She wasn't ready yet to become an orphan.

"If nothing more, Miss, it might make you feel a little more human."

Lena laughed then, a raspy half-laugh that escaped her mouth. "Do I look that bad?"

Gwen returned her smile. "I wouldn't be so bold as to say, Miss," she quipped.

"Very well," Lena said, "A bath sounds like a splendid idea. Maybe if you could ask the cook for a cup of broth and some crackers, that would be good too."

Rising, Lena donned a shawl, leaned down, and gave her father's cheek a peck. "I shan't be too long, father. Please know that I love you with all my heart."

Just as Gwen had predicted, the bath soothed her muscles, and the broth settled her stomach. She perched on the edge of her bed and closed her eyes, waking with a start. She threw on her shawl and hurried through the door. Passing the clock on the landing, she noted she'd been away from her father little more than two hours, yet she was feeling refreshed.

Staff had lit the lights along the corridor, the butler stepping out of her father's room just as she reached it.

One look at his face confirmed Lena's earlier fears. Wordlessly, she rushed past him and burst into her father's chambers. Not only was the room absent of the dreadful death rattle that had accompanied her father's last few days, but she also felt the absence of his essence. His mouth hung slack, his lips dark blue. Tears filled her eyes as she walked across the carpet. Several other servants hovered in the doorway, their hushed whispers falling away as she approached the bed.

She clasped his hand that still held the lingering warmth of life, her tears running steadily down her cheeks. She lowered into the chair that she'd occupied for almost a month and pressed the back of his hand to her cheek.

"I thought we had more time... I really wasn't ready for this, Papa. I wish you had taught me a little more about what I need to know... why didn't I ask you?" she whispered. She sniffed, laying his hand back down and pressing it gently into the bed. Regret mingled with the acute pain. "Why did you wait until I wasn't here, you stubborn goat?"

Behind her, Mr Brown stepped forward. "It was mere moments ago, Miss Lena. But he's at peace now."

"I do hope so, Mr Brown," Lena choked out, "because I don't know how I'm going to cope without him."

CHAPTER 8

$\mathcal{M}$ ill workers dotted the workyard, shivering under threadbare shawls, their breaths visible in the watery late January sunlight. The workers sat where they could find space, some leaning against the walls of the yard, others perched on crates and barrels, their bodies huddled together for warmth as they ate their lunch.

The fortunate few had retreated to their nearby cottages, stealing a few warmer moments out of the dusty lint of the mill. Libby stood in line with their other orphans, waiting for Mrs Reid to dole out handfuls of porridge directly into their hands. There were no plates, no spoons—luxuries like that would only add to her day's burdens with ninety children to feed and watch over. Libby stamped her feet to try and ward off the chill, eyes travelling around the cobbled yard, as she waited her turn. The fresh air made a welcome change to the steamy, lint-laden atmosphere of the mule room, and she kept drawing it in.

She watched a family meet in the yard, the mother reaching into the sack to pull out a bread slice. Tilly, one of the scavengers from the mule room, accepted it gratefully. For years, she'd always wondered what it would be like to have a family to go home to, knowing that her family were the children that shuffled along with her.

Mrs Reid, her grubby apron wrapped tightly around her plump belly, slapped the glob of thick porridge into her hand, and Libby sat against the far wall, biting into the cold stodge.

Usually, the allotted breaks were a chance for the mill workers to catch up; exchanging news and gossip, but today, a hushed pall had settled over the yard. Libby, like many of the workers here, had only known employment under Edwin Pemberton.

His sudden demise meant that things would change. This sent whispers of worry and discontent around the superstitious group as they speculated the fate that awaited them.

"She's not married," Jane Robertson said in a low voice.

"It's an ill omen," muttered Agnes Hart, her fingers gathering the cloth of her uniform unconsciously. "A Pemberton has run this mill for the past five decades."

"It'll be fine," said one of the weavers, a thread of assurance weaving through the uncertainty. "She's betrothed to a banker. Thomas Cavendish will take care of everything."

"Aye, but what do bankers ken about cotton?"

retorted an older spinner, his face carved with lines of scepticism. "It's cloth we're weaving, not coin."

His companion, a gaunt woman with lines of worry etched deep into her face, snorted quietly. "Marriage is no guarantee of happiness or prosperity. And it can't be good, leaving only a daughter in charge."

The calm weaver shook her head. "Money'll keep the mill spinning."

Agnes Hart let fly a disbelieving snort. "Money don't change the nature of a man. Not for their kind, anyhow. And I heard that the Cavendish family drives their workers harder than the devil stoking the fires of hell, wringing every last drop from us before we drop dead."

Other workers nodded, mostly quiet in contemplation.

"Ruthless they may be, but they know how to turn a profit," said another voice, this one belonging to an ambitious scutcher who had always aimed higher than the rafters of the mill allowed. "Maybe we'll see the fruits of it in our wages."

"Don't hold your breath, lad," the old weaver scoffed. "They might make the money but the likes of us will never see it. I say again – a banker knows nought about cotton and looms."

"Things might get better," Wilf Roberts offered. The young underseer was leaning against the wall a few feet away from Libby. He was quiet, kept to himself most days, and he had saved the girls he could by interrupting Mr Dower when he had a girl in the privy.

"How's that?"

Wilf's eyes narrowed against the weak sunlight. "Maybe Mr Cavendish will bring some of that Manchester progress here. And I wouldn't write off the daughter, either."

Libby's gaze fell to the grey mass in her hands. "She is a Pemberton, after all. She's grown up around the mill. She would want it to carry on." Wilf met her eyes and his mouth moved up into a small smile of solidarity, as the old spinner snorted again.

"I ask you, what does a young lass know of business and mills?"

"More than you, I dare say," Libby retorted, drawing a snigger from Wilf. Libby had seen Lena only from a distance. The younger Pemberton had always spoken to the girls if she passed by them in the yard, but Libby had never spoken to her. Still, she knew what it was like to watch a parent die. Her heart ached for her.

"She probably doesn't even know where the door to the mill is," the spinner wasn't to be swayed from his course. "More coins for Cavendish will mean a squeeze for the workers. It always does."

Speculation bubbled up like steam from a kettle as Thea settled in next to her. The girl bit into the cold porridge as if she hadn't eaten in days. Libby hid a smile as Thea quietly asked, "What do you think will happen to us if this place closes?"

Libby wiped her hand on her skirt, glancing about.

"Thomas Cavendish may indeed have his ways, but this mill... this is still Pemberton's. I think that has to count for something. It won't matter to me come the summer," she added as an afterthought.

"What's this about the summer?" Wilf leaned down, startling both girls.

Libby's chilled face pinked up. "None of your business."

"She'll be twenty-one," Polly added helpfully, earning a hiss from Libby and a wry chuckle from Wilf.

"What's so funny about that?" Thea asked him.

Wilf gestured about him. "How many of the girls here do you think dreamed of running off to the city for a bright future? Libby is good at what she does. No way will Mr Blackwood let her go, not if he has any sense."

"He won't have a say in the matter," Libby added heatedly.

"What's this?" Jane Robertson interrupted them.

The conversation had drawn the attention of those close by, including the older woman, who was nosey and opinionated. Years in the mule room also meant she was hard of hearing. Libby grinned, "Soon be Wakes Week."

A ripple of agreement spread throughout the corner of the yard. Libby heard Wilf's laughter again but waited until the worker's attention had drifted away from her.

"What?"

"You on about Wakes Week. Orphans like us never

53

get to visit the seaside. That's for families who can afford the travel. Come Wakes, you'll still be stuck in this mill with me."

Libby picked at the bits of dried porridge clinging to her skirts. It was true. The annual holiday when the mills all fell silent, and the workers were free to spend their time as they wished was but a dream for people like Libby and Wilf. For her, Wakes Week was not a holiday but a reminder of her solitary state—no family to speak of, no excursions to look forward to.

"I understand why you'll leave but..." Thea thoughtfully prodded the glob of porridge that had congealed in her palm.

"But?"

Thea lifted her eyes, earnest gaze meeting Libby's, "I always wanted a big sister. Or a sister. I feel that I... I have that with you. I shall miss you."

Libby's smile was genuine, and she put an arm around Thea. She still had to find a family willing to take Thea's child. She still had so much to do here before she left. With Polly being the next eldest, Libby would pass the torch on to her. The mill was more than a source of livelihood; it was a pulse by which their lives beat—a pulse now flickering under the shade of insecurity.

"I shall stay in touch with you and when you leave, you can come and stay with me," Libby jiggled Thea closer to her. "How does that sound?"

Libby encountered Wilf's gentle gaze. Like her, he'd worked at the mill long enough to know that dreams and hopes had a way of turning into cotton dust in places like this. The most Libby could hope for was that the mill survived long enough for her to discharge her indenture, granting her the freedom she yearned for. The bell tolled for the end of the break, and he acknowledged her with a slight nod as he tugged at the peak of his cloth cap before pushing away from the wall.

Libby rose with the others, their bodies sluggish, their spirits weighed down with doubts and misgivings. As they headed back towards the mill, grumblings persisted, albeit in hushed tones to avoid the notice of any overseers who might overhear such mutinous talk.

Libby felt the burden of the days ahead. Would the mill, the only community she'd ever known, survive the upcoming challenges? Or would they all be cast out in the name of progress? One thing remained certain—much like the unyielding turn of the mule spindles, the wheels of change would spare no one.

CHAPTER 9

*S*he'd watched the carriage racing along the driveway.

She had known exactly who it was inside, even before his dark head had emerged through the door. He'd thrust his gloves at James and issued a tersely barked order as he'd strode across the driveway, letting himself inside Hawks Manor without waiting for Mr Brown to greet him.

For three days, Lena had mourned the loss of her father alone. She heard the commotion beyond the library door – the room where her father favoured the most and she felt closest to him – and she waited. She steeled herself for his arrival and yet couldn't help the reaction her body gave when Thomas Cavendish entered, his eyes seeking her out. For a moment, she remembered the charming and dutiful person who'd lovingly courted her, the one who'd whispered sweet nothings into her ear, making her shiver with promised delight.

"My darling," he murmured, rushing across the room to sweep her into a hug. "I came as soon as I heard."

His touch, though gentle, brought back the revulsion she'd experienced at his ardent touch on Christmas Eve. She stiffened in his arms, even as apologies dripped from his lips.

She pulled back, her voice cracking as she asked, "Where have you been, Thomas?"

One side of his mouth moved in a half-smile and a line formed between his brows. "What does that matter? I'm here with you now. Here, come here," he pulled her tighter to him. Instead of the loving touch of a man who'd promised to cherish her, his arms felt cloying, suffocating.

She pushed against him until he released her, her anguish plea meeting his annoyed frown. "I wrote to you. Many times. My father…"

"Darling, the letters finally found me where I'd been staying."

Her lips parted as she looked at him. "Where were you?"

"Hunting grouse in the Highlands," he replied as if the answer had been an obvious one.

"The Highlands? Where? Staying with who?"

"At Balden Castle," he stated as if the answer should have been obvious to her.

A resigned sigh left her in a rush, and she shook her head. It was Amelia McMurray who'd written to Lena to tell her that she'd heard Thomas was in Scotland instead of his residence in London, where Lena had been sending his letters. "You've been staying with the Breckenridge's."

"Of course. Patrick and my father are old friends," he explained. "I spend every Christmas up there."

Memories of him flirting with the affluent Elizabeth at her father's party danced in her mind's eye. Instead of being jealous, she felt relieved.

Thomas closed the gap between them with a dry chuckle. "This is hardly the time for one of your suspicious fits, Lena. We have much to sort out."

"I wrote to you, Thomas. Many times." He shimmered through her tears of grief as she spoke. "I needed you here with me."

He cupped her face between his palms, pressing them uncomfortably. "I'm here now, my darling."

The door was opened by Mr Brown and James appeared with a tray. Lena realised then that the commotion she'd heard when he'd first arrived was Thomas already ordering around the house staff. *Her* staff.

Gwen followed behind James, a coal scuttle in hand, flicking nervous glances at Thomas as she tended the fire that hadn't needed any attention because Gwen had taken care of it earlier. Lena wondered if he even remembered the open threats that he'd made to the poor girl that night on the balcony. A maid's welfare probably didn't rate high on his agenda judging by the way he'd jumped straight into exerting his authority over the household. Lena didn't like it one bit, but her father's dire warnings echoed in her mind.

You have a responsibility to the people in the mill.

"T-thank you, James," Lena stammered.

"Anything else, miss?" The footman's expression was passive though she picked up on the edge in his voice.

A faint smile moved on her mouth as she felt a kinship with him; her staff were just as perturbed by Thomas' cavalier attitude as she was.

"No, that will be all, thank you."

She nodded at Gwen and offered a reassuring smile, patiently waiting until they were all alone with the door securely closed. Then, as she faced Thomas, a small mewl of horror slipped from her lips.

Thomas was sitting down at the wide walnut desk that her father used to sit at to write all his correspondence.

He spared her a glance whilst opening the drawers. "What?"

"What are you doing?" She demanded, "My father's body is upstairs, barely cold, and you're sitting at his desk. Have you no respect?"

"Your father was tight-lipped on his business dealings, Lena. If I'm to learn the machinations of how this place runs, I need to learn everything as fast as I can. Of course, we shall have to move up the wedding date now. There is no time to waste.

"Pour me a cup of tea, will you? Though you could have had one of those people do that for us – why else do you pay them? Honestly, this whole place needs a revamp from chimney to cellar," he searched a drawer, closed it, and opened the next, "I shall see to it that it's whipped into shipshape in no time. Things are going to change here."

She ignored his request and took a step towards him. "Thomas, stop. Mr Clark will be here for the funeral tomorrow. He has written to tell me that he is due here this evening and will bring me up to date with everything once the service is over."

Thomas snorted. "That's just the legal side of ownership – your father's solicitor won't have a clue about the business."

Lena squared her shoulders. "That's my father's desk. And the mill is *mine*."

His hands stilled as his gaze lifted to meet hers. His eyes turned flinty, but he still didn't move. Instead, he leaned back in the chair, linking his fingers across his stomach. "After we marry it will become *ours*. And you don't know the first thing about running a business, my dear, do you?"

The final two words were uttered with an undertone of menace, causing a tremor to slip along her spine.

She couldn't argue with him – she knew nothing, but watching how he simply occupied her father's place with such aplomb irked her. "Well, no, but I can learn. I am a Pemberton, after all."

Thomas shook his head and sat forward once more, dismissing her. "Darling, why trouble yourself? You are too pretty to be concerning yourself with such matters. What have you instructed the cook to prepare for tonight's guests?"

Her bottom lip disappeared between her teeth. She

hadn't even thought about the matter, trusting that her father's staff would see to it. If she could overlook such a simple problem, what hope did she have about learning how to run a complicated enterprise such as a cotton mill?

He glanced up at her, brow raised. "How many are staying here at the house for the funeral?"

"I don't know," she admitted with an out-breath.

He shook his head mockingly. "You can't even run your household, Lena. How can you even contemplate that your father would want the reins of his mill to fall into your inept hands?"

"He..."

Thomas Cavendish will be an invaluable ally in the coming years.

Her father had known that she couldn't cope. That knowledge felt like a betrayal, and the sting of it brought more tears.

Thomas came to his feet, his considerable height making her feel feeble and incompetent. "Do you know how many people are employed in that building across the lane, Lena?" He jabbed a finger at the window towards the building that rumbled relentlessly throughout the day. "What about how many mouths depend on production there?"

She shook her head.

"What about those who supply this place – when is the next shipment coming in? Where does the cloth go once it's finished? How many invoices are outstanding?" He advanced on her slowly, ticking off the questions with his fingers.

Shame crept over her, and again she shook her head. This business had fed and clothed her all her life – how could she not know more about those who helped make it work?

"This is business, Lena. People rely on it. One wrong decision by you will mean that these people lose their livelihoods, their homes... do you want their *deaths* on your conscience?" A small cry escaped her, and he pressed on. "Business is not choosing silk dresses from Paris or having a tea party with your friends to gossip. It's hard. Cut-throat. My father raised me to run a bank; business is in my blood.

"Your father chose me as your suitor because he knew that you wouldn't know what to do; he wanted me to ensure that this mill carried on because you couldn't manage it. And judging by your expression, I'd say he was right.

"There are many mills in this area, all waiting for Hawks Mill to fail. They're all waiting to rummage through the leftovers. Those men will pick your bones bare without a second's thought or consideration for your gender. You need to be tough, brutal, and ruthless," Thomas came to a halt in front of her. "You are none of those things. Now, be a lamb and go speak to the kitchen. I want those lazy staff of yours to be brought up to scratch. I'm certain that tomorrow will be busy. Your father knew many people. You need to see to it that they're well-fed and looked after. If you are to face them, you need to rest. You look dreadful. Ensure that I'm left alone in here to go through your father's documents."

Dazed, stricken, Lena stumbled out of the drawing room and into the passage. She leaned against the wall, her body heaving with silent sobs.

"Lena! I'm sorry it took so long to get here but the weather halted trains down south. I came most of the way by carriage," The chatty voice sounded far away, as if in a box, as sorrow crashed over her. Lena squeezed her eyes shut tight, torment and grief tossing her about so that when a hand touched her shoulder, she let out a strangled cry. She blinked through her tears before the kind face of Amelia McMurray swam into focus. "My aunt says I can stay with her... I was going to go straight to hers because I thought that you'd have a house full but had the driver stop by here to see if I can do anything for you...

"Are you quite all right, my dear?" Amelia paused, her eyes searching Lena's face.

Lena shook her head, unable to speak past the tight ball of misery lodged in her throat.

Amelia's hand stayed in place, her voice tinged with sorrow. "I'm so sorry for your loss."

Faced with her friend's sympathetic expression after Thomas' apathy, Lena collapsed into hopeless tears.

"Oh, my goodness," Amelia gathered her close. "Hush, now, my dear, come. Mr Brown? Where can I take her?"

The butler hovered impotently, James beside him with Amelia's coat and gloves in his hands. "The drawing room, miss."

Lena allowed them to fuss over her, relieved that

someone else was making the choices. The turmoil of the past month had been filled with nothing but impossible decisions. The same uproar didn't show any signs of abating now that her father had passed. Amelia guided her to the chaise longue, sat with her, and gathered her hands so that she could press them between her own.

"I'm sorry," Lena muttered. "I should be…"

"Be what?" Amelia asked her gently.

"Organised, I suppose."

Amelia's soft sigh brushed her cheeks. "You've lost your father, Lena. I would have come sooner had I known how grave the situation was."

Lena's lips flexed. "The doctor assured me that he would recover. I never thought…"

"None of us expected him to pass," Amelia voiced what Lena couldn't. "He's always been strong as an ox. Nothing could faze him. You're allowed to be out of sorts."

"Thomas says–"

"He's here?"

Lena nodded, accepting the handkerchief that Amelia gave her. "Arrived not too long ago."

"Well, that's something, I suppose. He was at the Breckenridge residence?" Lena bobbed her head. Amelia's mouth moved into a disapproving line. "Let's not dwell on that too much. Patrick Breckenridge is good friends with Alistair Cavendish. Now that Thomas is here, he can surely help you with things."

Lena wanted to share the burden, about how she'd

made a grave error in accepting Thomas' proposal, but doubts swirled in her mind.

She needed him.

The mill workers… they needed a capable hand and a strong mind, like her father's, like Thomas', to work under.

She knew nothing about running the mill.

"You'll be fine, Lena. You're made of stern stuff. Your father surrounded himself with capable, knowledgeable men. The mill will survive, and so will you."

Lena wanted to believe those words. Needed to believe them, but the ambiguity of a future with a man who hadn't even expressed his regret at the passing of her father yawned before her. And she felt hopeless, defenceless, to be able to stop any of it, wishing not for the first time that her father was with her to make it all better.

Knowing that she would never get the benefit of his counsel, of his sage advice, ever again saddened her more than the knowledge that she would never again hear him laugh.

CHAPTER 10

"What will happen to me, Libby?"

The question was soft, her voice filled with fear, sounding as if she were far away, not right next to her as they walked along the pathway that ran behind the apprentice's house.

Thea's body shape was already changing. Libby didn't know much about some things, but she'd seen and heard enough during her time at the mill to know that women's bodies changed as the baby grew. The poor girl was often uncomfortable at night, and it was already showing in the shadows under her eyes.

Libby knew that moving often helped during the early stages and that taking in fresh air would help ease her ailments. It was why she'd suggested that they take a walk.

The air was chilly. Mist clung to the trees that climbed up along the riverbank, cloaking the gloomy day in a damp haze. Droplets of water had formed on Thea's hair that poked out from under her cap.

Thea stopped walking, her mouth moving as if at war with the words that tumbled out.

"Am I going to die?"

The immediate denial sprang to her lips, but Libby held it back. Thea was a bright girl, and lying outright to her wasn't going to help the situation. But scaring the poor girl wasn't going to work either. Every mill worker family that Libby approached to take on a newborn baby had declined, whether due to financial needs or the fact that it was another Blackwood baby, she couldn't say. Polly had let out Thea's uniform dress slightly, and Mrs Reid was yet to spot the changes that were happening. They had time.

"Not if I can help it," Libby said, linking her arm through hers. "When the time comes, I'll be with you."

Thea grimaced. "I was there when my cousin was born. I heard my aunt scream down the house. She had a doctor. I won't have anyone!"

Hysteria made her louder. Libby turned to face her, pressing her face between her palms to calm her. "There are women here who've delivered ten babies, Thea. It can't be all that bad else there would never be any babies. Agnes Davidson calls herself a midwife. She'll know what to do to ease your pains. I hear even the Queen had chloroform for the prince."

Thea frowned, then rolled her eyes as she chuckled reluctantly. "Well, if it's good enough for the queen, then."

Libby smiled. "Exactly. I know you're scared. I know that none of this is your fault, but we'll get through this."

Thea's bottom lip disappeared as she nibbled it, and her blue eyes swam with tears. "What if the baby comes when Mr Dower is there? What am I to do then? I haven't seen a baby coming into the world, but I've heard the stories and my aunt– "

"That's enough," Libby interrupted. "Your mind is running away before we've even got there. Come on," she linked arms again and started walking, tugging an unenthusiastic Thea along with her, "let's get back inside. I'm as cold as a frog out here."

"Perhaps I should've just carried on with the douche, but I didn't like it. He told me to, every time. I didn't know what it did, but I didn't like it. It made me sore… down there," she said shyly.

Libby had heard of the practice where women washed themselves after being with a man, using vinegar and ammonia. The fact that the child's father was telling her to do such an act proved that he knew there would be consequences for what he was doing to the girls. Libby was about to press for the name of the father but held back when she heard the chatter coming from the yard ahead of them. They rounded the corner and sure enough, two figures emerged from the gloom.

It was normal for the mill workers to be out on a Sunday afternoon. After all, just like Libby and Thea, taking in fresh air made a change from every other day of the week, but Thea wasn't in the right frame of mind for company. Libby gently guided the young girl towards the door of the Apprentice house when Wilf called out, "Does Mrs Reid know you've escaped?"

With Thea sniffling next to her, Libby pasted on a smile as the two young men closed the gap. "Any day where I don't have to be standing, breathing in cotton dust is a bonus." She deliberately inhaled and made a satisfied sound as she released the breath, drawing a chuckle from Wilf, though he and his companion were watching Thea.

The young underseer looked from Thea to Libby, a line between his brows. "Is everything alright?"

Libby shrugged. "Aye. Just out for some fresh air." Libby focused on Wilf's companion, something familiar about him tugging at her memory. "Nab? Nab Rose?"

The young man had thick black hair that stood out poker straight from his head when he whipped off his cap. Even after he'd settled it, the tufts didn't flatten. "Hello, Libby. It's been a long time."

"What brings you down here?"

Nab looked to Wilf, who rubbed his chin thoughtfully. "We were..."

"I needed to show him –"

They spoke at the same time, and Libby's eyes narrowed. "What's going on?"

Wilf stepped closer to them, lowering his voice. "Can I trust you, Libby?" The girls exchanged a glance before Libby nodded. "Nab here tells me that they've had lots of workers knocking on the foreman's door up at Black Marsh Mill. Hawks workers, all looking for work."

"That doesn't sound good," Libby admitted.

"Why would they do that?" Thea asked.

"People are worried," Nab told her, his dark brown eyes roaming her face. With her watery eyes and her red-tipped nose, Thea was still as pretty as a picture. "With old man Pemberton gone, folks around here are hedging their bets."

"Nab started out working at Hawks Mill, though he left a few years ago now," Libby explained to Thea. "His Ma worked the looms with us. His father was a labourer."

Nab whipped off his cap again, running a hand through his uncontrollable hair. His fingernails were lined with black, and his clean face was made all the more obvious by the dirt that lined his ears. "Ma and Pa wanted more money. I wanted to move up, which you can't do with men like Blackwood and Pemberton in charge," he added bitterly. "I wanted more than a weaver's wage. I'm a stoker now," he said with a touch of pride.

"A what?"

"He keeps the furnaces stoked," Libby explained to Thea, staring at the young man with renewed interest. A stoker had one of the hardest and dirtiest jobs in a mill. It wasn't dirt that she could see ingrained in his skin, but coal dust. "It's an important job, too. Well done, Nab."

His chest puffed out a little. "Dirty work, but someone has to do it."

"Nab thought I should know," Wilf said.

Libby tilted her head. "Does that mean you're leaving too?"

Wilf lifted his shoulder. "I don't know, but if the mill closes, it's good to have options."

The door to the apprentice's house opened, and Polly's head appeared in the gap. "Libby! You're wanted in here."

Libby suppressed a sigh. She looked apologetically at the boys. "No rest for the wicked."

"It was nice meeting you," Nab said to Thea, interrupting them as they turned.

Thea smiled briefly. "You, too."

The young girl seemed oblivious to Nab's discreet admiration, but Libby quickly forgot about the boys and the impending changes as she guided Thea towards the door that stood open.

She could already hear the bickering voices and hurried to deal with it before Mrs Reid came in and they all had a good hiding for bothering the older woman on a Sunday.

CHAPTER 11

he funeral procession filled the lane like a seam of coal, stretching from the mill to the small church in the village of Birchleigh.

As she followed her father's coffin out of the church, she couldn't help but notice the empty pews towards the rear, and the mourners who had gathered to bid farewell to Edwin Pemberton were predominantly local, their modest attire setting them apart as they filed out into the foggy February morning. Her father had been a prominent and influential figure in the business world. Where were those who had once sought his counsel and guidance?

Bitter disappointment filled her, as she stated as much to John Sparrow.

"It's the weather, miss," he told her. His demeanour remained solemn, but she noticed his gaze shifting away as if seeking an avenue of escape. She watched her mill manager scurry away, leaving her little opportunity to ponder his feeble excuse further as she was urged into position by the vicar.

She was then swept up in her sense of duty as the world looked on. Pallbearers carried the casket along the gravel path towards the gaping hole in the ground.

Lena's breath shuddered as reality crashed in.

Thomas emerged from the gathering of mourners for the interment, but he maintained a certain distance. In this moment, when she needed him more than ever, he chose to be detached from her. With her jaw clenched, she observed the coffin's descent into the ground, an overwhelming sadness stealing her breath. When the sod fell onto the lid with a dull, resolute finality, Lena closed her eyes.

She felt utterly alone.

She stood in silent fortitude long after the others had dispersed; the mill workers returning to their duties, the villagers to their homes. Lena allowed her tears to flow freely. Amelia, eventually, slipped her arm through Lena's and gently guided her away from the cemetery and towards the awaiting carriage.

Gwen was standing outside the cab, and she laid a blanket over Lena's knees as soon as she was seated. Amelia sat next to Lena, her gloved hands patting her in a matronly fashion.

"W-where's Thomas?" Lena stammered, teeth chattering.

"I believe he's back at the house, miss," Gwen tucked the blanket around her and stood back, her hand on the edge of the door. "I shall meet you back there," she moved to close the door, but Lena stretched out a hand.

"You can come with me, Gwen."

The maid's brows moved in surprise. "In the carriage, miss? With you?"

"It's freezing out here, and you've been standing there waiting for me for goodness knows how long. And we're going to the same place."

The maid's mouth flapped as if to question the decision.

"Your father would never…" Amelia began, her tone uncertain.

Lena quite frankly didn't care what Amelia or anyone else thought of such transgression on the correct order of staff travelling with the employers. She gesticulated impatiently at Gwen. "Please, inside, now. I need to get back."

Lena noticed the peculiar expression the coachman directed at Gwen, but he'd closed the door before she recognised it for what it was: judgement.

In the past few days, as visitors came to offer their condolences for her father, it seemed as though these kinds of glances were all around her. They were waiting to see what Thomas would do with her father's business. Her father's dire warnings echoed in her mind once more.

She needed Thomas' acumen and connections to steer the mill out of this shark-infested waters of the business world.

Gwen settled on the bench opposite Lena.

She waited until the carriage was moving before

she asked, "Mr Cavendish is back at Hawks Manor?"

"Yes, miss," Gwen replied hesitantly.

Lena tucked her chin to her chest to hide her disappointment. Perhaps she was a fool for secretly hoping that she could rely on him in her hour of need. For wanting him to become the man she'd believed him to be when he was wooing her for marriage.

Amelia was arranging the layers of her black outfit over her legs. "I believe his father had summoned him back there," she murmured kindly. "The two of them seemed out of sorts. If I were to guess, I would say that Alistair was none-too-pleased about something."

"They were arguing?" Lena asked Gwen once more and the maid nodded slightly.

Her father-in-law could be fearsome when he chose and, in her fragile state, she wasn't sure that she could face him.

Too often, Thomas had grumbled to her about the control his father exerted over his life, but he would still toe the line for the older, more experienced banker.

Lena's gaze drifted through the window of the carriage, to the world shrouded in rain clouds and mists, where trees and houses loomed like spectres in the brume.

She'd face Alistair and his son.

She'd face the criticism and condemnation of those who would never approve of a woman inheriting, of allowing a maid to sit inside the carriage.

However, she couldn't stem the despair that closed in on her at the thought of facing it all alone.

CHAPTER 12

*S*he'd allowed Gwen to fuss over her, removing her damp clothing and tweaking her hair, but she wasn't sure she'd ever be warm again. The damp seemed to have sunk into her bones, pervading her body with endless shivers.

As she descended the staircase and looked down upon the sea of mourners, the morbid black that filled the room made her feel both breathless and boneless. The conversations stilled amongst the well-wishers, and Lena saw their fixed looks of pity as she rounded the bottom of the staircase.

It was Amelia who broke away from the group, the only genuine smile among them. "You look perished, my dear," she murmured, low enough for only Lena to hear. "Let's get you a drink and warm you from the inside out."

Lena allowed herself to be guided through the group, and with Amelia's assistance, she began to make the rounds, thanking people for coming to pay their respects. From the austere businessmen to the genteel locals, Lena listened to the banal stories about a man she thought she knew.

But each story had a continuous theme: her father was all about the business, through and through.

The man who would roast chestnuts over the fire and belly laugh over a word she'd pronounced wrong was known only to her, and she kept that little kernel of information close to her chest.

"Miss Pemberton," a subdued voice spoke behind her.

She turned to look up into the familiar face of her father's solicitor. Robert Clark was a bookish scholar who usually favoured brown tweed, though today he'd worn a darker suit. His hair was combed neatly into a middle parting. He'd arrived late last night, though Lena had been too exhausted by organising and dealing with people arriving to pay him much attention.

"Good afternoon, Mr Clark," she said.

"I'm very sorry for your loss," he said solemnly. His visits had always been concise, his language brief. Even now, his eyes were glancing around the room, as though looking for an exit. "Your father will be greatly missed, I'm sure."

"Thank you, Mr Clark, that means a great deal. And thank you for all that you did for my father over the years. I know that you were one of his most trusted advisors."

He acknowledged the comment with a head dip. "I was looking for Mr Cavendish."

Lena swallowed, trying to engage her spluttering mind. She hadn't seen Thomas since the graveside. "He's here somewhere."

"Um," Amelia interrupted. "He... he left, Lena."

Lena's lips parted. "I'm sorry?"

Amelia looked embarrassed at having to be the one to deliver the news. "About half an hour ago. He and Alistair had words, but they left together."

Lena fought for composure. "When is he coming back?"

Amelia could only shake her head. Lena looked around the room; the measured looks, the lingering glances.

Judgement.

"No matter," the solicitor's expression remained passive. "This concerns you, anyway."

Lena cast a pointed look around them, before meeting his bespectacled face. "I'm afraid now is not a good time, sir."

Mr Clark stepped forward, his voice low and urgent. "I must return to London immediately Miss Pemberton, and this matter is an urgent one that cannot possibly wait."

Lena's heart tripped over itself, and she gave a little nod. "Let's speak in the library."

Amelia began to follow but Mr Clark lifted a hand and sent an apologetic smile. "I'm afraid this matter is confidential. I must speak with Miss Pemberton alone."

A trickle of trepidation dripped down Lena's back, and she was aware of the gazes that followed them as they made their way through the crowd and into the library.

Mr Clark closed the door behind him, his hand resting on the wooden panel for a moment. "I'm sorry for taking you away from your guests on such a sad day, but this can't wait. Why don't you take a seat?"

Unfiltered alarm surged through her and she had to lock her knees to ensure that her trembling legs kept her upright. "You're frightening me, Mr Clark."

"I had rather hoped that Mr Cavendish would be here with us, if only to see you through what I have to tell you...perhaps even to explain some of the finer points that you might not understand... but considering the circumstances..."

Lena's patience snapped. "Please, Mr Clark, whatever it is, just get it over with."

She saw the crease of amusement briefly in his cheek.

"Perhaps all is not yet lost, Miss Pemberton. You sound exactly like your father." His hand fell away from the door, and he linked his fingers in front of him, a reluctant sigh filling the space. "For the past year or so, the mill has been floundering."

Lena waited a moment, brows knitted. "What do you mean, 'floundering'?"

"I'm not sure if you remember the changes in the law, the so-called Ten Hour Bill?"

She remembered the screaming headlines in the newspapers, the intense arguments that her father conducted in this very room, the protests in the cities where workers demanded fair pay for fewer hours.

She nodded, and he continued. "The changes have impacted many industries that rely on women and children, none more so than the cotton mills. Many of the people employed here at Hawks Mill are skilled workers; many of them are children.

"Owners use them because they're cheaper, and there is a never-ending supply of orphans and widows looking for an honest day's work."

Carefully, Lena folded her arms. "You sound like a chartist, Mr Clark."

His stare was bleak. "The changes in the law were meant to make things better for workers but, as some of the more astute mill owners predicted, there were some who found loopholes."

She nodded, rubbing her arms to ward off the chill despite a fire roaring in the hearth. "I remember. My father was vocal about the ambiguity of the proposed legislation. He pointed out several loopholes, as I remember.

"One of them was that mill owners would simply split the shifts to maintain production levels. My father was worried that he would have to cut wages to cover the loss in productivity, which would cause even further hardship for his workers. He said to me that millwork was better than starving to death more than once."

Lena recalled the dire warnings of the men who'd visited with her father, the heated discussions around the dinner table.

The mill's working day had been cut short by the government, meaning that women and children over the age of thirteen weren't permitted to work more than ten hours a day. Further amendments had curtailed the times that they could start working, and any Saturday work. Her father had predicted that workers would simply find a work-around, perhaps by working at two different mills, and that mill owners would be powerless to stop this from happening.

She remembered her father's anger at the textile being the only industry adversely affected by this because it was the only one with industry-assigned inspectors to monitor that the rules were being adhered to. Mining, iron and steel, glass, paper making, blast furnaces... those industries escaped policing, much to Edwin Pemberton's eternal disgust.

"I thought that the inspectors appointed by the government were meant to stop such occurrences?"

Robert Clark's thin brow bobbed. "Less than a half dozen inspectors charged with keeping an eye on every single mill in England? A seemingly insurmountable task, I'm sure you'd agree," he said dryly. "And yet..."

"Yet?" She prompted him when he went quiet.

He paused, and the air in the library seemed to still, his eyes betraying the burden of the words he was yet to speak. Lena found herself holding her breath, her hands clenched in the folds of her mourning dress.

He cleared his throat, the sound cutting sharply through the stillness of the library. "Mr Pemberton agreed to the split shift in principle but had instructed that they were to run as they always had. He ignored the new laws, believing that the inspectors wouldn't come this far out into the countryside. Your father also assured the inspectorate that no one started work at Hawks Mill before the stroke of six o'clock in the morning.

"Alas, it appears one of the mill hands contradicted this claim. The officials, acting on a tip, were outside one crisp morning, watching as the lights within flickered to life at the ungodly hour of five. They walked in to find women and children at work, leaving your father without a defence for breaking the law."

A silence hung between them, punctuated only by the ticking of the grandfather clock in the corner. "Hawk's Mill was fined for this transgression."

"On top of that," he continued with a grimace, each word a hammer to her heart, "the mill was also fined for failing to report an accident in the timely manner required by law."

"What accident?" she said with a slight shake of her head.

He blinked at her.

"What was the cost of the fine, Mr Clark?"

"Significant. The judge wanted to send a message to the textile industry that the new bill was not to be ignored. In ordinary circumstances though, the fines were not enough to cause pecuniary damages."

"I don't understand, sir. If the fines were not that much, why do you speak with such alarming perilousness?"

He shifted slightly, his gaze never leaving her face. "Black Marsh Mill, just up the road, has embraced the winds of change as your father resisted them. The other mill offers higher wages and better working conditions, in line with the labour laws. Consequently, Hawks Mill has been bleeding workers to them. This... exodus... has grossly impacted profits.

"Edwin was reluctant to modernise. He was convinced that continuing with the methods used in *his* father's time was best – after all, it was how the empire had been built in the first place. It isn't polite to speak ill of the dead when they're not here to defend themselves but," a quick smile curved the solicitor's lips. "He lacked your mother's vision for business."

Lena's heart thrummed as her eyes went wide. "You... you knew my mother?"

"Albeit, briefly, yes," he replied. "Your father was never the same after her death, most certainly in business."

Lena's mind raced.

Her father's legacy, once a beacon of industrious pride, was crumbling under her feet.

Fines? Accidents?

She pressed her fingertips to her temples to try and slow her thoughts down as the stark reality of the situation unfurled like a dark tapestry. The losses, the fines, the defecting of the workers—a litany of woes that painted a bleak portrait of the mill's future.

"You're aware of how the river here fluctuates?"

She nodded. The whims of the river had always

been a thorn in her father's side. "Of course. Production in the winter would fall sharply when the river levels dropped too low to power the wheel. But that was before the steam engine was installed to power the looms, as a safeguarding measure for those times when nature stood against industry."

The solicitor sighed. "The steam engine — coaxed by your dear mother's influence — was your father's only reluctant concession to modernity. I'm told it falters more with each passing day."

"Then repair it?"

"It is worn out, Miss Pemberton and the mill's coffers are too barren to entertain the thought of a new one."

Lena's mouth closed as the solicitor predicted her next suggestion.

He swallowed hard, the spectacles on his nose catching the light as he looked down, his next words seeming to pain him. "Your father, in his desperate attempts to keep Hawk's Mill afloat, leveraged all he owned against the business. Including the manor house. The mortgage is... suffocating."

The solicitor's eyes met hers, and in them, she read the unwelcome end of the story. "As it stands, you cannot hope to compete with the other mills that have adapted to the cheaper, more cost-effective ways of the age." A heavy stillness fell like a veil over the remnants of her childhood certainties. "There's no easy way to say this," he whispered, almost afraid. "At this rate, the mill—and with it, everything attached to the Pemberton name—will cease to exist within months."

The room spun, and Lena's legs betrayed her, folding beneath her as she collapsed into the chair. The workers, the lifeblood of Hawks Mill, faced a future devoid of security—starving, homeless, desperate. And all of it was now her responsibility. The enormity of her duty to them all threatened to crush her.

"There's nothing left?"

"I'm afraid you find yourself in the direst of straits, Miss Pemberton," he murmured, the finality in his voice like a coffin nail. "It would take a miracle to salvage it."

Or the finances of a bank, her mind whispered, a bitter revelation dawning on her. She understood now, the almost visceral reaction her father had shown over her wish to end her engagement to Thomas Cavendish.

The Cavendish fortune could very well be the salvation Hawk's Mill so desperately needed.

Nausea roiled in her stomach as she grasped the entirety of her plight. The dream of spending her life with a kind man, someone she chose, who loved and respected her withered.

She'd imagined – hoped – that now, without her father's insistence on the union, she would be able to break away from Thomas. That plan gave way to a bitter realisation: the future of Hawks Mill hinged upon her marriage to a man that she despised.

CHAPTER 13

*L*ena had been awake since before the echoing footsteps clopped along the lane at first light for the start of the mill's workday.

Mr Radford, her father's accountant, had confirmed the starkness painted by Mr Clark at her father's funeral when he'd shown her the state of the accounts. Her father had indeed sunk everything into the mill, despite his advisors wanting him to invest in more modern equipment. Now, his investors were beginning to realise the extent of his mismanagement of their funds and were furious.

In the days following the funeral, Lena had tried to make peace with the knowledge that she was going to have to marry Thomas Cavendish out of sinister necessity.

In the low dawn light, as she'd watched the bowed heads bob along the narrow lane and into the cavernous mill, it had occurred to her that she'd not paid much attention to the machinations of the mill yet ever since her father's funeral, and her conversation with Mr Clark, she'd become obsessed with it.

Those people were relying on her to do the right thing, to forgo happiness for the good of the mill.

They had a life here. A community.

They needed a job.

They needed her.

She'd tried to make peace with the fact that Thomas would be a philanderer. Letters had been arriving telling her of the many dalliances he'd shared with Elizabeth Breckenridge. She replied dutifully to each one, explaining away such behaviour by explaining the family friendship...but she knew the truth.

That he wasn't being subtle about his relationship with her was humiliating enough – and she needed to play along for the sake of those people making their way into the mill.

She'd waited patiently for his reply to her letter requesting that he return to Hawks Manor so that they could finalise the details of the wedding.

In the interim, she'd spoken with the house staff to apprise them of the fact that Thomas had wanted to move the wedding date up and that they would be having a new master sooner.

She'd taken the time with Cook to familiarise herself with the house accounts, dismayed to find that there were small debts that had accrued with many local suppliers – further evidence that her father had continued to display wealth far beyond affordability. Cook had smiled blandly when Lena had tried to reassure her that the funds were coming, that she could settle the accounts with the grumbling business owners soon enough, and that she wasn't to worry.

That morning, she'd taken the time with her appearance, choosing her favourite purple dress, and letting Gwen style her hair into a neat chignon at the back of her head, with neat curls that framed her face becomingly. She had left her breakfast tray, unable to face the thought of food as her stomach churned nervously.

Her heart was thrumming with anticipation as she spotted the carriage racing up the lane towards the mill, the black body gleaming in the watery sunlight. She shook out her skirts and pasted a bright smile on her face as Mr Brown opened the door for Thomas.

"Good morning, Mr Cavendish, sir," Mr Brown intoned dutifully as Thomas handed off his overcoat to James.

Thomas only nodded, his gaze sweeping over Lena's attire with a remoteness that made her feel ill. Uncertainty prickled at her skin, but she upped the wattage of her smile.

"Hello, Thomas, how was your journey?"

"Let's talk in the library," he muttered, striding past them all.

Lena swallowed, her breath shaky as she said, "Gwen, could you please fetch Mr Cavendish a tray of tea?"

"Don't bother," Thomas tossed out over his shoulder as he reached the library doorway, "I'm not staying."

Dread pooled like ice in her belly.

This wasn't how she'd anticipated the day going. In her mind, he would claim his stake in the house in his usual merciless manner. She'd wondered if he'd even try and hurry her to the marital bed sooner, but this detachment was most perturbing. She drifted into the library, fists balled, grinding to a halt when she came face to face with his cold fury.

He stood with his hands on his hips. "Shut the door," he said with a head jerk.

Obediently, she did, turning back to the room. She'd expected territorial and forceful, but this remote anger unnerved her even more. "What's the matter?"

"Why didn't you tell me?" he ground out.

"Tell you what?"

"That there was no money? You led me to believe that this was a viable business, that being saddled with the likes of you was worth it because of what you came with!"

Her mouth fell open. Her tongue flicked out as words failed her. She shook her head.

"I wanted to do this by letter, not waste my time coming here in person," he sneered. "My father told me everything! I had to go and look at the accounts for myself. Everything is mortgaged, Lena. Everything!" he roared.

"I-I didn't... I was just as in the dark as you, I swear, Thomas," Her voice cracked with emotion. "I had no idea."

"You're just as twisted as he was," he sneered and

flicked a hand over her attire. "This is for me, yes? Because you need my father's money – *my money* – to pull this behemoth out of danger. He won't do it, and neither will I. You were going to wait until after we were married before you revealed the truth, yes?"

"Well, I," she began but the deep red that travelled over her face told a different story. Hysteria clawed through her shame. *All those people...* She owed it to them to try.

"Please, Thomas...you said yourself that I know nothing about business. Surely, there must be a way. Mr Clark said that, with conservative management, there's enough to last until the year's end. The textile industry is still one of the biggest industries in the world. Black Marsh mill is just up the road – they're growing at a steady rate," She stepped forward, flooded with the information she'd gleaned from her father's team. "Under better administration, with the right kind of investment and modernising, we could..."

"There's no 'we' in any of this," his hand came up. He whirled away from her, then walked back, standing closer to her. "I never wanted you. This was what my father chose because *your* father made it look as if the business was thriving – just like every other cotton mill in the North – when in reality he was misleading us all, steering us down the same path as his investors. It will go to auction, Lena. The monies made will at least pay off what's owed to my father's bank."

"It can be saved, Thomas–"

"Your father's arrogance did this. He thought he knew better."

"You said yourself, I know nothing about business but there has to be a way," she pleaded.

He stilled and her heart slammed against her ribcage as the air around them charged. "Are you offering yourself to me like that?" His mouth moved into a reptilian smile. She swallowed and started to shake her head, but he closed the gap between them. Just like Christmas Eve, his hands were rough and painful as he grabbed at her. She twisted out of his grip and shoved him back with all her might.

"No!" She spat. "No, you cannot do this to me anymore, Thomas."

"Come on, now," he advanced, eyes alight with vicious spite. "The way you're going, you'll soon be at the docks with the rest of the fallen women, earning money on your back for this kind of service."

He grabbed for her again, twisting his hand painfully into her hair and she yelped in pain.

"Mr Cavendish!" The authoritative tone cut through their scuffling and Lena was pushed to the floor as Thomas rounded on the furious butler.

James stood next to him, fire poker in hand. Gwen brought up the rear with Thomas' belongings, her fearful eyes on Lena.

"Have you *quite* forgotten yourself, sir?" The reprimand was sharp, and a high colour fused Thomas's face.

He dragged the back of his hand across his mouth, tugged at the bottom of his jacket and smoothed down his blond hair, his angry eyes moving about the room slowly.

"It's fine, she'll be handing it out for a shilling by the end of the year. And you'll all be out of work and begging on the streets."

He snatched up his items and stalked out of the house.

The room, once a sanctuary for her, now felt like a tomb. She could feel the shock of Thomas' words still reverberating around the room as her staff – who'd stood by her for these past months – absorbed the implications.

Just the sound of her shaky breath punctured the heavy silence. Shame burned her cheeks and hot tears silently tracked down her face. Her eyes, brimming with anguish, finally faced the people who had been her strength through turmoil. They knew that she had failed them, that her father's legacy was no more, and that they now all faced the same uncertain and daunting future as she did.

CHAPTER 14

"*A*llow me, miss," Mr Brown hurried forward, gently assisting her up.

With the grace of a swan yet the fragility of porcelain, she lowered herself into a chair, the velvet cushion accepting her trembling form. Her fingers pressed against her bruised mouth—a physical indication of the harshness of Thomas's parting.

"Are you hurt?"

Words failed her, stuck in the dry wasteland of her throat. She shook her head helplessly, shoulders slumping, tears dripping into her lap. The first test of taking action to maintain the Pemberton business washed away in a tide of humiliation and shattered hope.

The bitter truth gnawed at her insides; Alistair Cavendish must have unearthed the precarious state of Pemberton's affairs as soon as Edwin was removed from the picture. It must have been why they quarrelled, why Thomas had abandoned her on the day of the funeral. Knowing Thomas as she did, he would want to see proof.

Not even the notion of being released from the claws of Thomas and his family could bring her solace now.

"Gwen, please fetch Miss Pemberton some tea," Mr Brown said briskly. "James, see to it that Mr Cavendish is off Pemberton property, hmm?"

"Right away, Mr Brown." Dutifully, they set about their tasks, leaving Lena to wonder how they could continue with their roles even as their world teetered on the brink of collapse.

"I've failed everyone," Lena confessed roughly. "You, Gwen... my father..."

The butler was adding a log to the fire. He turned to face her, his expression stoic, his loyalty unwavering. "I don't believe you ever could, Miss Lena," he said softly.

"I have, don't you see?" Lena said thickly. "I needed Thomas' money to save the house and the mill. Thomas said I would be down at the docks before too long, selling myself to pay for lodgings, yet I was prepared to offer myself to him here, in exchange for his money and his business acumen. I'm no better than a prostitute now, am I? Except I am in better surroundings!" Her laugh was cold and harsh as she gestured to the room at hand. "I couldn't even do that right. Now, everyone will suffer – staff, mill workers, businesses waiting for bills to be paid – everyone, because of my failure."

Gwen carried in the tray and dealt with filling a

cup, whispering about extra sugar for the shock before she left as quietly as she'd arrived. Lena picked up the cup, setting it down again when it rattled in its saucer. She curled her unsteady hands into a fist, a storm of emotions boiling inside.

"Everything must go to auction to settle the debts," Lena murmured, her gaze moving about the room before settling on the fire's flickering dance. "I'm not sure that there will be enough for me to live on. I shall have to find a job, though I don't know what. I have no skills to claim as my own, save how to dance at a ball. Perhaps I'll even end up in debtor's prison."

"Miss Pemberton, may I offer the counsel of a foolish old man?"

She looked at him, a faint semblance of a smile gracing her lips. "I think I would welcome it right now, Mr Brown."

"May I?" He gestured to the sofa opposite her, and she nodded, watching as he settled himself, the leather creaking under his careful weight. His hands came together, fingers interlaced.

"A man in my position – trusted, one might say... well, it means that I was privy to many conversations around this table, Miss Lena. Your father knew this was coming. The staff... they saw things about the house. We all hoped that he would..." The butler sighed.

"It pains me to tell you but... it could have been prevented." At her sharp intake of breath, he hastened to add, "I don't mean to speak out of turn or be disrespectful."

"I'm not offended," she replied, her voice steadier now. "I'm intrigued. How could it have been prevented?"

In the hall beyond the door, the great hall clock struck the hour. Mr Brown cleared his throat.

"I've worked for the Pemberton family for many years. I came to the post from your mother's household – did you know that?"

She shook her head and he continued, "I was a footman in your grandfather's house. Your mother... she could light up a room, even a cave, I'd say. She was always kind to me. I remember when she met your father. Your grandfather wasn't keen on the match, but your mother knew her mind, and your grandfather couldn't say no to the apple of his eye. Hawks Mill passed along to your father not long after your grandfather passed away. The marriage was arranged and when your mother was setting up the house, she offered me the post. Your grandfather's butler was apoplectic. I was a footman; what did I know about being a butler?"

"Papa rarely spoke of her," she murmured huskily, tea forgotten.

"He loved her, very much," he replied. "She made him happy."

She took that kernel of knowledge and tucked it away deep inside. The untrustworthy cad that people believed her father to be had known love, and that eased her heartache.

"Your mother and I worked to build up the manor house together. Your father hired the best in the textile industry. Money talks and he could charm the birds out of the trees when he so chose." Lena was struck by the depth of emotion that laced his words, the evident respect and fondness he held for her late father. "I'd hazard a guess that your mother influenced his choices over the men he hired.

"Your mother inherited your grandfather's ability for business. Whilst she wasn't ever allowed to speak out around the dinner table, she was behind many of the shrewder decisions that helped lay the foundations for the mill's success.

"When she passed…" Mr Brown paused and Lena was struck by the emotional impact that her mother's death seemed to have had on him, too. "Your father was never the same. He didn't have your mother to temper his rash decisions or push him into listening to the sound advice of his staff.

"I'd wager good money that many of those men chose to stay at Hawks Mill out of loyalty to her, not to him. Those men… they tried to persuade your father to replace the looms, to make them more efficient, but he always claimed the cost was too prohibitive."

The image of her father, a man of stubborn pride and fierce determination, was etched into her mind.

"The steam engine needed replacing years ago to counteract the fickle river flow, but he ignored that. One by one, the workers left. Some were fired. He pushed the workers beyond the laws, and, well, he lost the most experienced ones. Instead, the mill has been left with the young and the desperate."

"Why are you telling me all this now?"

Mr Brown met her gaze, eyes glistening. "Because, Miss Lena, you are a Pemberton. Your mother's intelligence and your father's charm... you have these traits and more. There is still a chance to save the mill."

She shook her head and sighed wearily. "It's a nice dream but I don't know the first thing about running a mill, let alone the textile business. I think that the prudent thing to do would be to cut my losses now. Sell everything off and pray that there's enough left over that I can live off of."

"Give up?"

She looked at him sharply, pride needling at her. The thought of abandoning something that had once been brandished locally as a beacon of progress hurt. But wasn't it pride that had led her father to the point of ruin?

"I can't run a business if I don't know how. I can't, in all good conscience, rely on pride and make more of a mess than I'm already in."

"You might not know how, but the knowledge to save us still resides within the walls of that mill," he pointed through the window. She followed the direction to the stone buildings beyond. "There are men in there who can advise you. The ones who hold the wisdom that your father shunned? Some of them still work here."

Lena felt something stir within her, a flicker of something she dared not name just yet. Still, the voice of reason doused it. "I can't..."

"Only because you've never been allowed, Miss Lena. I've heard the times you've been dismissed, not just by your father or that wretched Cavendish, but others, too. You know more than you think you do," he nodded. "There is hope. I believe it. So does everyone else downstairs."

Doubts swirled. Her gaze slid once more to the mill.

"You won't know if you don't try," he prompted. "That's what your mother once said to me before I came here. She believed in me then. Now I'm lending you a little of my self-belief. Try, Miss Pemberton. That's all any of us can ask of you." Mr Brown's gaze locked with hers, steady and resolute. With a determination that seemed to straighten his old frame, the butler pushed to his feet. "Your father kept his ledgers in his desk. I'm not one for figures though I know my way around a ledger book should you require any assistance. Not that you will, once you get the hang of it, I'm sure."

Lena blinked owlishly between her butler and the desk, her mind stuttering.

"Now, I shall get back to my duties. I'll send in Gwen for tea. Shall I tell Cook you want to eat supper in here?"

"I-I think that would be, uh, be fine, Mr Brown," she said, her voice a mix of trepidation and a burgeoning strength she hadn't known lingered in her spirit.

Mr Brown paused by the door and nodded encouragingly. "We're not done yet, Miss Lena. If there's hope, then the fight for Pemberton Mill is far from over."

In that moment, the butler stood not as a servant, but as a general rallying his troops, and Lena, the unwilling heiress, felt the mantle of leadership within.

CHAPTER 15

"Come again, lass?"

It had been years since Lena had stepped foot inside the mill. The walls and floors vibrated with the thunderous machinery and the mill manager had to raise his voice over the racket.

He leaned forward, forearms resting on the cluttered desk. "You want me to what?"

Lena firmed her lips, annoyed by the gleam of mirth in his bloodshot eyes. "Mr Sparrow, I'm not sure what it is about me that you find amusing."

His hands came up and he surged to his feet. "Where is Mr Cavendish?" he asked, peevishly.

"Mr Cavendish will not be joining me here," she was pleased that her voice didn't betray the quaking in her body. "Not today. Not ever. Now, sir, if you'd care to give me a tour of the mill…"

The office door was knocked and opened in quick succession, and the balding pate of Bert Blackwood appeared around the edge. He drew up short, his piggy eyes sending a questioning look at John Sparrow.

"Miss Pemberton," he nodded. "Good morning."

"Hello, Mr Blackwood," she murmured, hoping to find an ally within him but his perpetual look of distaste didn't alter as he closed the door and sat in the chair next to hers.

Ever since Mr Brown had inspired her to look within herself, she'd been reading as much information contained within her father's office as she could to try and familiarise herself with the business. But the butler was right – she had a wealth of experience right here in this room.

Where else better to look to learn all that she needed to know? And, as much as she didn't care for the foreman of the mill, right now, she needed his expertise and guidance.

"Thank you for joining us this morning."

He swallowed nervously, unsmiling, as he looked at his manager. "What's this about?"

"Miss Pemberton wishes for a tour of the mill," John Sparrow announced to the foreman.

Blackwood's eyes settled on hers. Lena returned his stare with a cool look. "A tour?"

"That's right," she replied. "I wish to learn all I can from you both, about the running of the business."

"I, uh, this is most unusual, Miss Pemberton," he muttered. "Will Mr Cav–"

"No," Lena interrupted him impatiently. "Thomas is not joining us. I am the mill's owner, Mr Blackwood. It is up to me to understand how it all works."

Both men exchanged a look and Lena's patience snapped. "What seems to be the problem?"

The foreman shifted in his seat. "It's just... the processes are complex, and... you're a woman..."

Lena's brows climbed her forehead, stunned into silence.

"Your father wouldn't want us to burden you or put you in danger," Mr Sparrow scrambled for an explanation.

Lena surged to her feet, incensed that she was being stone-walled by them simply because of her gender. What stung more was the knowledge that Thomas had predicted this outcome. Being a woman had her at a disadvantage. She tried to drag up some of that resolve from the other day when she'd been sat with Mr Brown.

"Well, gentleman, my father isn't here. The workforce in this mill is predominantly female. If they can handle it, why can't I?"

"Your father wouldn't like it," the mill manager tried again, and Lena rounded on him.

"I'm not my father, Mr Sparrow," she retorted, eyes flashing, "Like it or not, you have a new owner. It has fallen upon my shoulders to try and steer the mill through these changeable waters. If I am to do that successfully, I need to have at least a working understanding of how this place works."

Mr Sparrow stood, too, his expression serious. "They're true, then? The rumours? The mill is in financial straits?"

Lena didn't want to stir the pot. Instinctively, she

wanted to defend her father's memory and protect the reputation of the Pemberton name, but she also needed them to understand the severity of the situation. No doubt the industry would be rife with gossip, especially since Thomas had been quite vocal in their social circles already about their relationship ending so abruptly and the reasons behind it.

Trying to counter such tales with false promises would undeniably insult their intelligence.

She let out a breath, meeting their concern with what she prayed was a reassuring look. "I want to do right by the people who have kept a roof over my head for all these years, Mr Sparrow. Yes, the mill has some issues. But I am certain, with the right management and equipment that we can collectively steer the mill out of danger.

But I cannot do this alone, sir."

CHAPTER 16

*C*otton dust hung suspended in the air, dancing in the feeble beams of light that struggled through the grimy windows. Amidst the relentless clatter of machinery, Libby toiled alongside her fellow workers in the mule room. With meticulous precision, her movements followed the mechanical rhythm of the looms, adjusting tension and closely monitoring the delicate dance of warp and weft.

The rhythmic cacophony of the machines led her into a trance-like state as she focused on her work. However, her concentration was shattered when a flurry of movement caught her attention from the corner of her eye. There, she spotted one of the engine room lads, easily distinguishable by the sooty-stained clothing, engaged in an animated conversation with Wilf. A sense of unease trickled through Libby as she watched the exchange. She continued tending to the threads, her watchful gaze fixed on the argument, then on her underseer as he approached her mule.

"What's wrong?" She raised her voice to be heard over the din of the machines.

Wilf leaned closer to her. "Lena Pemberton is Sparrow's office. Reggie tells me she's coming to inspect the mill."

Libby's brow creased in surprise. She couldn't recall a single instance when the younger Pemberton had set foot in the mill. The novelty of the situation briefly amused her, though it didn't explain Wilf's obvious agitation until he clarified, "I can't find Mr Dower."

Turning her attention back to the loom, Libby checked her threads and waited for Pip to emerge from underneath it. "So?"

Wilf continued, "The floor needs proper supervision. How will it look if it's not being overseen? Mr Blackwood won't like it!"

"You're here, Wilf, and that should be supervision enough," Libby replied, even as her eyes travelled along the length of loomers, checking that everyone was where they should be as she said, "Besides, she needs to know that the men she's been paying to do their jobs have really been sitting on their laurels since old man Pemberton took to his sickbed."

She turned on a heel to check the room once more as she realised that Daisy wasn't on the line. That trickle of unease bloomed to panic within.

"Can you see Daisy in here?" She rose up on tiptoes. "Wilf, where is she?"

"Not in here," he muttered angrily, already making his way towards the privy in the corner.

"Polly!" Libby signalled to the other girl to man the looms before hastily following him, heart pounding with a mixture of determination and dread. She already had one pregnant girl – was Mr Dower responsible for Thea instead of Blackwood?

She couldn't help but wonder what the new owner of Pemberton Mill would think about these despicable acts of abuse of trust by the men who were paid to do their jobs.

Would she even care?

CHAPTER 17

The mill manager's office was a small room attached to the side of the mill, added almost as an afterthought. Behind it lay sheds and the warehouse that stored the rolls of finished products.

John Sparrow led the way from his cluttered office, with Mr Blackwood huffing behind her. Neither man was happy about her intrusion. She kept her face impassive, reminding herself that this was for their benefit, too.

The long red edifice of Hawks Mill stood proudly, its single chimney belching plumes of white steam into the already grey sky. She could already hear the thunder of machinery and feel it reverberating through her feet as they approached a narrow, blackened door.

"I'll start at the beginning," John Sparrow said over his shoulder. He paused at the door, eyeing Lena dubiously as if giving her the chance to change her mind.

She squared her shoulders and gave him a nod.

"This is the engine room," he explained.

The cacophony of mechanisation was near deafening as soon as he opened the door. The cavernous expanse of the room unfolded before her, the relentless thud vibrating through her bones. The great iron wheel rolled endlessly with a humming groan as it turned, driving the main shaft that erupted from the floor on one side. Water cascaded from the massive buckets within the wheel, its deluge contributing to the cacophony.

The air was humid and smoky, tinged with the odour of oil and hot metal from the furnace.

John Sparrow's mouth moved, but Lena had to shake her head and point to her ears; she couldn't hear a word he was saying. He sent her a look of annoyance and led the way through another door at the end that opened to a narrow staircase. "I was saying that since our engineer left for Black Marsh Mill, our mechanic has kept the machines turning for now."

Lena stared at him. "We have no engineer?"

The news didn't bode well for her success at the mill. The engineer was one of the highest-paid workers at the mill and for good reason. He was responsible for keeping all the machinery running smoothly, swiftly identifying, and repairing any breakdowns.

"The mechanic, Frank Simmons, knows what he's doing. Of course, he's trying to squeeze us for higher pay, or he'll walk, but that's a problem for another day," John Sparrow said dismissively.

Lena tried to dwell on his glib attitude, but he was already climbing the staircase to the next floor, and she was acutely aware of the repugnant foreman standing right behind her.

"We have boys who give the boiler the attention it needs, topping up the oil pots and such, and labourers that lend a hand when needed. There is a fireman to keep the burners going in the boiler, to ensure that the head of steam is sufficient to keep the engine turning under the load from the machinery," he continued. "A mill this size needs an engineer, but we can make do for now."

"I see," Lena murmured, as the enormity of the problems began to make her doubt herself.

Lena followed him through another door as he continued, "Cotton arrives in bales," he gestured toward the piles of hessian sacks neatly piled up against the wall. "It's collected from the docks in Liverpool, stuck on a barge, then put on a cart and travels by road right here to the mill.

"The first job is to clean the cotton. We have to get rid of any seeds, dirt, twigs, and the like. It gets fed into this machine here, the scutcher.

"Then," he explained, moving along the narrow row of machines that thundered around them, "These machines straighten the cotton into lines called slivers. This is called carding."

She watched as bristles attached to huge drums span in a blur. "Like brushing one's hair, yes?"

John Sparrow blinked before he nodded. "It ensures that the fibres all lie together neatly."

Lena watched the young workers as they moved between the machines, their fingers swift and nimble, tending to the downy streams of cotton that emerged off the drums. It was still hot and humid in here, perpetually gloomy as little light filtered through the grimy windows.

Mill workers averted her gaze, almost afraid to return her tentative smile and she couldn't help but think it might have something to do with the glowering men she stood with.

John Sparrow moved along the lines of machines, waiting for her at another door.

"This is the mule room, where we have most of our workers," he said, opening the door to a room where Lena had to squint to see inside.

At first, she thought that maybe steam was leaking from the floor below; the air was hazy and murky. Pulleys and belts twirled endlessly overhead, whipping and spitting, turning incessantly like sinews. As she stepped further inside, she realised that it wasn't mist she was looking at, but fine cotton filaments that filled the room, eddying on the air as it was stirred. She blinked several times as the gauzy air tickled her eyes, her nose, clogged her throat.

John Sparrow leaned in closer, pointing to the beasts that clunked and roared. "After carding comes drawing. The fibres are teased into strands and, depending on the quality of the cloth we're making, can be brushed again and again to make them even smoother and stronger. Calico, for instance, has a rougher yarn.

"The strands, or slivers, are drawn out – called drawing – then pulled through rollers that stretch and thin them until the fibres are all uniform, given a slight twist in the roving process, and wound down to bobbins.

"We have the spinning mule," he pointed out to a contraption with rows of bobbins atop a carriage. With the relentless clutter of shuttles firing back and forth, the pulleys and belts, a network of leather and iron, rose from the wooden floors to the ceiling and across, driving the looms with energy harnessed from the both steam and water wheel below.

Women and children, their faces grimy from their labours, monitored the looms with vigilance. Their attention was on the spindles, tending to the cotton as it emerged in thin, white lines. Lena was astounded by how young some of the operators were; she'd seen them, of course, but hadn't even paid much attention to them before. They each wore a grey shift, with a grimy apron, and a cloth hat. Everyone was barefoot.

She opened her mouth to question this, stopping as the carriage rumbled out into the middle of the room. She watched in horror as the smallest of the children darted under the moving machines with the agility of cats, their small hands plucking at the floor. She peered more closely, noticing that they gripped strands of cotton waste, moving quickly before they ducked back under as the carriage travelled back.

"If the thread breaks, it comes off the wages at the

end of the day," Mr Blackwood explained, and Lena tried to ignore the pride in his tone. "Nothing but the best here at Hawks Mill under my watch."

John Sparrow explained the difference between warp and weft threads and which machine did what job.

"They're all so young," Lena murmured, unable to tear her eyes from how the spinners, a mix of young and old women and girls, watched their charges carefully, mindful of the dance as they fixed the broken threads and removed the full bobbins before adding empty ones.

The productivity was constant.

John Sparrow nodded as if stating the obvious. "Paupers and orphans," he shrugged, and Lena was left with the distinct impression that he wasn't at all considerate of the people in this room.

"Why are they all barefoot?" Lena asked.

"Because the iron nails in their clogs can cause a spark," Mr Blackwood interjected. "The last thing anybody wants is a spark that could start a fire on these wooden floors. And the cotton can be slippery, too."

Consciously, Lena wiggled her toes inside her boots. Her feet were chilled even in her stockings and leather boots, and she wondered how the barefoot workers must feel.

"Each of the children is indentured until they're twenty-one," Mr. Blackwood explained.

"How many of them stay on at the mill after their apprenticeship is over?"

"Almost all of them," Blackwood replied, clearly affronted. "Working in the mills is a prestigious job."

Lena held her counsel, her gaze travelling over the people she was responsible for.

"Who is in charge of this room?" she asked.

John Sparrow's gaze locked on a young man with a thatch of chestnut hair who was eying the trio nervously. "That's the underseer, Wilf Roberts."

The boy didn't look old enough to shave yet. She frowned at the foreman. "And where is the overseer? Don't tell me he's migrated to Black Marsh, too?"

A look of indignation flashed across his face. "Wilf, get over here!"

The young lad flinched, quickly weaving his way through the workers. Lena felt several sets of eyes on her, though she offered the boy an encouraging smile as he whipped his cloth cap off his head. Up close, she saw he was older than she'd first thought, probably closer to her in age, just small. He had an angry-looking red mark down one side of his face.

"Yes, Mr Blackwood, sir?" His tone was deferential, subdued... scared? Lena eyed the foreman with renewed focus.

"Where's Dower?"

The young man stammered, his face flushing bright red. Lena dipped her head closer to try and catch his explanation, though her blood turned to ice in her veins when the horrific screams rent the air.

CHAPTER 18

*L*ena's heart seized in her chest, her gaze fixed upon a sight so ghastly that for a moment, the tumultuous din of Hawk's Mill seemed to fall away into a dreadful silence. A small boy, no more than a wisp of a lad, dangled from the roof, his hand ensnared in the merciless grip of a pulley above one of the mules. His terrified screams amplified when the blood started to run down his arm.

Panic surged through the mill floor like an electric current, and all around her, the workers sprang into action. John Sparrow, with his ever-present air of detachment, stood aside, his indifference a jarring note in the chaos. It was Wilf, however, whose presence of mind shone through the pandemonium.

"Libby! The clutch!" His command cut through the air, sharp and authoritative.

A young woman, her hair a wild mane of blonde, leapt toward the machinery, grabbing at a lever to disengage the machine. Everyone seemed to hold their breath as the gears and pulleys ground to a halt, the cessation of their movement bringing about a sudden quiet that was almost more terrifying than their constant clamour. Lena stood rooted to the spot; her horror mirrored in the faces of those around her as the dangers of the mill were laid bare before her eyes.

The mule stilled and the poor boy's screams got louder.

"Where's Mr Dower?" Mr Blackwood strode into the throng and John Sparrow finally had the presence of mind to try and steer Lena away from the gory scene.

The name echoed through the mill, a desperate call for the overseer who seemed to have vanished at the very moment he was most needed.

Lena twisted her arm out of the mill manager's grip, drawn to try and soothe the child whose cries were beginning to reduce to mewling.

"Help him!" Lena pushed through the crowds. "Quick! Something to stand on! Help him!"

"It's okay, Billy, we're here!" Comforting voices reached out to the boy as Wilf wasted no time in finding a ladder.

The overseer appeared, joining the foreman and mill manager, looking as red-faced as his underseer.

They all joined Wilf in carefully disengaging the child from gears and metal, lowering him into the arms of the waiting workers. The boy had lost consciousness, his small face whiter than the cotton strands he lay upon. Wilf took the apron that the blonde-haired girl had handed him and wrapped the mangled stump where his hand used to be.

"Quickly, he needs a doctor," Lena said, squeezing through to the group. "Now, Mr Blackwood." The child's face was ashen, and Lena reached out to brush his hair. When no one around her moved, she looked up at the foreman. "Did you hear what I said?"

The foreman nodded. "Boy's done for. Why waste your money?"

Outraged, Lena said, "I beg your pardon?"

"Seen it before," he muttered. "If he doesn't die from blood loss, the infection will get him in a week. Kinder to let him go now."

Lena gaped at the foreman, her gaze swinging to the mill manager who shrugged and said, "The dangers of the mill, Miss Pemberton. And while these mules aren't running, the mill is losing money."

Lena's lips thinned in fury. Were these managers so obsessed with coin and production to keep her father happy that they would allow a child to perish? She felt the blinkers fall away.

"Where are his parents?"

"H-he's an orphan, miss," the one they'd called Libby broke the silence, head ducked against the glare from the overseer and his comrades. "He lives in the apprentice house."

Lena's eyes travelled over the sea of grimy faces. Faces that were indentured to her business. "Libby, is it?"

The young woman nodded. "Yes, miss."

"Do you know this boy well?"

"Y-yes, miss."

"Good. You can come with him. I want him carrying through to the manor house." Lena pressed to her feet, silencing the protesting mill manager with a look as she stood up. "He is under my charge, is he not, Mr Sparrow? Then you and Mr Blackwood will help fetch him through to the house. *Now*, gentleman," she enunciated through gritted teeth.

Both men shook their heads exasperatedly, grumbling about the absurdity, and Mr Sparrow ordered the overseer to assist the foreman and two of the boys to lift the child.

Lena moved out of the way as the lifeless boy was hefted into the air. "Wilf?" The young man eyed her cautiously. "Please, can you run down to the village? Fetch Doctor Fitch – tell him it's urgent."

When he hesitated, looking to the overseer for confirmation, Lena injected more heat into her voice. "You won't have your wages docked. Go now, please – and hurry!"

By the time they'd carried Billy to the manor house, the men were puffing heavily from the exertion. Lena erupted through into the reception hall, calling urgently for Mr Brown.

"Quickly," she said to him, shrugging out of her coat and tugging off her gloves, eying the limp boy worriedly. "Take him through to the parlour."

She could have kissed her butler in gratitude as he followed her directives without question.

She followed Billy as they all crowded into the

parlour and set him not too gently down onto the velvet sofa. "We need something to stop the blood."

The butler took over, ordering Gwen and James to find him something to stem the bleeding and something to make a tourniquet with. The mill manager moved out of the way, glaring obstinately at Lena.

"You're wasting your time," he snapped. "The boy is done for. I've seen it many a time."

Lena ignored him, trying to keep her focus on the lifeless child. The butler took over, working quickly and efficiently, leaving Lena in no doubt that he'd had an experience of events as ghastly as this at some point in his life.

"Right, you lot, back to work," Mr Blackwood snapped his fingers at the gaping youngsters. "Can't have that mule standing still too long." He began to round up Libby and the two boys, but Lena stopped him.

"Libby is staying here with me."

"She belongs in the mule room, earning her keep," the foreman spat.

"I pay her wages, Mr Blackwood, not you," Lena spoke evenly. "I will send her back across when the time is right."

He looked as though he were about to argue with her again but then stomped out of the room, bellowing that the boys follow him.

John Sparrow's furious expression spoke volumes. "Your father trusted us to run the mill for him, Miss Pemberton. You'd do well to heed his ways of doing business and let us run the place as we see fit."

The room stilled and Lena rolled her lips. "We'll talk about this another time, Mr Sparrow, but please note that things will be changing around here." The mill manager slapped his hat on his head and snatched at the door handle, pausing only when Lena said, "I still want the remainder of the tour, Mr Sparrow."

"You'll get it," he told her, slamming the door on the way out of the house for good measure.

Lena let out a trembling breath, meeting the worried gazes of the others in the room. "Right," she dusted her hands against the skirts of her dress and turned to Libby. "Do you know how to build a fire?"

"Yes, miss?"

"Good," Lena nodded, "please tend to the one in here. Billy is so cold to the touch. Mr Brown, what else can we do until the doctor gets here?"

CHAPTER 19

"You wanted to see us, Miss Pemberton?"

Lena nodded as Wilf and Libby peered around the edge of the parlour door, a fleeting smile touching her mouth.

The fire snapped merrily in the hearth, its warm glow almost in defiance against the gloom brought on by the relentless rain that lashed against the long windows of the parlour. Lena had closed the curtains herself against the encroaching darkness, more for something to do than out of privacy. Gwen and the other servants had done things, seen things, well beyond their duties today.

As they stepped into the room, their gazes moved over the dark mahogany furniture and velvet that draped the room, before landing on poor Billy where he slept tucked up under the blankets on the sofa. His injured arm was lying across his chest, the stump where his hand once was bandaged heavily.

"Please, come in," Lena spoke softly. "You've both eaten?"

"Aye," Wilf rubbed his belly contentedly. "Best meal I've ever eaten, Miss."

"I'm certain Cook would be happy to hear that," Lena sat further up in her chair.

She had watched over poor Billy for hours, his small form still and silent in the deep sleep of recovery. She'd insisted on keeping Wilf here after he'd arrived with the doctor, knowing what fear looked like, recognising it in his face when Blackwood had burst into the room to insist once more that his workers return to the mill.

The images from the surgery, vivid and visceral, had been forever etched into her mind. Her thoughts were a tempest as fierce as the storm outside, roiling with the knowledge that all was not well within Hawks Mill and that the truth was shrouded by the men in charge who would resist her delving into matters to discover the truth. Her gut feeling was that this wouldn't be out of loyalty to the mill but for more selfish reasons.

Lena sat up higher, hoping that the two people before her might allow her a small window into their world. "I won't keep you both too much longer."

Wilf sent her a half-grin, gesturing at the richly adorned room. "It's not a hardship, miss. Good food and a warm house."

Libby hissed at him, elbowing the blushing Wilf as she sent an apologetic look at Lena.

Lena brushed away the cheeky comment with a hand.

"I wanted to thank you both for all your help today and...to speak to you about something," Lena studied them both, timid and out of place in the grandeur of the manor's parlour —Wilf, with his stocky build filling out his tunic, and Libby, slight and dainty as a bird.

"Was Mr Sparrow speaking truthfully? Has this sort of terrible thing happened before at the mill?" Lena's voice was steady, trepidation drumming in her blood.

For a moment, neither moved. Lena didn't know how but somehow, they seemed to seek tacit permission from the other before answering her. They nodded in unison, a silent affirmation that chilled her to the bone. "To a child?" she pressed further.

Again, they nodded, and Lena felt her heart constrict with sorrow.

"What happens to the injured children?" she asked, her voice husky with emotion.

"Without a hand, they can't work properly. They're no good to the mill so they get sent to the poorhouse, or they...they end up on the streets," Libby replied, her head bowed, the words falling heavily in the room.

Lena had suspected as much, but hearing it spoken aloud tightened the vice around her chest even further. *All this time,* she thought, *to children just like that poor boy.*

In my mill.

"Did either of you see what happened today?" she asked, her eyes searching theirs.

They exchanged a nervous glance, another silent conversation passing between them that Lena could not decipher.

She was worried that it had been her fault, that her presence in the mule room had distracted the boy, and that she was the reason he'd been mutilated so badly. Unease rolled off them as the shadows of the firelight danced over their faces.

"You won't get into any trouble; I only want to help."

Another look was exchanged, and Lena guessed that it wasn't her that they feared, but the men who'd helped to carry Billy into the house earlier.

Lena rose from her chair, her gaze settling on Libby. "I saw how you were with the other mill workers earlier," Lena said, her head tilted in contemplation. "How they all rallied at your behest. I can tell that they trust you. How long have you worked at the mill?"

"Since I was eight, miss," Libby answered.

"And you, Wilf?" Lena asked gently.

"I was nine, miss. My pa died at the docks, and my ma left me at the poorhouse. I waited, but she never came back," he said, and she heard the sadness in his tone. She'd felt it herself already, and she'd been older when she'd been orphaned. Libby moved closer to him in a show of solidarity, and Lena felt a small pang of envy at their simple gesture of comfort.

"I know that we don't know each other very well

and that you're worried about consequences that might come–"

"We like our jobs, miss," Libby said quickly, "Mrs Reid looks after us all…very well."

Lena accepted the answer with a single nod. "Whatever you say here to me tonight, you have my word that it won't go any further." Lena linked her fingers in front of her, her gaze divided between them. "I want to help make the mill a better place, you see. I need to understand what went wrong today…" Her gaze drifted to where Billy lay.

"Is he going to be okay?" Libby asked softly.

Lena nodded. "The doctor said his hand was crushed beyond repair—that amputation was his only chance at life."

"And will he? Live, I mean?" Wilf asked tentatively.

"God willing," Lena replied with a soft sigh. "We must all pray for him. He'll stay here, of course."

"At the manor house?" Libby blurted out, her hand flying to her mouth as if she hadn't meant to let the words slip out.

"Yes, the doctor will come by tomorrow. He assures me Billy will regain consciousness, but we must wait," Lena said, not wanting to offer empty assurances like those she'd received about her father. She pulled her thoughts from that path when her eyes stung with bitter tears.

Lena continued, firming her voice. "I want to help make the mill safer, so these accidents don't happen. I must confess my ignorance about the mill, the business…but I am taking steps to make changes. I was in the mule room today to see for myself, to try and make sense of the facts and figures in my father's books," Lena stopped herself before she admitted anything more, though the confession seemed to unsettle them.

"Mr Sparrow is the one who will be able to tell you all of that," Wilf hedged.

Lena's mouth twisted and she turned to the fireplace. "I suspect Mr Sparrow will only show me elements that he thinks I need to know about. I want to understand what happened," she looked back at them, "I want to know if there's something I could do so that another person on my payroll doesn't get a life-changing injury for the sake of a pair of curtains!"

They went back to their noiseless dialogue once more. Lena dug her fingers into her eye sockets, pressing at her hot, gritty eyes, exasperated at the continuous blocks she was coming up against in her efforts to find the truth.

"For the love of all the saints," Lena muttered, throwing her hands wide, "just say what's on your mind! I can see you want to tell me something!"

"Guards."

Lena's hands dropped and she frowned at Wilf. "What?"

Wilf tempered his tone, still hesitant in answering her. "Guards…on the machines?" he said in gentle explanation at her blank look. "It was made law that the machines have covers over the pulleys, the belts, the cogs."

"Has the guard broken?"

Wilf's sigh moved his big shoulders. He gave a little shake of his head. "None of the machines had them when I was young. After the law changed, there was talk that we'd have them. A job like that must cost a pretty penny."

"The engineer should fit them, yes?"

"Aye, that's true enough. And the machines on the other floors got the guards fitted... just not the mule room."

Lena gnawed at the inside of her cheek as she considered their answer. Grimy, ghostly faces swam before her eyes, and she recalled the words of Mr Sparrow. "There's mostly women and children on that floor," she surmised.

Wilf nodded.

Lena's gaze slid to Billy. Mostly children, who were indentured to the mill. Children who relied on the overseers and the like for food, for protection. Children would do as they were told and not protest too much because they were frightened about losing their jobs if they stepped out of line. She tried to marry up the suggestion that her father was aware of this gross manipulation of the law and came up short.

"Most of the machines on the other floors have them, so that when the inspectors are here –"

"It looks as though the law is being followed," Lena finished for him. Mr Clark had said that her father had been fined, and she wondered if it was for this infringement. Hawks Mill had done enough to push back on the laws. "Is it costly to fit the guards?"

"Not in the right hands," Wilf replied. "We used to have a good engineer, but he is no longer here."

"I heard he went to Black Marsh?"

Libby snorted. "Not that old coot. He wasn't worth a spit."

"Libby," Wilf patted his companion, who eyed him back.

"It's true enough," Libby muttered. "Old Jenks was a good engineer. He'd see to it that the machines ran well enough 'til he... well, he died. Old Jenks would turn in his grave to know that Hawks didn't have an engineer now."

"He was a good man?"

"The best," Libby declared, a hitch in her chin defying Wilf to correct her now.

"Folks say the mules slow down with the guards," Wilf said instead. "The law says that we're supposed to stop the machines when cleaning under them, or when we have to piece together the broken ends of cotton but stopping the machines means a loss of production.

"I'm sorry to say that I didn't see what happened to Billy... but if the machines had protectors, it wouldn't have been quite so..."

"He might have lost a finger, but he'd probably still have a hand," Libby chimed in.

"And he could still work," Wilf finished.

It seemed such a simple answer to the problem. "Do other mills have them?"

Cautiously, Wilf said, "I hear that's the way, aye."

Lena's brow knotted. "What would it take to fit them? You said an engineer could do it?"

"Aye, the right one."

"The right one is expensive, yes?"

"I'm afraid that's a question for the mill manager, miss," Wilf replied, twisting the cloth cap in his hands.

Or my father, Lena tacked on the end. She didn't want to think that her father had foregone something as simple as a guard for the sake of running the mill, but then thinking about the state of the accounts and the mounting debt, she knew it to be true.

"Have you heard of *The Workers' Review*?"

Lena shook her head at Wilf's question. Wilf explained it was a publication filled with articles about the changes workers were trying to bring about. "There will be lots of information in there about the ways you can help make changes. Campaigners are pushing for changes not just in the textile industry, but across all of them – mining, and factory work, too. The working folks are talking, miss."

Inspired, Lena asked, "Where would I find a copy?"

"The village shop but..." Wilf swallowed, measuring his words.

"But what?"

"Some people around here wouldn't like it if they thought that you were a chartist, miss," Libby said what Wilf was reluctant to.

Lena surmised who the 'some people' were in that statement.

Mr Sparrow.

Mr Blackwood.

Wilf shook his head. "It's not just that. It might... open your eyes to unpleasant things."

"More unpleasant than this?" She pointed to Billy.

"I meant that it's mostly about how the workers view their employers," Wilf said, "and I'm afraid that Hawks Mill has one of the worst reputations."

CHAPTER 20

*T*he flickering glow of oil lamps cast warm, amber light across the room, creating dancing shadows on the plain, whitewashed walls. The air was filled with the faint aroma of a simple, home-cooked meal that had been shared earlier.

Mrs Reid, the house matron, looked up from the scarred kitchen table, a deck of cards arranged out across the surface.

"Well, well, look what the cat dragged in," she huffed, eying Libby spitefully.

Libby bowed her head. "I… I was–"

"I know where you were," she spat. "Lording it up in places you had no business being."

Libby swallowed nervously as the house manager pushed to her feet, the chair scraping loudly against the stone floor.

"Mr Reid told me all about it, how you stuck your oar in, playing up to the new boss like you owned the place," Mrs Reid shuffled across from the table, eyes glinting in the lamplight.

"I just did as I was told," Libby said quietly.

Mrs Reid came to a stop a hair's breadth away. "Mind you do, Libby Baker. What did she say?"

"Miss Pemb–"

"Yes, Miss Pemberton!" she bellowed. "Unless you have been dining with the ruddy Queen!"

"She th-thanked me for helping and she, uh, sent me back here."

The older woman's eyes narrowed to slits. "You expect me to believe that when you've been gone hours? Leaving me to feed them ungrateful sods by meself?"

Libby flinched when Mrs Reid poked a finger towards the ceiling. "It's the truth," she whispered, waiting for a blow.

It never came. Mrs Reid shook her head, stepping back. "You mind yourself, Libby. I got my eye on you and I'm not the only one. Mr Reid says that changes are afoot, and I won't be losing my job because of some stuck-up cow that thinks she knows business!"

Mrs Reid hobbled up the narrow stairs, unlocking the door. She pushed it back.

"Straight to bed with you, no dilly-dallying. Or you'll have nothing but gruel for a week."

Libby nodded obediently and slipped into the dimly lit bedroom. Many faces of the mill workers turned to her in the darkness, their eyes reflecting curiosity and eagerness. Libby pressed a finger to her lips, urging silence as the key turned in the lock.

They waited in silence until the receding footsteps of Mrs Reid moved down the hallway. Then the girls sat up in their beds, eager to know what had transpired during Libby's mysterious absence.

"Where were you?"

"At the big house," Libby whispered, tucking her clogs under the foot of her bed.

"Is Billy alive?"

"For now," she replied, pulling her work shift over her head. Her skin puckered as the cold air shivered over her. "He's lost a hand."

"He's done for then," came a voice in the darkness.

"Doctor says differently," Libby replied, peering through the gloom, relieved when she spied Daisy in her bed. "Paid for by Miss Pemberton." She heard the shock of this revelation roll around the room as she tiptoed across the floor Polly announced in a hushed whisper, "Mr Dower was good and furious. Got his self a right dressing down from Blackwood."

"I thought they were going to scrap," added someone else.

"I think they could both do with a good smack," Libby muttered as she gingerly lowered herself onto Daisy's bed. "You okay?"

Daisy nodded, gratitude shining in her moonlit eyes. Her face was marked by her tussle with Dower earlier. "Having you and Wilf interrupt him stopped him before he went too far. I can't believe he walloped Wilf like he did."

"No man likes to be interrupted," Polly chimed in with a snigger.

Libby didn't want to think about the apoplectic rage of the overseer earlier. She would never forget the desperation that streaked across Daisy's face when Wilf had burst through the privy door.

Daisy hugged Libby. "You saved me."

"Aye, for now," Polly's tone was laced with scepticism. "But what about next time?"

Libby's thoughts drifted to her encounter with Lena Pemberton in the mill, the unexpected kindness she had shown and the hint of genuine concern. She described the house, the hot meal, and the warmth of the kitchen, and how the servants had treated them both with unexpected kindness.

"If I didn't know any better, I'd say she's different to the other rich folks. She seems to care. When Wilf told her about *The Review*? It bothered her." Libby sighed, her mind still reeling from the events of the day. "Hopefully, things are changing, for the better."

But Polly couldn't shake her cynicism. "She's still a Pemberton, Libby. Don't forget that. She'll either fall beneath the pressure of running this place, or the mill will fold, just like everyone is saying. Either way, we're all doomed."

Libby, however, held onto a secret hope. She tiptoed back to her bed and slipped under the thin blanket, tucking herself into a ball, as the whispers of the room lulled her weary body.

Regardless of what the others thought, she wanted to believe that Lena Pemberton was genuine in her concerns. She'd listened to Wilf, to her – no one had ever simply let her talk so freely before now, save for the girls she lived with. She prayed that Lena would be the one to bring about change. In that dimly lit room, amidst the sighs, Libby clung to the small belief that perhaps, just perhaps, a brighter future was within their grasp.

CHAPTER 21

"*I* wish I could have brought better news to you."

Lena sighed, eying the accountant. They were seated in her father's study. The morning sun cast a gentle glow across the oak-panelled walls, dust motes dancing in the shaft of light like tiny, carefree spirits.

The past few weeks had been an unremitting and harsh education for Lena in the running of the mill. She'd sat through exhaustive meetings with the mill's accountant, the solicitor, the manager, and others who had come to offer her advice. Each session had simply served to reveal more of the dire financial straits Hawk's Mill faced. The figures on the ledger were unyielding, and the path forward was shrouded in uncertainty.

On the desk sat a copy of *The Worker's Review*.

Following Wilf's caution, Gwen had procured it from town for her, with an air of secrecy, as though the pamphlet were a seditious tract rather than a magazine filled with voices calling for reform. The magazine lay open, and Lena's eyes traced the printed words, each line of the article painting a damning portrait of life at Hawks Mill. Just as Wilf had said, the mill's reputation was in tatters and hinted at a legacy hanging by a thread.

A letter from Amelia lay beside the magazine. It was bathed in a bar of sunlight on the mahogany desk, almost mocking her. She'd penned a flowing script of London life filled with gilded ballrooms, glittering dinner parties and elegant soirees. Reading about her friend's life, of the gossip and the engagements – a life she herself had nearly led – Lena felt a pang of something she could not quite name. Whispers of her broken engagement had spread like wildfire. According to Amelia's latest news, Thomas had wasted no time in finding comfort in the arms of Elizabeth. All of which seemed trivial amidst her current predicaments.

"The most that Alistair would agree to was a six-month offset, but he is demanding a hefty sum to be made by May to show good faith on your part against the bulk of the loans." Mr Radford's despondency was infectious. He'd approached the banker to negotiate a better interest rate on the loans, or to delay the repayments whilst Lena saw to the necessary repairs within the mill.

"We always knew that it was a long shot," Lena murmured. She imagined Alistair Cavendish wielding his power like a new toy now that Edwin was no longer here to counteract the demands. "If only there was a filthy rich distant relative that no one knows about to help us out."

Mr Radford didn't smile at her feeble joke. "Robert has suggested liquidating some assets."

Lena shook her head. "There's nothing left. Our only hope is to secure a large order, which we cannot meet at our current production levels. We need to upgrade our machines. Buy a new engine to boost productivity when the water levels drop in the river. To do that, we need an injection of cash."

Mr Radford spread his hands helplessly. "Cavendish laughed when I expressed how you were looking at ways to secure work for the mill."

Lena met Radford's skittish look with a steady one of her own, as annoyance simmered in her blood.

It irked her that neither Thomas nor his father believed that Hawks Mill could be saved. Perhaps they were right, but she owed to the workers to at least try.

"He told me to give you some advice."

Lena's brow soared up. "Am I going to like it?"

"He told me to tell you that you must sell the mill now, and this house. And then for you to marry and leave business to people who understand the situation better than a woman can."

"No, I don't like it. It's a shame he's not here in person so I can tell him what he can do with his 'advice,'" Lena muttered, pushing out of her chair, too wired to sit still.

The accountant coughed to hide his discomfort at

such rudeness. She could care less about offending his delicate ears. She crossed to the window, staring out across the expanse of Pemberton lands. She'd been so immersed in ledgers and strategies for rejuvenation these past weeks that without her noticing, spring had begun to unfold across the countryside.

Spikes of daffodils pushed through the softening ground, their yellow trumpets defiant against the lingering chill, a visual fanfare to the sun's tentative forays into the lengthening days. The last vestiges of winter had vanished, making way for a new beginning. One that felt filled with uncertainty and dread.

Yet, there was hope.

The boy, Billy, had woken up, much to everyone's relief. By Lena's express permission, Libby had been visiting him regularly, her presence a comfort to the injured child and a balm to Lena's conscience.

At night, her dreams were haunted by the echoes of Billy's screams. He was sweet and brave, even though his life had been altered thanks to a machine in her mill.

The gravity of the situation weighed heavily on Lena. She'd tallied losses and liabilities, the numbers telling a grim tale of a business teetering on the brink of ruin.

She'd hoped to appeal to the businessman in Cavendish but had also expected him to deny the request. The mill and its people needed more from her. Lena knew that refinancing was essential, and for that, a substantial order was needed. Although the dismissal from Cavendish Bank stung her deeply, she was getting used to the reluctance of others to deal with a woman in business.

It was during one of her many heated discussions with Mr Sparrow that Lena had come to understand the stubbornness of old ways. She had argued relentlessly with him about fitting the looms with guards. At first, he had been rude and contemptuous, his retorts sharp as the winter frost.

"We've managed for years without them," he had retorted with a flippant wave of his hand at her from behind his desk. "The expense to fit them would be colossal. I don't need to tell you that we don't have the budget. Besides, the boy got what he deserved for not minding his place. We can't be nursing fools, or we'd have accidents aplenty."

Lena, armed with the newly acquired knowledge of impending changes in the law and a growing sense of responsibility, would not be deterred.

But John Sparrow's obstinacy was as rigid as the iron machines he defended. "We have to turn the machines off – if they're not running, we're not producing and, the way I hear it, you cannot afford that!"

Lena hated that he was right.

The cruel dismissal of the boy's injury still troubled her, along with Wilf's reluctant admission that Mr Sparrow had brazenly dismissed sub-inspectors from the mill, choosing to conceal the liabilities rather than address them shocked Lena to her core.

She brought a clenched fist to her chin, impotency scraping her temper. "I want to make changes, Mr

Radford. Make Hawks Mill a shining beacon for safety. But hope alone won't work. There must be another way," Lena turned back to the room, the sun at her back making the man have to squint at her.

He considered his answer. "People are reluctant to sink any money into a business that has a reputation for missing deadlines, and for producing lower-quality products. Your workers need to be up to the task, and so does your machinery," the solicitor paused, leaning forward. "We could approach other enterprises with a proposal of collaboration, providing that we could show that our safety records are improving, and the productivity has increased. You need to better machines—"

"—or repair the ones we have," Lena finished for him.

He nodded, sitting back in his chair. "That's the cheaper option, certainly, but I'm not sure that you'd be able to bring anyone in, considering many of our skilled workers have already left us behind. Even if you found someone, we wouldn't be able to offer much in the way of wages—"

"Not yet, anyway," Lena said, renewed determination flowing through her. "Please, help yourself to the tea on the tray. I just need to do one thing quickly." She hurried out of the study and into the hallway, the portraits of her ancestors gazed down at her with reticent expectancy. Her steps were rushed. Out through the front door into the warm spring sunlight.

Wilf, the young lad who had shown such courage and heart, had been more forthcoming than anyone else at the mill. Perhaps he would know of a man willing to pull Hawks Mill back from the brink. She rounded the edge of the building, drawing up short when she came face to face with a glowering John Sparrow.

CHAPTER 22

$\mathcal{A}$t the mill manager's insistence, Lena found herself standing in his cramped office. With a cursory glance, a cold pill of dread settled in the pit of her stomach. Some of the shelves, which the other day had been filled with knick-knacks and detritus that Mr Sparrow and his predecessors had accumulated during his years of service, were now mostly empty. Only a few ledgers and logs remained.

John Sparrow was fidgety, demonstrated by the way he tapped the edge of a bulging envelope against his desk.

Uninvited, Lena sat in the chair on her side of the desk. Her hand flattened, smoothing out the pleats of her dress as the bubbles of her earlier excitement dissipated. "What is it that was so urgent it could not wait, Mr Sparrow?"

If he was offended by her clipped tone, he didn't betray it. "This is my resignation, and I'm tendering it immediately."

The envelope plopped loudly onto the scarred desk, and Lena stared at him, astounded. Of all the insults and incidents that she'd encountered so far, this was certainly not expected. "Excuse me?"

John Sparrow's elbows hit the desk with a thud. He leaned forward. "May I be frank with you, Miss Pemberton?"

Mimicking one of his flippant hand waves, she indicated that she was listening, even though her heart thrummed against her ribcage.

"I've been a faithful servant to both your father and Hawks Mill all my life. And until recently, I would have been content finishing up my days as mill manager here. But things have changed." He sat back, his wooden chair protesting loudly at the weight shift. "I have worked tirelessly for this place. I have stood alongside your father – defended him… and now, it's as if my word bears no weight here whatsoever."

"My father made you a wealthy man, Mr Sparrow. I've seen the accounts – your annual income is handsome compared to some," Lena replied, her voice husky with temper.

John Sparrow snorted. "It's no secret that Hawks Mill is in trouble, and through no fault of my own, it doesn't seem that the tide will be changing anytime soon. I have extensive experience in the textile industry, and to *some* people, that makes me an asset. A valuable one, at that."

Lena's brow shot up as he enunciated 'some', the insult striking home. The statement left no illusion that he'd been lured away by one of the competitor mills.

"Which one is it?" Lena asked. But as he was about to answer, she stood so abruptly that her chair toppled over. "It doesn't matter, not really."

A mill without a manager was like a ship without a rudder. Just at the time she needed help and guidance, he was leaving. Her mind raced over the implications this would have now. She snatched up the envelope and used it to poke the air as she spoke.

"You may be laying the blame for the demise of the mill squarely at my father's feet, Mr Sparrow, but it has come to my attention that you have skirted— no, blatantly flouted —the laws in favour of production, and the safety of the mill workers, resulting in hefty fines being levied against the business."

"That's preposterous," Mr Sparrow spluttered, his outrage colouring his response. He surged to his feet. "Your father was the one who instructed me to keep the inspectors out. He knew the value of keeping workers in line and ensuring that productivity was at its peak. I can't work with the owner ignoring my instructions. On your head be it! Hawks Mill is going down, Miss Pemberton, and I refuse to hitch my cart to it."

Lena gritted her teeth, holding back any further scathing retorts. She pivoted and grasped the door handle, paused in the doorway to look back at the obnoxious manager. "You can peddle your lies all you like to whatever mill has been unlucky enough to buy into your narrative, Mr Sparrow. But one day, your true nature will reveal itself." With that, she slammed the door behind her.

Still fuming, she barrelled through the mill to the engine room. Workers scattered as the door burst open. As she reached the floor of the mule room, she stormed into the space, searching for Wilf. Once again, the overseer, Dower, was nowhere to be found. Her anger bubbled over when she considered that he was just another cog in the lacklustre management. Perhaps Sparrow's resignation was the best thing that could happen, rather than an omen that they were past the point of being able to save the mill.

She peered through the murky clouds of cotton mist; the young mill girls eyed her fearfully as she stalked past them. The mechanical clunk and hiss of the machines clamoured, pressing in all around her. Worried that she was causing too much of a distraction, she shouted, "Don't watch me, watch the bobbins!" She moved through the group of girls, pleased to see that they were following her instructions as their attention turned back to the clattering mules. She spotted Wilf further along the line, with his head bent close to Libby's, the two of them deep in discussion.

Stomping over to them, they sprang apart, just as she bellowed, "Where on *earth* is Mr Dower?"

"I-I don't k-know," Wilf stammered, wide-eyed at the fury rolling off her. Lena looked at Libby, at how her eyes slowly, deliberately slid towards the narrow door in the middle of the wall behind Lena.

The privy door.

Lena hesitated. The man was allowed to take a natural break, after all. She took a breath, trying to calm her temper down.

"I'm sorry," she amended her tone. "I didn't mean to shout. I wanted to speak to you in private, Wilf."

"M-me, miss?"

"Yes. It's a delicate matter," she began, though her attention diverted and swung behind her at the stricken look that crossed Libby's face.

For a moment, Lena's mind stumbled. A young girl had tipped out of the privy door, tears having carved a clear path into her grubby cheeks. A trickle of blood leaked from her nose, but it was the look on her face that gave Lena pause. She recognised the panic, the fear, in the girl's eyes because she'd experienced that fear herself.

On Christmas Eve, at the hands of Thomas Cavendish.

Arthur Dower emerged behind her, looking very much like the cat who'd got the cream.

Until his gaze clashed with Lena's one of white fury. His face fell. He quickly hitched up his trousers, wiping at his nose, and Lena could almost hear the weasel rooting around in his head for an excuse.

Lena leaned towards Libby, instructing the young girl to stop the machines. Libby pushed the clutch lever, and the ensuing silence was deafening.

Lena folded her arms, glaring at the overseer, daring him to lie to her. "Care to explain yourself, Mr Dower?"

"I, er, had to search the girl," he swiped a thumb

across his chin, nodding to himself as if satisfied with the explanation. "They, er, they steal, miss. Mr Sparrow has me checking, you know, up their skirts, where they hide things."

Lena blinked once, twice. Above her, the floored chundered with other machines but in the mule room, no one moved. "I see. So, you were… just doing your job then, Mr Dower?"

He tugged at his waistband once more, the movement more like a shrug. "That's right. Why, what else did you think I was doing, Miss?"

The challenge in his tone was like salt in a scald. Lena looked at the trembling waif next to him. The blood had smeared across her pale cheek where she must have wiped at it. "And how did her nose become bloodied so?"

He looked at the girl casually before meeting Lena's hard stare. "She resisted. A thief don't much like to be caught now, do they?"

Libby was watching the young girl, her expression creased with concern. When Lena quirked a brow at her, Libby gave a slight shake of her head.

"If that will be all, miss, Mr Sparrow don't much like it when the mules have stopped, neither."

Realising that he was dismissing her, Lena's finger shot out, halting him in his tracks.

She tilted her head at the girl, gentling her tone. "What's your name?"

"Effie," she checked with Libby before replying. "Effie Wilson."

"Effie, I want to ask you a question. You won't get

in trouble, no matter your answer, but I want you to tell the truth."

After hesitation, Effie nodded.

"Are you a thief, Effie?"

Her eyes popped wide, white in the already pale face. "No, Miss! Me ma would skin me alive!"

Dower snorted derisively, throwing his arms wide. "She'll hardly admit it now, will she, miss? The place is full of thieves. Mr Sparrow insists that we check everyone, make sure what's made in here, stays in here."

Lena slowly looked around the room, travelling the sea of faces. The older ones stared at Dower without outright disdain; others had their heads bowed. Icy fingers of understanding, at what was going on in her mill, with these young girls, slid through her belly. They had no one to protect them. Lena's gaze came around to the overseer as he began to urge the workers to return to their jobs.

"Wilf, can you please take over here? I need a word with Mr Dower alone."

The overseer jabbered his protests as Wilf sent the machines into motion once more, but Dower followed her outside.

"I was just doing my job," the man snivelled as Lena rounded on him, "nothing untoward. It's how we've always done things. They hide things up... you know..."

"Things are changing at my mill, Mr Dower. Your services are no longer required."

The man visibly baulked, paling before he

exploded with indignation. "You're sacking me? For what?"

Lena nodded sagely, her voice cold and final. "You're paid to oversee, not assault vulnerable young girls, Mr Dower."

He waved his arms in the air, advancing on her. "She was asking for it, they all do! Begging for a man to take up with. That's how all you women work!"

Lena kept her face passive and had to lock her knees so her legs wouldn't give way as his fury erupted.

"Hell, half the girls in there are Blackwood's spawn! Bastards, the lot of them! I have rights!"

"I imagine you do." She tried not to react to his claims and resolved to get to the bottom of it all.

Saddened, she wondered if her father had known about the terrible situation and had turned a blind eye to this, too, all in the name of profit. She vowed that she wouldn't do the same. "I'd be happy to explain my findings to any sub-inspector or policeman of your choosing. I'll make sure that each of those young girls in there is given a voice. Would you like me to call Sergeant Platt, the village constable?"

He shook his fist at her, lips peeled back, "You can't sack me! Wait 'til Mr Sparrow hears about this! He won't stand for it - you'll see!"

Dower began stomping away from her, but Lena's laugh stopped him. "What's so ruddy funny?"

She gave him a pitying head shake. "John Sparrow doesn't work here anymore either."

CHAPTER 23

*L*ena's anger dissipated slightly as she stormed back into the mule room and saw that Wilf and Libby had set the machines back to working order. Perhaps her instincts about him were right, and he could be relied upon after all. The absence of Mr Dower must be confusing the workers, their uncertainty palpable as they exchanged furtive glances.

Determined to instil some semblance of security amongst them all, Lena beckoned to Wilf. "We need to talk. Come with me to the manor," she instructed firmly.

"Libby," he called out with a brief nod towards the other workers, "I shouldn't be too long." Their look was meaningful, lingering. It occurred to her that he too might also be worried about his future at the mill as he followed her into the interior of the house, though he wisely remained quiet.

She led him into her father's study where Mr

Radford was ensconced in the deep leather chair at the corner, the *Workers' Review* magazine open on his lap. He looked up, startled, as Lena burst into the room, cheeks flushed.

"I have dismissed the overseer from the mule room," she declared, shutting the door behind Wilf. "Mr Sparrow stopped me on my way to the mule room. He has found informed me this morning that he has had an offer of work elsewhere."

Both men looked at her in incredulity.

"What have you done, Lena?"

Thinking about what Dower had claimed about her foreman, she said, "I'm not done yet, either."

"We need them," Mr Radford protested. "Especially at a time like this."

"We don't need men like them," Lena retorted firmly. The abuse she suspected within the walls of Hawks Mill was unspeakable, and she was resolute in her next move. "I'm cutting out the cancer in this place, starting from the top."

The solicitor was horrified. "You can't possibly hope to run this place without knowledgeable men from the industry."

Lena indicated Wilf, who was still in the corner of the room, wide-eyed, wringing his cap in his hands. "This is Wilf, Mr Radford. He runs the mule room. I do not doubt that the mill floor will flourish under his skilled guidance in his new role as overseer."

"Blimey, Miss," Wilf stammered. "I... I don't know what to say."

"You're capable of the job, aren't you?"

His head lifted; shoulders squared imperceptibly. He swallowed but nodded firmly. "I believe so, miss. Thank you."

Lena made her way over to the desk, needlessly fiddling with the items on top. "Don't thank me, Wilf. We're not out of the woods yet. But I do need your help. We must make Hawks Mill safe and competitive.

"We'll start by repairing what we can and planning replacements where necessary. Our workers' safety is paramount, and I need a management team that I can trust, who knows their craft." Leaning over, she snatched up the magazine from Mr Radford's lap and held it out. "I've read what is being said about this place – about its former glory in my grandfather's days. I want to restore that legacy. I want to make it that way once more."

Hope flaring in his eyes, Wilf nodded in understanding. "Repaired machines will yield better work and the workers... They'll follow your lead if they believe in the future you're building."

Inspired, Lena's lips curved slightly. "I need a manager, Wilf. Someone who knows the industry, who understands what improvement to make in the mill. I see people talk about managers in these articles," she waggled the paper. "The managers probably command steep fees."

Wilf pondered a moment before responding. "My uncle, Albert Simpson, may be interested. I couldn't speak of fees, miss. He might box my ears for suggesting a thing, mind. He's a foreman in Sheffield but has spoken of returning home one day."

Lena hastily wrote down the details as Wilf gave them. "I'll write to him today. Is he a good man?"

"He's fair, miss. Honest and hardworking."

"And what of an engineer?" Lena inquired, her voice betraying a hint of anxiety. "Would you know of one?"

Wilf shook his head. "They're scarce, and their services don't come cheap. They've studied at school and the like, they're time-served in their trade. It's why they're among the highest-paid in the mills."

Lena's heart sank; the mill's funds were already stretched thin. She had ideas for raising cash but had little to spare.

"What about this Henry Wickham I read about?" Mr Radford interjected, tapping the magazine where Lena had set it down. "He redesigned a mule for efficiency at a mill in Yorkshire. He's renowned for innovation. Didn't I read he hailed from Overleigh?"

Memory glimmered in Lena's mind. Overleigh was the next town over, where Black Marsh mill was located.

"That's right. A local man who's done well for himself. I remember him being mentioned in several articles. He's been quite vocal about the reforms for safety in factories and mills, as I recall. Do you know him, Wilf?" She looked across at the young man, but her optimism dimmed at his regretful expression.

"Aye, he's local," Wilf conceded, "I never met him myself…but those articles… they aren't always current."

Her brow rippled. "What do you mean?"

The cap was swapped between his hands. "Mr Wickham... he has, um, he left the industry."

Undeterred, Lena's resolve hardened. "Then it is upon us to present him with a challenge he cannot refuse. Hope is not yet lost, gentlemen, not while we still draw breath to fight for Hawks Mill.

"Where would I find him?"

Wilf sighed. "The Borough Gaol in Walton, miss."

CHAPTER 24

*D*ying embers of sunlight lit up the walls of the mill with gold and oranges. Libby didn't notice. She hurried out of the mule room, her mind spinning with all the changes of the day. Much like a ship cast adrift in a storm, she wasn't sure which course Lena Pemberton had set them down, but faint hope warmed her as much as the sunshine did.

She burst in through the back door of the Apprentice house, startling the girls seated around the kitchen table eating the supper of watery stew.

"Scared me good an' proper," Polly exclaimed, clutching her chest.

"Mrs Reid was asking where you were," Daisy said as she spooned up more stew.

Libby shut the door, leaning back against it. For a moment, she didn't move. She simply looked about the kitchen.

"What's wrong?" Polly demanded, looking up from her supper.

Libby finally pushed off from the door, making her way towards the stove. She deftly lifted a ladle of watery stew out of the pan and tapped it into a pewter dish.

"You'll never believe it," Libby nudged Effie along the crowded bench to make room for her. Spoons stilled and she felt the expectancy in the stares.

"Well, come on then," Polly urged impatiently. "What's got you in such a state?"

"Miss Pemberton has made Wilf an overseer!" she exclaimed, savouring the giddy excitement that rolled around the table. Smiles and gasps of delight greeted this news, all except Polly, who was staring at her open-mouthed.

"What? Where's Dower?"

"Gone!" Libby laughed. "Sacked. Marched off the premises by Angus and the others so that there would be no trouble!"

"Blackwood won't like that. He's going to be hell to work for now, more than ever!" Polly muttered, her brow furrowing in worry.

Libby, undeterred, shook her head confidently. "Doesn't matter," she said, her gaze scanning the faces of her companions before continuing, "Because he's been sacked, too. And Mr Sparrow has upped and quit."

The room fell into an eerie stillness as the girls stared at Libby, their expressions a mixture of disbelief and uncertainty. Thea's stricken, down-cast face confirmed what Libby had suspected—that Mr Blackwood was responsible for her current predicament.

"He's truly gone?" Effie asked, her face still bearing the marks of her scuffle with Mr Dower.

Libby nodded solemnly. "He has. I heard the almighty row between Blackwood and Miss Pemberton. I bet they heard it all the way over in Manchester. He was hopping mad."

Libby had been in the house to see Billy when she'd happened upon the argument. It had been vicious and combative as the foreman had fought his position, claiming lies and rumours, and calling Miss Pemberton the most distasteful names. Yet she'd held her ground, matching the foreman's wrath with a temper of her own.

"Miss Pemberton threatened him with the law, and he ran away with his tail between his legs," Libby quipped.

Shocked silence was punctuated by two of them starting to cry. Glances were exchanged as they took in the news and sudden turn of events.

Daisy, with a worried look, whispered, "What will become of us all?"

Libby understood their trepidation. The men who had run the mill had been cruel taskmasters, but their familiar presence had provided some semblance of security. She tried to offer reassurance. "We're going to be fine. I don't know how, but now we're free from them all."

Polly, however, remained sceptical, standing up and carrying her plate to the sink. "It's all right for you, Libby," she said, her expression grim. "You've only got until the summer to work. Some of us have years left to work off our indenture. I don't want to end up in the workhouse or begging for alms in the streets. I want a proper job so that I can feed me kids, not like me Mam who was worn out before she was twenty."

The plate sloshed into the bucket before Polly turned to address the room, her tone sombre. "Who-ever heard of a cotton mill without a manager? We have no engineer. No foreman, and now an overseer who's still wet behind the ears?

"Has she lost her mind? I'm telling you, this doesn't bode well for any of us."

CHAPTER 25

"*D*id you manage to get the letter posted?"

Wilf smiled and nodded. "After I had Thea's help to write it, yes."

They were walking through the thicket of trees that bordered Pemberton lands. Mists swirled, muffling their steps on a dreary Sunday afternoon. She'd met Wilf on her way back to the mill.

"Do you think your uncle will accept the position?"

Wilf kicked at a stone, lifting his big shoulders. "I told him in the letter that Miss Lena was trying her best to make changes, that she wasn't like other bosses. I tried to let him know that he could make a difference here but… it's his decision at the end of the day."

"Is he a good man?"

A wistful smile touched his mouth. "I remember him that way, aye. Haven't clapped eyes on him for many a year, mind. But he has my mother's blood in him. I reminded him of that."

Libby sighed, digesting the information. "'Miss Lena'? Does she know you call her that?"

Wilf grinned. "That's what the house staff call her."

"Have you called her that?"

"Not likely," he chuckled, and Libby smiled. "What do you think of her?"

She took a moment to think about her answer. "I want to believe in her. The way she stood up to Blackwood, even as he was shouting and calling her for everything under the sun? She stuck to her guns.

"And the way she is with Billy. She has a..."

"A kindness," Wilf supplied, and Libby stopped him, nodding enthusiastically.

"Yes, a goodness. I believe her heart is in the right place but whether she will be able to pull it off?" She shook her head sadly. "That I don't know."

In the days since Miss Pemberton had sacked her management team, the mill had flailed whilst she was brought up to speed. More workers left, a stream of people seeking the security of work in mills where the management wasn't decimated. Libby's enthusiasm for the changes had waned slightly as the tales of woe and threats of impending disaster swirled around them all. It was hard to stay upbeat in the face of it all.

Wilf had decided to shore up the chances of getting his uncle to take the job by writing to him and giving him an honest assessment of what was really happening at Hawks Mill.

"We're a long way from being out of the woods

yet," Wilf started to walk again. "We need an engineer… at least a foreman to supervise the three floors, but my uncle could do that standing on his head. I mentioned Henry Wickham to her–"

Libby grabbed his sleeve, bringing them both to a standstill again. "Henry Wickham? *The* Henry Wickham?"

"Yes," Wilf enunciated.

"But isn't he in…?"

"Gaol, yes," Wilf shook his head, "but that doesn't seem to bother her. She says she's written to the master at Walton, requesting a meeting with him, because Wickham has returned her letters unopened."

Libby wasn't sure about the logic of seeking out an engineer such as Henry Wickham. "Do you think that that is a good idea?"

Wilf looked affronted. "Miss Lena trusts me. She asks for my help. I've never… never had that before, you know, people listening to my opinion. She wants to help us all."

Libby thought about Thea's predicament and wondered how far the mill owner's benevolence would go. Helping an unmarried mother, maybe?

"What are you thinking?"

Libby eyed Wilf, knowing that Thea wouldn't like her private business being common knowledge, though it probably already was. Most of the apprentices knew of Thea's pregnancy, even though her belly was well hidden beneath her tunic still.

"Thea…"

"What about her?"

Libby decided that she needed to check with Thea before seeking out support from people like their employer. If Miss Pemberton was inclined, she could send Thea to the workhouse as soon as she found out. She shook her head and began walking. "Never mind."

"Is she alright – Thea, I mean," Wilf said.

"Why do you ask?"

"She seemed… I don't know… sad, I'd say."

"We're all worried," Libby hedged, ducking under a branch. "Lots of changes. Polly is vocal that they'll all be stuck with the consequences of these changes. I keep telling her that we're all in this together but–"

"Polly is like a terrier with some things. God help the man who marries her. He'll be in for a lifetime of earache with that one. At least with Thea, a man would be able to hear his own thoughts."

Libby eyed Wilf thoughtfully. Was he sweet on the pretty Thea, too? And if he was, why did that make her feel annoyed?

They climbed a stile, Wilf turned and held out a hand to help her down. "Where will you go? In the summer, I mean, when your indenture expires."

The dew-laden grass soaked through her boots, chilling her feet, as she struck out across the field. The chimney stack disappeared into the low-lying clouds, the mill sat in silence.

"I don't know," Libby answered truthfully.

But for the first time in her life, she wasn't sure she wanted to leave this place.

CHAPTER 26

igh walls of the Borough Gaol loomed into the misty morning. The dressed brick facade was flanked by square towers, and the gates yawned open like an iron maw as Lena and Wilf walked through them.

Though the building was relatively new, the narrow corridors carried a miserable stench of despair. The distressed sounds of humanity—groans and coughs—echoed through the structure.

Lena's stomach coiled with tension as she met the forlorn gazes of the occupants in the rooms along the passageway they walked down. The guard's keys clinked with a heavy finality as he led the way. It filled her with dread to know that such an eventuality could be in her future if things continued as they were at Hawks Mill.

That morning, Wilf had filled the awkward silence on the carriage ride into Liverpool by telling her how sometimes families were allowed to remain together, even if it was the father who'd accrued the debt. But also, oftentimes, the owners of the gaol charged for the privileges of these accommodations, meaning that families were stuck inside these places for years.

The guard stopped outside a room. To her surprise, the door was open.

Inside, Lena could see the cell was bare save for a simple wooden frame bed and a rickety stool. Using the iron key in his hand, the guard rapped twice on the wooden cell door. A small, barred window, high on the wall opposite the door, allowed scant light through, casting an ominous bar of illumination upon the stone floor. Through the dimness, Lena narrowed her eyes, trying to discern the shape of a man in the shadows.

"On your feet, Wickham," the guard snapped. "It's your lucky day."

The shape on the bed moved, morphing into a man as he rolled onto his back and then to the edge of the bed. "No day can be considered lucky when I have to look upon your pocked face," the voice was raspy, as if rarely used.

The guard met Lena's harried gaze. "Are you sure you know what you're doing, miss?"

Lena set her shoulders back, refusing to be cowed by this dreary man. "You can wait at the end of the hall," she said starchily, dismissing the guard by stepping further into the cell. She waited until the guard had ambled away, consciously unrolling the fists she'd made at her sides. "Mr Wickham?"

The man didn't move, but she felt his gaze on her.

She felt it in the way her skin prickled with awareness.

"From what I've read about you, sir, you're not an ill-mannered man. Yet you've returned my letters unopened and now you ignore me."

He moved then, rolling off the bed and into the middle of the floor in one smooth motion, with such pace that she took a fearful step back and collided with Wilf. Where he'd stopped, he was standing in the pool of light. His dark hair was a mass of curls, a scraggly beard concealed his jaw, but his eyes blazed not with hatred, but intensity. "What do you want?"

Lena's chin lifted a fraction. "My name is Lena Pemberton. I own Hawks Mill in Birchleigh. I require an engineer."

His gaze wandered indelicately over her attire, blatantly rude, leaving her momentarily breathless. "Then you're a long way from home. What brings you to my humble abode?"

"I wish to offer you a job, Mr Wickham. My mill needs an engineer, one with a knack for innovation and a commitment to safety protocols. I believe you're the right fit for such a position."

The intensity in his eyes flickered with loathing. He spread his hands wide, a gesture at odds with his confined state. "As you can see, I'm slightly indisposed at the moment."

"I am aware of your situation, Mr Wickham," she said, hating the way her voice hitched over the words, especially when his gaze met hers. The man disconcerted her, and she didn't care for it. "I am prepared to settle your debts and offer you employment."

Henry Wickham spun away from her, and she flinched. "Not interested," he muttered curtly.

He dropped back onto his bed, lay down, stretched out his legs, and stacked his hands behind his head.

Lena glanced at Wilf, who shrugged and shook his head in reply. She turned back to the surly man, "Do you understand what I'm offering you? It's a way out of here."

His eyes remained shut. "You have a job that you want me to do. And I'm telling you, I'm not interested."

"Mr Wickham, I don't have much time or the patience for this. Word is that you are the best in the business, and I—"

His torso lifted in a swift motion as he sprung off the bed and prowled across the floor once more. Instinctively, this time Lena retreated until the wall met her back. His hands came up either side of her head, though he did not touch her.

"I know your mill, Miss Pemberton. I know that your father is a man who cuts corners. You're here to offer me a job because your mill is probably near bankruptcy and you're out of options, especially if you're here seeking to offer me work."

Lena's tongue slipped out to moisten her lips. "My father is dead."

His gaze held hers captive, and he took some of the sharpness out of his tone, "For that, I am sorry. I never met the man himself. Losing a parent is hard."

His hands dropped to his sides. "But I'm done with the industry."

Lena tried again. "I'm trying to salvage what's left of my grandfather's legacy. I'm making changes at the mill, but I need experts. I've had doors slammed in my face constantly. I'm prepared to settle your outstanding debts and give you a job. The position would come with accommodation, and food, if needed—"

"The rot at Hawk's Mill is deep-seated. I won't attach my name to anything there."

"I sacked the overseer, my foreman, and the mill manager has left of his own accord in the past month," Lena said firmly. "I know exactly what's been happening at the mill. I want to change it, but I can't do it alone."

"It's all true. Every word she says," Wilf spoke up for the first time when Wickham continued to watch her. "A boy was injured in the mill. Miss Pemberton took him in and has been nursing him back to health. She paid for a doctor, despite Mr Sparrow's objections. She's even planning to make it so that Billy can keep working once he's fully recovered. No one else has done that before, and you know it. I've seen the changes myself, Mr Wickham, sir."

"Wilf is the overseer in the mule room now," Lena said softly.

"He's just a scrap of a boy; he can't manage running the mule room," Wickham scoffed, finally stepping back from her. Lena placed her hands across her stomach to try and steady the fluttering within. "If this is all you have, no amount of experience will save your wretched mill."

Wilf drew himself up. "I'm twenty-three, sir."

Lena found herself rushing to Wilf's defence. "He may be young, but his advice has steered me right so far. And I trust him, which doesn't come easily to me. Besides, many of the workers have gotten wind of the changes in Pemberton fortune, and the rumours that it comes with, and they've left."

"With the right equipment, workers, and a better steam engine to help, we could do it," Wilf said. "The workers who are left are behind her plans."

Henry's dark eyes flicked between them, landing on Wilf. "What steam engine do you have?"

Lena said, "A single-cylinder beam engine."

Henry shook his head, exhaling noisily. "An antique these days."

"I can get you a better steam engine," Lena said quickly, knowing that she didn't have the finances to make such an outlandish statement, but vowed that she would find a way. "All I need from you is to make the looms we have more efficient, the same way you did for the ones in Lancashire."

Pain moved in the dark depths of his eyes, replaced by temper once more. "You wouldn't want to attach yourself to a debtor, Miss Pemberton. Not if you're looking to secure finance to pull your mill from the depths your father left it in."

"You do know about the Pemberton name and Hawks Mill then," Lena murmured. She wondered if she would ever be free of the pity and scorn that she'd faced from people in the past weeks.

"Aye, I do," Henry said roughly. "I know all about your father's ways. But I can't go back to Birchleigh, of all places. People know me there. They'll know I'm in here. How could I face them?"

"Mr Wickham, I don't much care for the circumstances that brought you here. But if I don't turn things around by the year's end, I'll be joining you in the next cell. Please, help me. I can't do this on my own." Her voice was a whisper of vulnerability, a plea for an ally in a battle she was afraid to face alone.

He turned his head, staring at the cell window, at the grey sky beyond it. Lena held her breath, waiting. Just as she was about to plead once more, Henry Wickham turned back to her and sighed.

Then nodded once.

CHAPTER 27

*H*enry had woken long before daylight. He'd stood at the small bedroom window in his cottage and watched the sun crest the horizon, lessening the sky from black to pink, bathing the Lancashire countryside with April warmth as it rose.

The cottage was small and functional, with white-washed walls and a thatched roof, right at the edge of the village. It had been sparsely furnished with a threadbare sofa and two worn chairs. The bare wooden floors bore scuffs of past residents. The kitchen contained a stove and a sturdy oak table that was bigger than he needed and, judging by some of the deep gouges in the surface, it had served as a workbench more than once. The stout cast-iron stove was meant to heat the place as well as cook his food. The brass bed frame behind him must have cost a pretty penny, and the mattress was much more comfortable than the one in the gaol, yet he'd not slept well.

The mill, with its tall chimney, was easily discernible. The long building with numerous windows rumbled like a sibilating beast, even at this early hour. Behind it was Hawks Manor, like a sentinel watching over its domain, elegant and stately with tall windows that shone in the sunlight.

Last evening had been spent acquainting himself with his new quarters, tidying up the remnants of autumn's leaves and layers of dust, following his adamant choice to journey on foot to the village, declining Lena's offer of a carriage ride upon his departure from the gaol. He'd had tasks to attend to, ones that he wanted to keep out of prying eyes, but those errands did little to alleviate his lingering sense of guilt—a feeling he realised would now be a constant companion.

He hadn't yet fully comprehended his newfound liberty, his freedom from debt nor the fact that he was now resuming an occupation he'd resolutely walked away from, especially after what had happened.

Yet here he was, now indebted to a pretty mill owner who, despite her appealing exterior, seemed woefully out of her depth with the task ahead.

Had he not learned his lesson?

He looked out over the patchwork of slate rooftops and chimney stacks poking out of the tree-tops, the cobblestone streets tucked at the foot of the rolling hills. He'd grown up looking at the hills from the opposite side in the neighbouring village of Overleigh. He'd left for an apprenticeship, convinced that he was going to change the world and never come back.

Guilt twisted his gut and he moved away from the vista. He had changed the world for one family. He scrubbed his hands down his face, now free of the beard. It served as a reminder that he'd made a choice, albeit out of compassion for a young woman seeking help and trying to make those changes. Maybe it had spoken to the inner mutineer in him, the one who'd long since been silenced when the reality of change had come crashing down on his head.

He knew one thing for certain: once Lena Pemberton knew the truth, she wouldn't want him at her mill.

As he made his way down the narrow staircase, a knock rattled the back door, reminding him that fixing the door latch was at the top of his to-do list. He yanked open the door, expecting Lena, but was met by a stranger instead. Inquisitive hazel eyes swept over Henry, leaving him with the distinct feeling of being thoroughly appraised. The man wore a neat suit, though upon closer inspection, Henry noted crude repairs in the fabric, suggesting the man couldn't afford new attire. After a quick evaluation of his own, Henry pegged the man as working class, likely having something to do with the mill.

Henry's brows arched in inquiry.

"'Ow do," he greeted, the thick Yorkshire accent of the visitor was accompanied by a hand being thrust towards him. "You must be my new engineer."

Henry accepted the hand. "Henry Wickham."

"Albert Simpson," the man replied.

Silence fell between them, with Henry bracing for a judgment that didn't come.

Albert's eyes roamed over the facade of the cottage. "How is it?"

Henry nodded. "Better than what I've known for the past year."

A hint of a smile touched the corners of Albert's mouth. Henry knew there was no point in skirting the subject of his time in debtor's prison. "Do you know who I am?"

"Aye," Albert said slowly. "I know you're from Overleigh and that your work is well spoken of in these parts, and that there's not much you can't do with a piece of machinery."

Henry shifted his feet, awkward under the firm gaze the mill manager was giving him. This was a man with whom Henry would have to work closely with. "High praise, indeed," he muttered as he broke the watchful gaze, looking instead at the mill.

"You don't get as long in't tooth as me in this industry without learning a few names," Albert said. "I want you to know I don't judge a book by its cover. I make my own mind up about a man based on how he treats me and those around him. If you're straight by me, I'll stand by you."

Henry's gaze moved back to Albert. This outlook was a refreshing one. "I can live with that," he responded with a nod. "Does anybody else know?"

"You can't keep news like that under wraps, son,"

Albert said. "But anyone in my mill will live by my rules."

Henry indicated the manor house with a nod. "And Miss Pemberton?"

Albert shrugged. "I've only been here a few days. Can't speak for her, but I will say, she's fine. She wants the changes and wants the mill to succeed.

"I won't lie to you—financing it is going to be a tough, uphill battle for the lass. But she keeps finding the coin when I ask her for it. She'll question it, mind, but what owner wouldn't? She's dismissed the overseers who took advantage of their positions, and she's doing right by the workers. In my book, that's good enough for me."

Henry hesitated, shame clogging his throat. That wasn't what he was asking about. He hated that the opinions of his peers mattered to him, hated it more that he wanted to erase what had happened in his past. It was one of the reasons why he'd walked away from engineering.

Albert sighed as he guessed where Henry's thoughts were. "I don't pretend to know all the details of what happened to you. If that girl up there knows anything, she hasn't said a word to me. You do your job, Wickham; that's all anyone can ask of you."

Henry wished it were that simple but nodded anyway. He unhooked his coat from the back of the door. "Best you show me what is needed with these looms, then."

CHAPTER 28

The clatter of machinery filled the vast mule room. They navigated between the looms and spindles, their path illuminated by shafts of weak sunlight filtering through the grime-streaked windows. The machines rumbled and groaned, watched over by lithe fingers.

The tickle of the dusty air and the scent of oil all seemed to soothe his agitation.

Soon, Henry was focused on the job at hand. It grieved him that corners had been cut. He could still see the dark stain on the rough floorboards where he was told a child had lost a hand because of the lack of guards.

Albert was a wellspring of knowledge, a natural fit in the surroundings of the mill. But the rumours about the Pemberton mill were true, and together they began to cobble a list of areas that needed the most urgent attention first.

As they turned a corner by the carding machines,

Lena Pemberton emerged from the din, a vision of understated elegance and a stark contrast to the workers in their labour-worn garb.

Gone was the fancy navy frock that she'd worn at the jail. Now, Lena wore a simple purple dress that softened her presence, and while modest, it did nothing to mask her beauty or the keen intelligence that sparkled in her eyes. Her dark hair was styled in an unassuming manner, tucked neatly away from her face, lending her a practical air.

Henry's gaze was wary. He'd seen for himself the miserliness and harsh cost-cutting that had been going on here. He had to remind himself that she was seeking to make changes. Henry stood by quietly while Albert and Lena exchanged greetings.

"I trust your lodgings are satisfactory, Mr Wickham?" Lena leaned closer so that he could hear her over the racket of the looms.

Henry caught the gentle scent of perfume, which must have clung to her from a delicate dab along her neck and a vivid image rushed through his mind. "Yes, thank you, Miss Pemberton."

If she found his response curt, she didn't show it.

Albert, unaware of any underlying tension, joined in the conversation. "I've been showing Mr Wickham around, allowing him to cast his eye over the equipment. We have a few ideas where we could make some immediate changes, right, Miss?"

Lena's gaze met his. "I imagine there are lots of changes to be made. I'm looking to make the mill as safe as possible with a minimal amount of cost until I can secure enough finance to bring everything up to a standard where children and everyone can work safely. I want to build a business that we can all be proud of, Mr Wickham."

"There are more than a few changes needed," Henry remarked. "My only hope is that this isn't mere lip service, being offered by a Pemberton simply to pass inspection."

Lena met his gaze with quiet authority. "I am not my father, Mr Wickham. I seek to mend what has long been neglected here."

The admission was unexpected, and Henry felt his defences falter, just a fraction. "Guards should be fitted on all machines to prevent clothing from catching in the gears, perhaps even prevent the loss of a limb."

Lena nodded. "Of course. It's a necessary expense for the workers' safety."

"It's not just about safety," Henry said, his voice lowering as he leaned closer to one of the machines, inspecting its movements. "Well-guarded machines are less prone to cause disruptions. Guards offer protection from debris falling into the moving parts," he indicated the myriad cogs and wheels. "It's efficient, and it will save the mill money in the long run."

A glimmer of understanding shone in Lena's eyes. "I see," she said. "I hadn't considered the financial benefits. I appreciate your perspective."

Surprise flickered across Henry's features, quickly masked by his usual stoicism.

Lena's attention drifted to the workers, her

expression one of genuine concern that seemed to strip away any remnants of her father's reputation.

"Then we will make fitting the guards a priority. How quickly can they be installed?"

Henry's eyes narrowed. "With the right funds and hands to assist, I could begin immediately."

"Then that needs to be your first task."

Unable to help himself, Henry asked, "And what of the cost? I need to order materials and tools."

"The cost is secondary to the safety of my workers. I will not have another child maimed if I can help it. I would also like a guard placed up around all the pools, not just the millpond. It was noted by the last inspector, and I want to show that we're taking the recommended steps. Can you see to that?"

Henry had already taken note of the guard rail encircling the pond. The weathered wood was splintered and swayed in sections where it should have stood firm.

Henry felt the barriers of distrust beginning to crumble. "I will ensure it's done properly."

"Very good. Mr Simpson? You will see to it that any of the labourers will assist where possible if we can spare the manpower.

"If not, perhaps you would be kind enough to source some labour from the village," Lena said, scanning the breadth of the mill's interior, taking in the duck and dance of looms and workers. "I'm told that the children's schooling hasn't been completed as mandated. Mrs Reid claims to be struggling with her duties. I suspect the lion's share of taking care of all the apprentices falls on her shoulders, instead of being shared with her husband." Her keen gaze pinned her mill manager. "What would your advice be here, considering the pressures of funding an additional wage?"

Henry and Albert exchanged a look.

"Managing the apprentice house is hard work, Miss," Albert acknowledged. "At my last mill, the children were given two hours in the morning. It was more efficient because they'd just had their grub, and their heads seemed screwed on better at that time.

"Or you could see if there was a woman in the village who could read and write."

Lena inclined her head thoughtfully. "That could work. Bringing in someone just for the education. There are a few possibilities to consider there. Shall we continue?"

As the trio moved through the mill, Lena listened with focused intensity. She didn't scribble notes or indulge in frivolous comments. Instead, her questions seemed to cut to the core of the matter, revealing a mind that was following every word, every suggestion, and seeking ways to ensure that their suggestions for improvement melded with her tight budget.

Henry found himself explaining the finer points of mill engineering to her, and she followed his explanations with a keen interest that belied her lack of technical background. It revealed a mind attuned to the intricacies of her new role, one that sought to learn and understand what was needed.

Henry felt stirrings of cautious optimism and was forced to acknowledge that, on the surface at least, she seemed to be keen for change. And rather than changes to line her pocket, it seemed to be to better the lives of Hawk's Mill workers. Just as Albert had predicted, he felt a kernel of appreciation flourish deep inside. She might just be the salvation this place needed.

They moved down to the heart of the mill, where the great wheel turned with labouring creaks, its structure worn from years of use. Henry's trained eye was thorough in inspecting it, pointing out the fatigue in the mechanism and the wear on the paddles that dipped into the churning water of the pond.

"As predicted, the wheel is worn out," he remarked, running a hand along the grain of the wood from the top railing.

"Will it need to be replaced?" Lena inquired.

"The cost would be considerable," Henry replied. "And with the way the industry is changing, my recommendation would be to invest your money where you'll see the most profit right now." He led the way to the steam engine room. Inside, the steam engine clunked, its pistons heaving with an uneven rhythm, spluttering, and coughing like an asthmatic in the depths of winter.

"It's as we anticipated," Albert turned to Lena. "This one has seen better days, like some of us."

"I would say it would be a false economy to try and fix it. It's old, probably beyond repair," Henry added.

Lena watched the great beast of steam and iron. "What would be the cost of a new one?"

"Well, I've been out of the industry for a year or so; the prices may have fluctuated a bit," Henry hedged.

Her gaze was resolute as she pressed him.

Henry delivered the figures—a sum that would have made even the most hardened industrialist wince.

To her credit, she didn't flinch. "Then would you at least try to repair it first?"

Henry hesitated, unwilling to give her any false hope. It was Albert who patted him on the shoulders. "Of course, he will try, Miss. If anyone can fix it, it's young Henry here."

Henry wished he shared Albert's enthusiasm but found himself nodding.

Lena seemed to sense his hesitation. "I would appreciate it if you could try, Mr Wickham. If not, then I shall simply have to find the means for a new one.

"If Hawk's Mill is to be considered competitive and on an even playing field with the likes of Black Marsh and beyond, then it must run as smoothly as the finest silk thread.

Her mouth flattened in resignation. "What's next?"

CHAPTER 29

When Albert Simpson had accepted the job of mill manager, Lena had been nervous to meet him; there was no need for worry. Albert had an easy way about him and a quick smile, a complete antithesis of John Sparrow.

Just like his nephew, Albert was well-versed in engineering and the textile industry, and Lena found herself enthralled as he explained the intricacies and mechanisms of running a mill as complex as Hawks. Under Albert's tutelage, Lena began to explore the possibility of utilising one of the sheds as a weaving shed, so that they could produce goods in-house and boost profits. What was perhaps most distressing was his revelation that the ledger where all accidents at the mill were meant to be recorded was not accurate. She saw for herself that Billy's accident had been noted – the ink dark and fresh – though it neglected to mention the severity of the boy's injury.

Prior entries were faded as though Hawks Mill

didn't experience accidents. She knew first-hand that they had happened.

This statement, corroborated by Wilf, crushed her with the knowledge that her father had prioritised profit over the welfare of his workers.

Lena immersed herself in the politics of the industry as she sought ways to raise capital. Husbands dismissed her but Lena soon discovered that their wives were just like her; trying to get their voices heard, too. The wives she spoke with gave her the same nodding tacit encouragement as Mr Brown.

It was heartening, at least, to see that the changes she was implementing at the mill were starting to have a positive effect. Since John Sparrow's resignation and the dismissal of both the overseer and Mr Blackwood, the foreman, it seemed she had stemmed the haemorrhaging of staff to other mills.

Henry Wickham was also a surprise.

He'd insisted on making his own way to the mill from the gaol, though she had suspicions that his reluctance to travel with her had more to do with him being in a debtor's gaol than being seen in public with a Pemberton. He had taken up residence in a quaint little cottage on the edge of the estate.

On his first day of work, Lena almost didn't recognise him. The scraggly beard was gone, though he'd done little to tame his unruly curls. His clothing was that of an engineer: a simple cloth shirt and grey woollen waistcoat, with trousers often smeared with oil.

He and Albert had delved into deep conversations

as Lena and Albert had shown Henry around the mill. At times, Lena had trouble keeping up with them both and had to remind them that she wasn't an engineer; they needed to explain things in terms she could understand. As expected, the list of necessary repairs at the mill was long and, thus, very costly. As such, her days were filled with meetings and visits with various businessmen as she tried to secure investments, promising to reward shareholders with future profits.

Quite often, Lena would be in the mill and catch sight of Henry, his sleeves rolled back to his elbows, a canvas bag of tools open by his feet as he worked on the looms.

There was something about her engineer that gave Lena a frisson of excitement in her stomach whenever he was near. More than once, she'd felt those dark eyes assessing her, though he'd never behaved inappropriately. Instead, he was always...aloof.

Alone, she would often think about how he'd towered over her in the gaol, holding her captive without once laying a finger on her. Unlike with Thomas, she'd not felt scared by him.

She'd been almost...exhilarated.

More than anything, she was struck by his intelligence. Just as forecast, his skills were boundless. It seemed the locals were coming to help, too. Mr Simpson had sourced extra hands from the village in exchange for offcuts of cloth they could repurpose. This gave Lena the idea of transforming that cloth into something sellable. Albert had welcomed the plan, claiming 'even a dripping tap fills a bath'.

She appointed a salesman, a man by the name of Saunders, for the mill so he could liaise directly with local weaving sheds and those companies who required cloth that was not quite good enough for the finer fashion houses but available at a lower cost for those families who needed it.

Lena had also visited the apprentice's house. While she couldn't help the children being two, sometimes three, to a bed—the house was too small for more, and funds were too tight to accommodate additional beds—what she could do was ensure the children were warm, clothed, and fed properly. It pained her that they seemed afraid of her, with most of them sitting, heads bowed, not meeting her eyes. Others glared at her defiantly, and she wondered how much more happened at her mill that she was yet to discover.

She had already begun searching for a teacher. She knew other mills sent their children to school, but she wanted to ensure those at Hawks Mill were not treated differently because of where they worked.

Lena looked up at a sharp knock. The door to the drawing room opened, and Mr Simpson preceded Mr Brown, who announced his arrival.

The mill manager's jacket glistened with rain-drops. In surprise, Lena glanced at the window. Rain ran in rivulets down the panes, the spring rain in full swing, and she hadn't even noticed. A fire crackled warmly in the hearth, and she was grateful to Gwen for lighting it.

"You wanted to see me, Miss?" Albert inquired.

Lena, seated at her father's desk, gave him a warm smile. "Would you care for some tea?"

With Mr Brown dispatched to fetch a tray, Lena waited for Mr Simpson to take a seat on the sofa before joining him on the one opposite. "Thank you for coming over so swiftly. I would've come to you, but I'm afraid I got carried away with the accounts once more."

Albert smiled, his eyes roving over the pile of ledgers on the desk. "I trust everything is in order?"

"Actually," Lena began, hesitant, even though the idea seemed clear to her. She'd come to value Mr Simpson's opinion. "I have an idea and I wondered if it had merit. I thought I'd run it past you first."

"I'm all ears."

"I read about this split shift working pattern that some mills are employing," she explained. "We would have some people working in the morning and some in the evening. I know my father was greatly opposed to such a thing, but I've been looking at the workload.

"We could work the mill for longer, continuing production and managing our wage bill better. It would also easily comply with the ten-hour legislation, allowing the children to attend school. You pointed out that most accidents happen when the children are tired at the end of long shifts.

"Accidents would be reduced if they were not working those gruelling fifteen or sixteen-hour days. We could even bring in additional workers. What do you think?"

Albert's smile was genuine and warm. "It could be

open to abuse, but in my opinion, it is the way forward. We could start one shift at six and it would work until three, then the next shift would start at three and work until eleven."

Lena returned his smile. "Of course, it would be easier in the summer when we have more daylight hours. I know Mr Clark was also worried it would be open to abuse, with people coming in from other mills and the like. But with our lower staffing numbers, that's not something we need to be concerned with just yet."

"I agree."

Lena felt herself relax a little. "I was just wondering about the logistics of implementing it?"

Albert smoothed his hair down to his head as he gave it some thought. "It would require additional overseers, which would come at a cost. We have a handful of young lads who are ready to step up, and we could place them in more of a supervisory role, instead of overseers. They would answer to an over-seer who was managing two floors."

"So, similar to the underseer?" Lena asked.

"Aye," Albert said, his quick grin confirming. "Just like an underseer."

Lena felt buoyed by Albert's enthusiasm, and together they hammered out the details of which workers they could approach for such roles. Lena had already sought advice from both Wilf and Libby about the workers who were capable and experienced, and a plan began to form.

Implementing the new ideas felt like an eternity,

but three weeks later, Mr Simpson rushed into the room, his enthusiasm infectious as he plopped the accounts book on her desk.

Curiously, Lena looked up at him. "What's this?"

Albert pointed a crooked finger at the ledger, a grubby fingernail tapping the final column.

"Three weeks with this new shift, and productivity is up by eleven per cent already. It's working."

CHAPTER 30

"*L*ibby!"

The sharp cry pierced the rhythmic clatter of the machines. Libby snapped her head towards the sound, but it was the sight of Thea bent at the waist that sent her heart sinking into her stomach.

Without hesitation, she pulled the clutch on the loom and hurried over to the young girl.

Thea's face contorted with pain as she moaned, "Something is wrong."

"Is it the baby coming?" Effie joined them, followed by Daisy.

Libby placed a hand on Thea's back. "It's too soon," she murmured anxiously.

Between breaths, Thea managed to say, "The pains... They've never been this bad."

"It's okay," Libby found herself saying, even as Thea slowly lowered herself to the floor, writhing in pain.

"What is it?" Wilf approached them, concern

etched on his face as he looked at Thea. "Is she injured?"

Libby hesitated, torn between secrecy and the need to get her friend some help. Finally, she leaned in and whispered to Wilf, revealing Thea's secret. She saw the shock of new knowledge cross his face as his gaze dropped to Thea. Yet he nodded and said, "Take her back to the apprentice's house. I'll make sure your loom stays running. Get yourself back to work as soon as you can."

Libby was reluctant to do that, but the dusty, filthy floor of the mule room was no place to lay down, let alone birth a baby. It also meant that Matron would now find out the secret. Time was running out, and Thea needed her help.

Polly and Daisy helped her to get Thea to her feet. The young girl was scared, crying softly as Libby led her out of the mule room and into the fresh air. Libby had to stop every few steps as the pain gripped Thea, her low moans rolling around the stone walls of the yard. Libby offered the girl plaintive reassurances even as her fear pulsed through her.

Thea let out a sharp yelp. "Oh, it hurts!"

"You're almost there," Libby encouraged her to move forward a bit further until Henry appeared, sweeping the young girl up into his arms. Without a word, he strode across the yard, ducking under the arch that led through to the apprentice's house. He moved with pace and Libby had to trot to keep up with him.

As they approached the apprentice house, Lena

Pemberton appeared in the doorway, and Libby's heart skipped a beat.

"What's the matter with her?" She called out to Henry, who shook his head. "Libby?"

Libby was terrified that Lena would now send the young girl back to the poor house. She started to babble incoherently, stumbling over the words as she tried to think of an excuse – any excuse – to explain the young girl's condition. Lena held up a hand, urging Libby to calm down and clarify what was wrong.

Henry stopped outside the door, looking back at Libby. "She's pregnant?"

Libby bit her lip and gave a slight nod.

Mrs Reid's wail of shock was mirrored on Lena's face. "The father?" She asked weakly.

Libby gave a shake of her head just as Thea groaned, clutching her stomach once more.

Lena's expression was pinched with worry. Libby saw the evaluations move across her employer's face, even as the matron started pronouncing how unrelenting her work was, and how the girls took advantage of her.

Miss Pemberton ignored her, focusing on the struggling girl in Henry's arms instead.

"Go and fetch the doctor, Libby," she told her. " Mrs Reid, please, calm yourself! Henry, please bring Thea to the manor house. There's more room, and she'll be more comfortable there. Go now, Libby – as fast as you can. There's no time to lose."

Libby didn't hesitate and took off, running towards Birchleigh village.

WILF HAD to call her name twice to be heard across the din in the apprentice kitchen. Libby looked up in surprise, her heart giving a little jump at the sight of him poking his head around the edge of the kitchen door. He beckoned her with a gesture and then vanished, leaving her to follow him out the door.

She closed the door to a group of cackling and whooping young girls, giving an amused shake of her head.

"You'll start rumours if you keep calling 'round the apprentice house for me," she told him with a smile.

"How's Thea?" He asked, without preamble.

Libby glanced back at the door then pulled Wilf further into the yard, away from listening ears that might be pressed against the windows.

Moonlight bathed the yard, still apart from a few stray cats chasing rodents. She folded her arms to shield against the cool night air and recounted the drama of the day, how she'd fetched the doctor and stayed with Thea whilst he'd examined her.

"She hasn't lost the baby, but he says she needs to rest. There are no signs that she's going to lose it, but he's given her some milk to help her sleep. She's still across at the big house. Billy is happy because he has some company."

"What did Miss Lena say?" Wilf inquired, his brow creased with concern.

Libby sighed, her breath forming a small cloud in the crisp night air. "If she was cross, she didn't show it. If anything, I'd say she was shocked. She made me tell her who I thought the father was." She glanced at Wilf and said, "An unmarried girl, pregnant by her foreman isn't a good situation. At least she hasn't sent her away."

"I don't think Miss Lena would do that," Wilf replied. "From everything I've seen so far, she seems to want to help us. Albert says that she believes making the mill a better place for us will help her grow the mill in the end."

Libby wanted to believe it. She'd seen some of the changes for herself – hadn't Lena paid for a doctor to see to Thea? – but still wasn't quite ready to trust this new feeling of optimism that sparkled deep within.

"We've taken on more workers today – two have come back from Black Marsh, including Nab in the engine room."

"Nab Rose? Is back working at Hawks?"

Wilf gave her a lopsided smile. "Aye. We needed a stoker, though Henry has had the steam engine in bits more often than not. Seems the tide is turning for us all. More hands to help."

"Seems like."

Mrs Reid's sharp voice was heard through the door, drawing their attention.

"You'd never lose her on a dark night, would you?" Wilf murmured and Libby laughed.

"I think she's mad at us all about today. She's naggier than usual. I think she's worried that Miss Pemberton will expect her to look after the baby because she's been griping about all the work she has to do already."

"A girl as pretty and as clever as Thea won't be alone for long."

Libby was hit with a pang of envy. Wilf was kind and gentle, and a hard worker at that. He would make a good husband for the right girl, she thought.

"Mrs Reid was spitting mad, of course. She pretended to Miss Pemberton that she knew about the situation but, as good as admitted to us all that we were sneaking around behind her back. I'd best get back," she looked towards the house. She turned to go back inside but was stopped by his gentle touch on her arm.

"You're a good friend for looking out for her. Thea is lucky to have you on her side," he said earnestly.

Libby's gaze drifted over the softly lit windows of the apprentices' house. "They're my girls," she replied. "I'm the closest thing that most of them have to family."

She left Wilf standing in the yard as she walked back into the house. A house that had been her home for many, many years, and yet the closer she got to the time of her leaving, the less inclined she was to go.

CHAPTER 31

"*M*iss Pemberton?"

Lena turned in the portico of the manor house, plucking off her gloves. The carriage she had just alighted from was moving off, causing her to miss what Henry had said. She was still stewing over her earlier conversation with Mr Radford and had envisioned half an hour's peace in the silent library. That image evaporated as Henry approached.

It wasn't like her engineer to seek her out unless the matter was urgent.

"Is everything alright?"

Instead of his usual tool bag, Henry held a sheaf of papers in his hand, and Lena's heart sank. Papers often meant something official, and in her limited experience, that seldom boded well. "I tried to catch you earlier, but you were out."

She forced a smile onto her face. Though eager to unload the frustrations of the morning, she knew

Henry couldn't help her with Mr Clark's latest setback. "I've just this second got back."

"I can wait if you'd prefer?"

"By your expression, the news isn't good. I'd rather get it over with now," she muttered. She followed him down the steps and across the yard, ducking through the clematis-clad archway that led to the mill.

Workers stood around, munching on gruel and pieces of dried bread—it was lunchtime. A few of the orphans called out to her. She stopped to say hello to them, and she felt a sliver of her irritation dissipate as she looked upon their friendly faces. It was a reminder of why she was doing what she was doing. If Henry's curious looks made her question how she spoke to the children, he kept any comments to himself.

He opened the door to the engine room and held it for her, to which she murmured her thanks as she stepped inside. The lunch break meant that the looms were paused, and she welcomed the silence, grateful they wouldn't have to shout at each other to be heard.

The tang of oil and hot metal filled the room. Below their feet, water tumbled through a series of tunnels, diverted now that the wheel's power was not needed. Henry made his way over to the iron beast, and Lena was dismayed to see several flat pieces of metal laid out on the floor.

"This doesn't look too promising," she said resignedly.

Henry's grimace confirmed her fears. "Steam

engines like this take a while to heat up, and they require regular maintenance,"

"Which hasn't been done, I take it?"

Henry's stark gaze met hers before dropping to the pieces of metal by his feet. "It's as I feared. You see, we could tighten the piston rings here," he indicated, "but it's a stopgap.

"When the steam leaks in the supply, it affects all the cylinders leading to steam wastage. As a result, we end up using more coal to compensate for the loss in steam pressure. Maintaining consistent steam pressure and water levels is challenging, particularly when the machine is undergoing maintenance. This affects mill productivity since the water wheel only has a limited water supply each day due to fluctuations in the river level."

"In layman's terms, Mr Wickham?"

Henry stood straighter. "You need a new steam engine. The metal is too porous and won't hold any repairs I attempt to make. It's an old machine, and technology has advanced significantly. New machines are much more fuel-efficient, meaning the energy we use from the fuel isn't wasted."

"I understand what you're saying, Mr Wickham but…"

"Finances," he guessed, and she nodded grimly. "What about finding an investor?"

"That's what I've been trying to do. Reaching out to past acquaintances of my father's and seeking input. Promising a share of proceeds. Of course, I get turned away when they realise who I am. The reputation... well, you know yourself."

"You need to find up-and-coming people. Those who are looking for innovation. Or those who have money but don't know what to do with it. A widow, perhaps."

Lena's sigh was long and drawn out. Frustrated, she spun away from him and walked towards the water wheel. Her attention was on the water cascading down, and she welcomed the fine mist of droplets that sprayed her face as she stood next to the rumbling wheel.

"I did try to fix it," Henry's voice was low, coming from right behind her.

Lena didn't turn. She felt the strains of her exasperating day and pinched the bridge of her nose. "I do not doubt that you've tried. It's just that some days, it feels like I'm taking two steps forward and then get pushed three steps back.

"Sometimes I wonder if I shouldn't do as Mr Clark and all the other naysayers are telling me and sell the whole place."

Henry moved closer again, and she felt the weight of his look in her periphery. "But you've changed so much here already. Why give up now?"

A ghost of a smile touched the edges of her mouth. She looked up at the ceiling and shook her head. "Some days I feel like giving up. But then I see the children and how happy they are with the improvements we've made so far. No accidents in almost two months," she said, turning her head to meet his dark, unreadable gaze.

His head tilted slightly. "That's an improvement worth writing home about."

She laughed out then, feeling a little tension ease. "Thank you, Mr Wickham. It feels like quite some time since I've laughed."

He watched her for a few moments. Under his direct stare, she felt the trill of awareness prickle at her senses.

She was desperate to change the subject. "Have you always wanted to be an engineer?"

He followed her lead as she walked back to the steam engine. She reached for one of the parts, ignoring his warning about getting her hands dirty. "I've worked for as long as I can remember. When I was eight, I was selling bread door-to-door. My mother died when I was young," he said. "The winter was harsh, and it took my younger sister, too. My father worked as an overseer. He died of cotton lung."

Lena couldn't help the pitiful sound she emitted. Cotton lung was a prolific, nasty disease that claimed the lives of many within the mill.

Henry continued, "I followed him into the mill over at Black Marsh. There was an engineer there, a man named Victor Robinson. He had a sharp tongue and a quick hand, but I was relentless in pestering him to teach me what he knew. My mother and father had made sure that I could read and write, and that set me apart from many of the boys in the mill room."

"Did you work your way up to being an engineer?"

"Not at Black Marsh," Henry said. "There was no room. I worked as much as I could with Victor, learned from him whenever I got the chance. I went to Manchester first, where I studied at the Mechanics Institute. Victor put in a good word for me there which got me in through the door.

"Then I had to keep up with the learning. I worked on the Bramhope tunnel construction. Eventually, I ended up in Milton Hill, fixing and installing looms and improving the systems they had to make them more efficient. Several mills after that."

Lena nodded. "Quite a journey from such humble beginnings. I'm sure your father would be very proud of what you achieved, had he lived."

Her smile was met with a bleak expression, and aggrieved shadows moved behind his eyes before they shuttered once more. Lena realised she had said something wrong.

Henry held out the paperwork towards her. "I'm sure if you forward this to Mr Radford, it has all the details required to show the funds we need for your new steam engine. My recommendation is a double-beam engine. They have one in a mill at Warden near Rochdale. It's a great example of fuel efficiency and they're reliable."

Lena was left blinking at his back as he hurried away.

In the month or so he'd been in her employ, Lena had been careful not to mention where they'd first met. Debtor's prison was a shameful subject for anyone, let alone a man as prideful as Henry Wickham. However, it did leave her wondering how an educated man like him had fallen so far from grace.

With the paperwork clutched tightly in her hand, Lena pondered the riddle that was her engineer. She had gleaned much about his skills and intelligence but knew little about the man himself. It was evident that he had once climbed a difficult ladder, only to tumble down under the weight of circumstances that she could only guess at.

She shut the engine room door behind her and made her way back to her office. Henry had vanished and she held back a sigh. She'd invited him here as a means to an end. An engineer was pivotal in her endeavours to restore the mill. Lena believed that this job could now offer him a chance to rebuild what he had lost, and for that she was glad.

She was growing accustomed to the men in her employ, but Henry Wickham had piqued her curiosity in a way that none of the others did.

Her respect for him was growing every day. Now, his hidden past was a part of him that she felt compelled to understand.

CHAPTER 32

The commotion drew her attention first. She made her way out of her bedroom and along the landing, drawn along the manor's hallway that echoed with the sound of raised voices. They seemed to grow louder and more intense as she neared them. She heard the low rumble of Mr Brown's reasonable tone, but her belly turned watery when she recognised the velvet accent of Thomas Cavendish among them. Frowning, she rounded the newel at the top of the stairs. Sure enough, Thomas was in the foyer, towering over Mr Brown. Gwen and James stood behind the butler, each looking equally annoyed.

"What are you doing here, Thomas?" Lena demanded as she descended the stairs, her gaze fixed on them. All four faces swung towards her.

"Mr Cavendish claims he has an appointment to see you," Mr Brown began. "I tried to dissuade him of this, but he insisted on coming in."

"Pushed his way in, more like," Gwen grumbled as Lena reached the bottom step.

Lena was acutely aware of Thomas's appraising stare, her skin crawling under his gaze. "We don't have an appointment, Thomas," she told him firmly. Fear sidled into her blood, and she momentarily wondered if somehow the news of the plan that she'd made at Henry's suggestion had gotten out even though she had been stonewalled at each turn so far.

Would Henry have betrayed her?

Thomas's hands spread as wide as his crocodilian smile. "I wanted to see you, Lena," he said. "Is that a crime?"

Lena was annoyed most of all by his air of entitlement.

Reluctantly, she allowed him in, thinking that the faster she dealt with him, the sooner he would leave.

In the library, surrounded by shelves of leather-bound books and the scent of aged paper, she faced him. "Say what you came here to say, but then you'll have to go. I have a very busy day ahead."

Thomas, unabashed by her cool reception, flashed a charming smile. "You look more radiant than ever," he stated, his voice dripping with sycophancy. "That dress is very flattering."

Irritated, Lena sighed loudly. "I don't have time for inane fawning. Please state your purpose and then leave."

Her heart gave a jolt as something sinister slid into his eyes. Just as quickly, it was snuffed out, though the effect made her skin crawl.

He tilted his head, lips flickering with humour. "I see the modifications at the mill aren't the only things that have changed. I must congratulate you on the good things I've been hearing about you and your endeavours here."

She thanked him stiffly, discomfort evident in her posture. "I'm surprised you know," she added.

Thomas clicked his tongue, with a slight head shake. "Cavendish Bank is invested in your business, Lena. Besides, your interim loan payment is owed soon. I'm doing my due diligence," he explained, his eyes scanning her with a calculated gaze.

"We have another four weeks yet," Lena informed him, her voice confident despite the quivering sensation in her belly.

Thomas began to prowl slowly around the room, picking up knickknacks and inspecting them, his presence making Lena feel sullied and invaded. "I'm curious, Lena. Making the changes you are implementing requires a lot of financial input. Yet, we can't seem to find out who else is investing in your mill."

"What makes you think there are investors?"

Thomas bounced a paperweight in his palm, set it back on the shelf, and moved again. "Your father liquidated his assets. Your business doesn't have many options... Unless you've picked up your father's habit of manipulating the truth to suit your own needs and you have been hiding assets from us?"

Lena's chin lifted defiantly as he neared. "I have a good team behind me," she asserted. "I've spent time learning. The changes mean that profits are growing, albeit slowly."

"Where did you get the money from?" he pressed.

"It's not your concern, Thomas. Your only concern should be that you'll get your payment," she retorted.

"You're making waves in the industry, Lena. Ignoring the advice and the trends of other mills. Taking on workers as other businesses are crumbling under the pressures," Thomas's expression shifted to one of sly amusement. "It's all anyone can talk about at parties. Your mill's growing success is becoming quite the topic."

"I'm sure they'll move on to something much more interesting soon enough," Lena replied, swallowing hard as his journey around the room culminated in him reaching her. She remembered the last time they were alone and silently prayed for Gwen to interrupt them once again. Her pulse slammed in her ears, and she tried hard to remain calm in his proximity.

"How long do you think you can keep up this charade?"

Her brow creased. "I don't follow."

His gaze lingered on her uncomfortably. "You're not a mill owner. You're a woman playing in a man's world. If you'd like my sage advice, it would be that you sell now. Salvage what you can before it's too late. You can't possibly think that this will all work out. Let me handle the sale for you. That way, if you cut your losses now, you'll have a little income to draw on. You won't have this grand house, of course, but I'm sure you'll make a fine enough mistress for someone."

"I think I'll take my chances all the same," she said evenly.

Her whole body tensed as Thomas reached out, slowly trailing a hand down her face. "Maybe I was too hasty in calling off our engagement. Seems I overlooked the lioness inside of you. I like a woman who can fight back," he crooned.

Lena recoiled, pulling her face away from his touch. "I don't care for your vulgarity, Thomas. You'll get your money."

He leaned in, untroubled by her agitation judging by the smirk playing on his lips. "Or perhaps you've found... alternative ways to raise funds?" he insinuated. "The old-fashioned way, spreading your legs like one of the girls at the docks."

Furious, Lena's retort was interrupted by the door opening. Expecting Gwen, she was even more relieved to see Henry Wickham standing there, his presence an unexpected but very welcome intrusion.

"Mr Wickham." Relief rang warmly in her voice.

Henry's eyes narrowed as he took in the scene. Thomas didn't move though Lena was aware of a shift in his demeanour.

"I wondered if I might have a word, Miss Pemberton?" he asked, his dark gaze moving between the couple.

"Don't they knock where you come from?" Thomas snapped.

Henry merely brokered him with a stare. "I was invited into this house, unlike some."

Lena stood a little taller, bolstered by the engineer's timely entrance. "This is Mr Wickham, our new engineer. It's largely down to his remarkable skill that we've been able to make lots of changes successfully."

"Ah, yes," Thomas drew the words out. "The criminal. I suppose a woman in your position must scrape the barrel, Lena."

Lena's mouth fell open as Henry's face darkened. He took a step toward Thomas, but Lena quickly intervened. "I believe you've made your point, Thomas, just as I have made mine. You'll get your payment on time."

"And if I don't, Lena?" Thomas was still looking at Henry, now more watchful because of the vibrating fury that rolled off Henry in waves. When his attention slid around to Lena, his mouth lifted sadistically. "I shall be sure to come and collect in person, just as the others have been. I'll see myself out."

Thomas scurried past Henry, ducking under the engineer's glare. Lena waited until the front door slammed shut and the waiting carriage was in motion before she risked a glance at Henry.

The silence pulsed with expectancy. She swallowed, her tension dropping a little when he met her pained expression.

"So that was the mysterious Mr Cavendish."

Her sigh was full of disappointment. "I'm sorry if he offended you. He's... impossibly arrogant."

A cynical smile twisted his lips. "Why are you sorry? He was right. I am a criminal."

She scanned his face. "I suppose I don't see you like that."

A muscle twitched in his jaw. He crossed to the window as if checking that Thomas had indeed left. "You'd promised yourself to *him?*"

She rubbed her chest with the heel of her hand, trying to ease the tight band there. "Turns out he was not the man I thought he was." Flashes of last Christmas burst into her mind, and she sat on the sofa. "I tried to call the engagement off, but my father wouldn't allow it. Thomas was the one to end things when he realised that Papa had emptied the coffers, and the mill was on the brink of collapse."

When Henry didn't reply, she looked across the room at him. He met her eyes moodily. "I can assure you if he'd been with you that day you came to find me, I wouldn't have taken the job."

She smiled at that. "Then I'm glad for it, Mr Wickham."

CHAPTER 33

*H*enry knew he had no right to entertain anything other than a professional concern in Miss Lena Pemberton. After all, he'd just seen for himself the type of man that could hold her interest.

Thomas Cavendish, a wealthy banker, was aeons apart from a grubby engineer like him. It served as a reminder that although he was beginning to see Lena in a more respectful light, admiring her keen and intuitive mind, they were still worlds apart.

It didn't help that he'd been acutely aware of the fear in her eyes when he'd interrupted them, and he made a note to thank Gwen for bursting into his workshed and begging him to intervene. Gwen had been almost frantic with worry.

Without question, he'd followed the young maid into the house. He wasn't sure what had transpired before, but both Gwen and Lena seemed nervous around the smarmy Thomas Cavendish, and he would wager a week's wages on the reasons for that. He'd met men like Thomas Cavendish before, lurking around the docklands pubs in their extravagant suits and polished carriages, tossing out coins like rainwater, yet sitting on their golden thrones in judgment over the working man.

He could tell she was shaking, her arms wrapped around her waist as if trying to hold herself together. Not wanting to scrutinise his motives too closely, he still wanted to ease her obvious agitation.

"If you're feeling up to it, I have something to show you."

It took her a few moments to pull her mind back to the present. "What is it?"

"It's something I'm sure will make you feel better. Why don't you meet me in the mill shed in a few minutes?"

She agreed, and he made his way back to the mill, cursing himself for harbouring fanciful thoughts. It was his penchant for aiding damsels in distress that had gotten him into trouble in the first place, and he had to keep reminding himself that she was his employer. It wasn't his job to care about her feelings, only to ensure that her mill was profitable. He was sure that as soon as he had all her equipment up to scratch, he would be looking for his next big project.

Surely, once he had his debts paid off to Lena, he would be free to find work elsewhere.

By the time she made her way into the far shed, he had refocused his mind on the project. He told

ANNIE SHIELDS

himself not to notice the way she wore her hair or the faint smell of honeysuckle that trailed behind her.

The shed was cluttered, the detritus of workers long gone cluttering the place. Cobwebs draped over parts of machines. The mud floor had dried, and dust stirred in the light winds drifting through the open doors, which let in the warm sunshine that bathed the lush green landscape beyond. A riot of colour exploded behind her, yet his eyes were only for her. He watched her carefully as her eyes moved around the space, finally settling on where he had draped the cloth.

"Is this what you wanted to show me?"

Unable to help his grin, Henry nodded. "It is." He pulled at the edge of the sheet, his smile widening as her frown deepened. "I found this loom in one of the sheds. In my spare time, I've reworked it so that it will be more efficient for us."

"Forgive me, Mr Wickham, I know what a loom looks like, but I'm still not entirely sure how it works."

Henry chuckled. He explained to her as he went, pointing out the spindles on the bobbins, and the strings woven between them all before he engaged the clutch.

The loom came to life, the rhythmic ticking as the shuttle flew back and forth, fascinating Lena.

She smiled and nodded. "What am I looking at? It looks just the same as the others."

Henry paused, his finger extended. "Just wait."

The shuttle flew back and forth for a few more

minutes until it suddenly stopped, the ensuing silence deafening.

But Lena reacted just as he'd hoped, her eyes widening in surprise as she met his gaze. "It stopped automatically?"

"Exactly that. You see here, the warp thread has broken. The loom stops until it is fixed. It will do the same when the bobbin runs out of thread. The mechanism here will eject the depleted pirn and stop until a new one is loaded."

Wonderment was written all over her face. "Henry, that's incredible."

Hearing his name on her lips for the first time gave his heart a little skip, and he had to hide his happiness.

He broke the gaze, trying to collect his scattered thoughts. "It will make everything more efficient because we won't need as many workers."

Lena stepped closer, her eyes travelling over the machine. "It means it's safer."

Delighted by her insight, he grinned. "That's exactly what it means. But don't get too excited; this is still only a prototype. The Dutch have something similar already, so I've taken their technology and applied it here. Buying in more looms would cost a pretty fortune..."

"But if there was a safety shut-off, it would mean that we wouldn't need as many workers to watch over the looms. Can you do this to all of them?" Lena's eyes sparkled with the potential of what Henry's innovation could mean for the mill.

"Some," he agreed cautiously. "This one is old, so I've had to fabricate some of the parts myself. It would also mean taking one loom out of commission while I modify it." As he spoke, Henry could almost see the cogs turning in her mind, calculating the possibilities.

"One worker watches four looms now. We could have more looms working," she mused, her eyes lighting up with understanding.

He grimaced slightly at the thought, the implication of doing other workers out of pay weighing on him. "That's right."

When Lena turned to face him, her face was illuminated with a beaming smile. All the shadows that had lingered from her encounter with Thomas seemed to have vanished. At that moment, he realised it was worth it, just to see her smile again.

"Thank you, Mr Wickham," she said with genuine gratitude. "And not just for the work you're doing in here but also... for coming into the library just then," a rosy blush flooded her cheeks, and her self-conscious smile made her more becoming. "It was a nice change for me to see Mr Cavendish out of sorts for once."

He murmured his acknowledgement, his eyes lingering on her as she left the shed. The echo of her footsteps faded, leaving him with a yearning to hear her say his name just one more time. He stood there for a moment longer, the musty air of the shed filled with the remnants of her excitement, and then he turned back to his work, a faint smile on his lips.

CHAPTER 34

*T*he air was cool and damp, still carrying the scent of recent rainfall, as Libby watched Nab and Thea returning down the track that wound through the heart of Pemberton lands. Mist clung to the trees, muting the light and enveloping the surroundings in a hushed, serene atmosphere on this Sunday afternoon. A sense of relief washed over Libby, and she broke away from the other workers who were enjoying their day off. Taking shelter under the stone archway, she waited as Nab and Thea walked towards her, their paths diverging onto the cobblestone road that led to the workers' cottages.

"Where have you been?" she inquired, her voice tinged with worry. "You've been gone for quite a while."

Thea wore a faint, contented smile on her lips as she turned to watch Nab's departing figure. "Nab showed me the Temple Woods," she explained, her tone softening with pleasure. "It was lovely – the birds singing, and the rain hitting the trees above. So peaceful. I've had a wonderful time."

Libby bit the inside of her cheek to keep from laughing. For the whole time that Thea had been gone, the rain had been coming down in sheets. She knew the woods; she knew the places where a person could shelter – and just how cosy those places could be with more than one person inside.

"He's a nice man, isn't he?"

Libby pushed aside the anxiety that had initially filled her, thankful that the young girl hadn't run into any trouble in the woods. She absentmindedly rubbed her hand along Thea's arm, seeking reassurance. "I suppose he is. Come on, you should rest while you can. The doctor may have given you the all-clear, but I agree with Miss Pemberton – you shouldn't push yourself too hard. We're all invested in this baby now."

Thea allowed herself to be led into the yard, casting a final glance back at Nab as he hopped a fence and made his way across a field as a shortcut back to the cottages.

Libby leaned in closer, her curiosity getting the better of her. "He's certainly been making an effort to keep you company these days."

Libby had discovered Nab and Thea spending time together in the parlour of Hawks Manor after she'd finished her shift one evening. She had been pleasantly surprised to find that the young stoker had been visiting with Thea often while she convalesced. Although Thea had been back at work for a little over a fortnight, Libby felt obliged to keep a watchful eye on her. Lena might have made arrangements for her to return to work and assigned her a job where she could sit as needed, but Libby remembered how frightened she'd been the day Thea had collapsed.

"Why do you say that?" Thea asked.

Libby cocked her head. "A man like Nab Rose won't sit in the library just for the good of his health, you know. He likes you."

Thea's frown deepened. "Oh no," she replied. "Nab is a hard worker, but I don't think he's interested in that way."

Libby reached the back door, sending her friend a look of doubt.

"Don't look at me like that. A girl knows when a man is interested in her, and I'm not getting that feeling at all."

Libby sighed and put a shoulder into the door to open it. "He likes you."

Thea chuckled softly and shrugged again, stepping into the kitchen, and walking to the stove, holding out her hands to the warmth. "He was asking about you a lot," she pointed out. "Perhaps he's trying to gather more information from me to get closer to you."

Libby snorted. "Nab Rose is too young for me," she said with a playful grin.

"Age is but a number. I know many women who marry a man younger."

Libby stood next to her at the stove, bending down to check the fire within. "Widows who need a man to take care of them. I don't need a man like Nab to look after me."

Unbidden, her mind filled with the gentle manners and sparkling brown eyes of Wilf Roberts. She knew then that he had captured her heart in a way that she couldn't deny.

CHAPTER 35

"*T*his way," Gwen indicated, gesturing along the foyer. "She's waiting for you."

Libby followed the maid, returning her friendly smile, even as her mind raced with what could have prompted Lena's request to see her on her own. She racked her brain trying to think if she had done anything wrong to warrant such a summons. Gwen gently knocked on the door to the library, and at Lena's response, she opened the door and announced Libby's arrival.

Libby had visited the library on several occasions, and yet she was still in awe of this stunning room. Books filled shelves that stretched from floor to ceiling. There was always a pleasant aroma of leather and parchment, and she often found herself wishing for a quiet afternoon to sit and peruse one of the many leather-bound volumes that graced the shelves.

However, as Lena stood to greet her, Libby's

throat felt dry, so she could only nod in response when Lena offered her some tea.

"Please, won't you sit down," Lena gestured.

Grateful, Libby settled into the chair, tucking her hands under her legs as she waited for whatever news Lena had to deliver.

Lena offered a warm smile in return. "Thank you for coming. I know it's a bit much to ask after you've worked all day, but I wanted to speak with you away from Mrs Reid and the other apprentices."

"That's quite alright," Libby replied huskily.

"I wanted to talk to you because I've been making some headway into a project that has been on my mind for the past few months. You see, Mr Wickham suggested that I reach out to wealthy widows who might be an easier way into speaking with businessmen who are in a position to help the mill financially," Lena explained. "Through this, I've become involved with a group of women who are campaigning for women's rights. It's a troublesome subject, as you can imagine," Lena said with a rueful smile.

She paused, waiting while Gwen carried in a tray laden with teacups and a plate of biscuits. Lena dismissed the young maid with a warm smile, then poured them both a cup of tea. She set Libby's cup on the table to her right.

"Where was I? Oh yes. These women are familiar with the barricades I have encountered. It seems that because we are the fairer sex, with fewer opportunities than our male counterparts, we have been ignored. In fact, even Queen Victoria believes that we should remain where we are and allow the men to be the providers, so... It's a battle," she admitted.

The information intrigued Libby, and she leaned forward, listening intently.

"The good news is that these women are keen advocates of education and most interested in my idea of having a school, specifically for the apprentices here at Hawks Mill," Lena said. "A few of them have offered to pay for a teacher for a year and to supply necessary materials for such an endeavour, provided I can find a room for them to use somewhere here on the property. I have found such a room in the chapel. Albert has set about making any repairs required to get the room into decent working order. We've had to make do with an old stove, as the fireplace in there is older than the hills, but... it's a start."

Libby's eyes lit up with delight. "That's wonderful news," she said, elated by the prospect of the apprentices being given an opportunity that she never had.

Lena rested an elbow on the table, choosing her words carefully. "I want you to be the teacher," she said.

Libby's eyes widened with surprise. "How – how can I?" she stammered, her nerves surfacing at the idea. "I'm not a teacher."

Lena leaned forward; her tone gentle but firm. "Wilf informs me that you can read and write, yes?"

Libby gave a hesitant nod, her thoughts swirling with doubt and uncertainty. "Not as well as Thea. She would be much more suited to such a role."

Lena spread her hands in a placating gesture. "The children trust you, Libby," she said. "I've seen how they are with you. They would listen to you, and while I would be happy to support Thea in the future, for now, I believe you are the right person for this job.

"One of the widows, a lady called Mrs Richmond, mentioned that there is a college for girls in London called Whitelands College, where women can obtain a teaching certificate. With proper training, you could teach effectively."

Libby's thoughts tumbled over one another, a mixture of trepidation and excitement. The idea of helping her fellow apprentices was incredibly appealing, but the prospect of becoming a teacher was simply daunting.

Lena pressed on. "I'm keen to help my apprentices, Libby, but I can't do this alone. I know you're coming to the end of your indenture soon. This would mean an opportunity for you to stay here at the mill, if you wanted it, that is.

To have a career and be part of something that would endure, making a future for generations to come here. What do you say?"

CHAPTER 36

*W*arm summer air vibrated with the melodies of music from the jaunty violin players and the cheerful cacophony of villagers revelling at the annual village fete.

Brightly coloured ribbons adorned the houses and walls, and the bunting flapped gaily in the lazy breeze. Busy stalls brimming with handicrafts and sweetmeats filled the village grounds as jubilant voices and laughter filled the air. Servants from all the local big houses mixed with the lads and lasses of the farms, rubbing shoulders on the steam gallopers and swing boats, and dancing a jig to the lively organ grinder tunes.

Lena made her way through the bustling crowd, the scent of freshly baked pies wafting enticingly.

She had chosen to wear her new gown today; its sunny blue hue matched the mood of the day. The delicate fabric flowed gracefully around her figure, the intricate lace accents along the fitted bodice accentuating her slender waist.

She wove her way through the crowds, greeting families of her mill workers who were all enjoying the day's pleasures. She was surrounded by people, yet she felt a pang of melancholy amidst the glee and joyous shouts. It had been years since she'd attended the fete, the whims of her stern father ensuring she kept her distance from such exuberant frivolity.

His firm belief that the workers were mere cogs in the industrial machine to be used, instead of an integral part of the mill's success, saddened her greatly. Now, she knew he would never have approved of the decisions she'd made to stay afloat, even though the mill was starting to clear itself out of debt under her guidance.

Escaping the merriment, Lena's tension eased as the noise faded further behind her. She made her way along the cobble path, ducking under the evergreen archway, and escaping into the lush gardens of Hawks Manor. She wandered along the manicured parts of the meandering paths, her hand brushing against the soft rose petals that bloomed with abandon. The fragrant lavender scented the air as she traversed the gravel pathway.

Boxwood hedges marked out the geometrical patterns that the gardener had designed for her mother. The flower beds were vibrant with marigolds, peonies, and chrysanthemums, their colours a feast for the eyes and a balm for her soul.

She climbed the stone pathway, past the gazebo

draped with ivy and wisteria, and made her way into the thicket of trees that lined the edge of the garden. Instead of the rumble of the mill, the splashing of the river made a pleasant backdrop. The light sparkled on the water under the glorious sunshine. The ancient oak spread its boughs, casting a welcome shade, and she found herself drawn to a spot overlooking the sparkling water.

A kingfisher blue flashed on the other side of the bank, a fat silver fish in its beak. She took in the scene, the grounds of the manor house and the mammoth mill that dominated, silent today.

Tears, unbidden and long-repressed, filled her eyes as she thought of the years that she'd been denied the simple pleasure of community.

So many of the villagers had called out to her that day, making her feel welcome, sharing tales and introducing family members, ensuring that she was included in their happiness.

A sudden snap of a twig behind her shattered her meandering train of thought. She swung; eyes wide. Henry Wickham lingered in the dappled sunlight underneath the shade of the oak.

"Mr Wickham," she acknowledged with a gust of breath. She turned back, all too aware of her damp cheeks and vulnerable position. "What are you doing away from the celebrations?"

Henry extended a folded handkerchief towards her. "Are you okay?"

Gratefully accepting it, Lena dabbed at her eyes. "Yes."

In his usual equable manner, he simply stood in the silence until she felt compelled to explain. "I did not expect to find myself quite so moved by today's extravaganza."

Henry indicated the bench that her parents had thoughtfully installed alongside the riverbank. He settled beside her, not too close, yet near enough for a palpable awareness.

"It's a good turnout. I haven't been to a fete with as much exuberance as this one for quite some time," he murmured, a sheepish smile on his lips. His dark eyes sparkled with the reflections of sunlight on the river.

Lena deliberately looked away. It would do her no good to study the intricate pattern of light and shadows that played upon his face.

"I haven't been for years, either. I was a child the last time I was permitted to join in," Lena admitted, his handkerchief clutched in her hand. "It makes me feel sad, all those years lost to my father's indifference."

"You're here today. That's the *difference*."

A smile ghosted over her mouth. She broke his all-encompassing look. It was easier to look away than to try and fathom out what he was thinking.

"My father would never approve of the changes I've made. I can sometimes hear his furious discourse in my dreams."

"You're not your father. You don't seem to share his views. You respect skill and labour. It's a fresh perspective for all."

Lena smiled. "I've been welcomed so... the good-will of these people humbles me."

"Your people," he amended.

"I think that you may be right," she murmured, concentrating on the handkerchief.

"We are in a new era, Miss Pemberton," Henry said softly. "One that welcomes the humanity behind the labour. That's why you've been welcomed as such today. It's not a weakness to mourn what was lost. And you're allowed the time to rejoice in what you're rebuilding."

Lena found an unexpected understanding in the depths of his dark eyes. "Thank you, Mr Wickham. I'm not sure I could have done any of it without you."

"I'm certain you would have found a way," his deep voice had grown softer, more intimate.

He'd been her biggest surprise. After Thomas, she wasn't sure she would ever be interested in another person again. Yet here she was, almost vibrating in alertness of his proximity. There was something about this man that brought her to life, made her feel things she had no right feeling.

Sitting there, under the shade of the ancient oak was a tranquillity in the space between them that she hadn't expected to find. The revelry of the fete seemed to fade away, her blood thrumming with emotion.

"Do you know," Lena began, frowning to gather her thoughts and regain control. "As an only child, I've become accustomed to solitude, but it's a lonely thing to bear the weight of all these expectations.

"The livelihoods and survival of many of those people just beyond that stone wall depend on the success of the mill."

Henry shifted in his seat, his dark gaze roaming her face before settling briefly on her mouth. The corner of his lips curled up in a half-grin. "It's the price of leadership, making decisions that others may not understand or agree with. It's not possible to be both an effective employer and a friend, yet you seem to be pulling it off with such aplomb."

"Are you flattering me, Mr Wickham?"

His eyes blazed down at her, and she felt more alive than she had in years. "It's the truth."

Their eyes met, and for a moment, the world around them seemed to fall away. The intensity of his gaze grew, and it seemed to stall the fluttering inside her.

She wanted him to kiss her.

The realisation stunned her.

The silence between them stretched on and she felt the friendship for this man deepen into something far more significant – reliance, a trust that had blossomed into something unbidden.

Her tongue moistened her lips. Her voice was husky as she murmured, "You've become quite indispensable to me, Mr Wickham. Your advice, your... companionship, it's something that I value."

His eyes focused intently on her face. He moved, adjusting his position to lean in towards her. His hands lifted, hesitating in the air as if he meant to bridge the gap between them with a simple touch.

Lena's heart quickened, her breath hitching as warmth suffused her cheeks. His eyes were on her lips as he closed the gap between them imperceptibly.

The moment was shattered as a cheerful voice called out, "Henry! There you are!"

Spell broken, they pulled apart and both turned to see one of the loom workers approaching, sunlight dancing in her blonde hair, her cheeks rosy from the festival's excitement.

"Sally," Henry's deep baritone was rough, and Lena had to refrain from fanning her warm cheeks.

The young girl was both young and pretty, a coquettish glint in her big brown eyes as she approached them, though she only had eyes for Henry.

"I've been looking for you," she said as she made her way towards them.

Henry quickly rose, as if to draw attention away from the situation they had been found in, sitting alone with his employer. His smile was polite. "You found me."

"I've come to collect on your promise," Sally said, fingers linked as she swept the skirts of her simple blue dress around her legs. "You said you'd try your luck at the ring toss for me."

"You're right, I did," Henry cast a look at Lena, his expression as unreadable as ever.

Lena wished she could understand the emotions he seemed to mask so well, but Sally had already looped her arm through his, her familiarity with the engineer unmistakable.

If Henry was self-conscious at the obvious attention of the loom worker, he didn't show it.

"Are you coming back to the fete, Miss Pemberton?" he asked.

Lena's smile was as warm as she could muster. "I think I'll sit here a while longer, bask in the peace and quiet. Please, enjoy yourselves. Today is all about fun, after all."

"Come along, Henry," Sally urged, pulling at his arm eagerly.

Lena watched them both walk away, Henry's attention now on the young woman at his side and a pang of something unpleasant twisted in her chest. Leaning against the bench, the wood pressing into her back, she watched the young maiden bounce happily alongside him.

And why wouldn't she? Henry Wickham was handsome and clever, a combination that would lure any woman.

Lena's gaze moved back to the sparkling river, trying to push away the pangs of loneliness pressing on her.

The connection she felt with Henry, the ease of their conversation, was all in her mind. These feelings she was experiencing didn't change the fact that she was his employer.

Any interest he showed in what she was doing was for the business alone. Certainly, Henry Wickham would only be interested in young, unfettered girls like Sally.

CHAPTER 37

*S*tars winked in the inky black sky overhead, the mill silent after the long workday. Dusk had brought with it a dampness that chased a shiver down his back as Henry locked the engine room door. He hefted his workbag and struck out across the stones; his mind fixed on his stew supper as he made his way towards the archway. He noticed the soft glow of lamplight in the office window and, frowning, altered his direction. Thinking that Albert must have forgotten to extinguish a lamp before he left for the door, he barrelled into the office, drawing up short when his gaze clashed with Lena's startled one.

"Oh," Henry stopped, hesitating at her bleak look. "Pardon… I – I thought Albert had left a lamp burning."

The small smile that brushed her mouth vanished just as quickly. "I sent him home an hour ago."

Thinking he ought to leave her be, he touched his cap. "Very good. Good night, miss."

Her distracted response as she stared despondently at the ledgers spread over her desk made him hesitate in the doorway. She was so engrossed in them that she didn't look up as she exchanged one book for another, her deep sigh igniting sympathy in him.

"I don't wish to over-step here, Miss," Henry said. "But are you alright?"

The fleeting smile was back again. He'd come to recognise it as one that she used in defence.

She didn't quite meet his eyes when she nodded. "Nothing for you to be concerned about, Mr Wickham," she said briskly. "Have a good evening."

Head bowed; she swapped ledgers once more. Sighed, again.

Henry reluctantly backed out of the door. However, as the door got closer to shutting into the frame, he heard a tell-tale sniff that made his stomach clench. He paused, his hand on the door handle, debating.

He had no right to be concerned about her welfare; it was none of his business. Yet, he couldn't help the small squeeze of concern in his gut. He'd been in a position where he felt as if he was swimming against a tide that was determined to drag him under, no matter how hard he fought. She had been the one to rescue him when he hadn't wanted it.

He was well aware of the harsh gossip that had been circulating about her. For months, she had carried the weight of countless decisions on her slender shoulders. Although she'd had access to sympathetic listeners, they were people that she employed.

For the most part, she was alone.

As he pushed the door open once more, his heart stalled at the sight of tears glistening in her eyes.

He'd seen her stand her ground with angry men; ardently defend her position and push for change without a misstep.

Twice in a week now he'd found her alone and crying.

Expecting her to dismiss him so that she could gather her emotions, he decided to pretend he hadn't noticed.

"The foreman in my first job was a man named Sharp," Henry stepped into the room and shut the door. "Which was fairly ironic, as he was about as sharp as a spoon most days," he set his bag next to the door, taking his cap off and rolling it up neatly as he spoke. "He had a favourite saying: 'a problem shared is a problem halved'. Naturally, when one of us shared a problem with him, he could keep a secret about as effectively as a rusty bucket can hold rainwater," he drew a chair out and sat down without being asked. He leaned forward, his forearms resting on his knees, giving her a direct look. "I don't proclaim to be the cleverest man, but I've kept my fair share of secrets in my time. I'm a good listener. Please, tell me what's wrong."

He waited, seeing the internal debate warring as various expressions moved across her face in the soft lamplight. The soft expulsion of her breath heralded bad news. "Oh, very well. I've had a letter from Mr Clark this afternoon. I'd put a request for a loan extension to Alistair Cavendish, you see. It's his bank that holds the various loans that the mill owes. He regretfully declined," the bitter tone signalling the derision that he imagined was included in the letter.

Henry sat back in the chair, watching her carefully.

Lena steepled her fingers, returning the look. "I presented him with what I considered a fair argument. Just as Mr Radford suggested, I gave Alistair the sales figures to date, with a projected uplift that would offset any risk of him extending the loan. He simply stated that with me at the helm, the mill was in greater jeopardy than with my father running it."

She sniffed again, swiftly wiping her cheeks to capture the tears that escaped.

"His words, as harsh as they were, infuriated me. I've sat here for hours, trying to seek out a way an alternative way to bridge the shortfall."

"I'm very sorry, Miss,"

Lena stood, shaking her head vigorously, frustration erupting. "I'm here again – the same two steps forward, three steps back that I told you about. Only this feels more of a shove because it was a Cavendish, I suppose.

"I'm doing everything that everybody is suggesting. I've secured funds from..." Her gaze met his and slid away too quickly for him to interrupt and ask where before she rushed on, "...from elsewhere, but I can't keep doing that. I'm raising standards here.

Production is increasing and yet Alistair and his cronies insist that I'm incompetent. I don't know if it's because I am Pemberton, or because I'm a woman, or both," she ranted, fists clenched.

In that moment, he couldn't recall having ever seen a comelier woman.

"I'd hoped that making the payment in May would show him that I was a reliable gamble, yet he seemed to laugh at me. Being a mill owner is hard enough, but when the doors won't even open for me without even giving me a chance, what am I supposed to do?" Lena continued, oblivious to his admiration. She leaned over and flipped an open book closed. "I've been in here all afternoon, raking over those columns in the hopes that I would be able to raise extra money for the steam engine. We need better looms. That costs money.

"I said as much to Cavendish in my letter, but his trite response was that one good working loom does not a mill make. Wretched man," she muttered, dropping unceremoniously back into Albert's squeaky chair.

As if the wind had dropped out of her sails, she wilted. She sniffed a few more times, staring glumly at the paperwork. "I can't keep doing this."

Henry had seen the books for himself. He knew the productivity was as high as it could be, and the profits couldn't be squeezed much further without compromising safety once more. "How much is the next repayment?"

Lena eyed him dubiously. "I dare say it doesn't

matter if you know, soon we'll all be out of a job. No doubt, at the end of the year I shall be just where I found you, Mr Wickham," she stated sullenly.

He tried not to take heart at the choice of words. She was bitterly disappointed and when she told him how much the payment was going to be, he could see why. It would surely empty any savings she'd managed to scrape together with the uplift in productivity in the last few months. "But you can make the payment, can't you?"

"Fat lot of good it will do," Lena said. "It will empty the account with nothing left for investment or improvements."

"Would you care to hear my two pennies worth?"

Her eyes shifted. She sat up, pride momentarily forgotten as she brushed at the lint on her skirt. "Certainly, Mr Wickham," she said, primly, her demeanour snapping back into her usual self-controlled businesswoman mode.

"Cavendish isn't the only private bank that we have here in England. There are many banks, not just here, but abroad also. People are making money from railways and mining across the Atlantic. There is new money that is being invested in businesses there. It is possible to negotiate with these people, with a projected forecast and a well-documented business plan."

Lena's gaze flickered thoughtfully. "I'm not sure I fully understand what you mean."

"You can approach another bank and ask to borrow money from them," his hand rolled through the air as he explained. "You would ask them for the capital that you owe to the Cavendish bank, plus any interest accrued, less your payment. You can include what else is needed for you to buy your steam engine. You could seek lower interest rates than the Cavendish bank is charging you, which would lower your repayments too."

"Do businesses do this?" Lena frowned. "I'm not sure that Cavendish would agree to this."

Henry lifted a shoulder, his mouth moving with the shrug. "I can't say for sure," he said. "But I know business and I know money. Private banks - all they care about is getting their money back with interest. If you have a way of paying him off –"

"– I find a way of being rid of Cavendish for good," Lena said, her voice hardening. "Mr Wickham, I do believe you may have just answered my prayers."

Her sentence sent a thrill through his mid-section which he tried to ignore. She quickly flicked open the books, jotting down figures as she went, already absorbed in a new cause.

"I shall leave you to it then," he rose, and, unfurling his cap, settled it on his head.

"Mr Wickham?"

Henry paused in the doorway, his gaze lingering as he turned to look back at her.

A beatific smile graced her face, making his stomach tighten.

"Thank you. You have no idea how much that has helped."

Henry dipped his head. "You're welcome. And please, call me Henry."

She paused, lips flickering as she considered him. "Isn't that a little improper?"

"About as improper as a woman in business, miss."

Her chuckle followed him through the door and out into the burgeoning night, an echoing smile dancing over his mouth as he left her to it.

CHAPTER 38

"She's managed it again," Albert stated as soon as Henry stepped into the office.

Henry closed the door on the busy yard and the rumbling of the mill, lifting a brow at the statement. "Who's done what now?"

Albert leaned back in his creaky wooden chair, fixing Henry with a look as if he was soft in the head. "Miss Pemberton. Did you not see her in the yard? She just this minute left."

Henry had noticed her, of course, but he wasn't about to admit to Albert that he'd been looking for her all day. Nor would he confess that he'd been worrying about her when she'd not returned last night. Gwen had claimed that it was because she'd had extra business to attend to in Manchester after meeting with Cavendish yesterday to make the payment.

"No, I didn't even notice she was gone," Henry lied. "What did she have to say for herself?"

"Well, you should know that after she'd paid the next payment on the Cavendish bank loan, she renegotiated for a lower rate with another bank. I didn't see that coming," he said, tapping his fingers on the desk.

Of all the mill managers Henry had worked with, Albert Simpson was a different kettle of fish compared to what he was used to. The man was fair yet firm, and as far as Henry had seen, wasn't one to delegate anything he wouldn't do himself. His only downfall was that he was a bit of a gossip. This type of talk made Henry deeply uncomfortable, having been the subject of such talk himself.

Still, when the topic was salacious talk about the pretty mill owner, Henry couldn't help but be intrigued. Henry grunted by way of speaking, and stared out of the window, making a show of being disinterested by watching the draymen unload the cotton bales from the wagon.

All the while, his mind was churning. Had she followed his advice? He hid the small smile that wanted to erupt on his face.

"I don't know how she's done it," Albert was saying, shuffling paperwork on the desk behind Henry. "Once she'd made the payment to Cavendish, she already had someone else lined up so that she could move the loan away from that ex-fiancé of hers. I wonder if he'll be forcing his way into the house again after this. I can't say his type will like being outsmarted by a woman."

Henry made a noncommittal sound of agreement.

He knew all too well the palpable fear that had shrouded Lena when he had interrupted her and Thomas in the library. He dreaded to think what would've happened had he not intervened. The Cavendish family were powerful and influential in the world of finance. He guessed they wouldn't like having a controlling interest wrestled away from them.

"She has a knack for finding funds when we need them most. It's been a lifesaver for the mill."

"Who's the new investor?"

Albert spluttered, shuffling papers faster. "I don't go asking things like that. All I care about is the wages being paid. Why do you ask?"

Henry feigned disinterest. "Just curiosity."

"Curiosity killed the cat," Albert warned him. "You'd do well to keep your nose out of that."

"I just like to know who I'm getting into business with," Henry said, turning back to gaze through the window.

The glorious August sunshine bathed the lands in endless blue skies, chased by fluffy cumulus clouds with a gentle summer breeze. Leaves rippled in the light, catching in the skirts of the workers as they hurried about in the yard beyond the office window.

Albert huffed. "Why don't you ask Miss Pemberton? She seems to have taken a shine to you."

Henry snorted. "Who told you that?"

"No one," Albert replied. "Just an observation from a man who's seen more sunsets than you have, son."

His chuckle was like rocks in a rusty bucket, and

Henry's lips twitched despite himself. "Your observations are fading as fast as your eyesight, old timer."

A sly look crossed Albert's face. "But you have to wonder, don't you? Where's all this money coming from? I mean, she's supposed to be out of funds. Maybe it's as they say, and her father lied and had money hidden away from that Cavendish chap. What do you think?"

"I think you're paid to manage, not speculate."

It seemed that the manager was determined to get whatever was on his chest out into the open. "Come on, Henry! You've been around mills long enough to know that not all the money she's coming up with can be from investors. People are saying she must be using... other means to finance the company. Untoward ways, if you catch my drift."

It burned Henry to know that the mill manager was echoing the same thoughts he'd once had over where Lena was coming up with the funds. He didn't like thinking of her resorting to seedy means to pay his wages.

Or perhaps it was thinking about Lena with another man that he didn't like.

Henry gave Albert a stern look over his shoulder. "You're like a gossiping fish wife."

Albert raised an eyebrow, a knowing look in his eyes. "My eye! You've seen how she's turned this place around from the brink of ruin. It's not just business acumen. There's talk she's been seen with some well-to-do gentlemen in unsavoury circumstances."

Henry's expression hardened and he deliberately turned away from the dopey grin on Albert's face. "People will always talk, Albert. Doesn't mean we have to listen or give it any credence."

"Just what people are saying, Henry. You know how it is."

"Everyone has secrets – even someone like you," Henry turned to face his manager. He could see the comment had hit home from his expression. "Whatever means she's using to secure these funds, I'm sure they're legitimate. She's done more for this mill and its workers than anyone before her. She's saved our jobs. That's what matters."

Albert leaned forward and lowered his voice. "Of course, of course. Just idle chatter, I suppose. But you have to admit, it's unusual. A young woman like her, doing all this on her own?"

"How she raises the funds is her business, and I trust her judgment," Henry advanced on Albert and had the satisfaction of seeing him lean back once more in his chair as if trying to put some distance between them again. "You'd do well to stay on her good side, Albert. She's sacked better men for less."

Albert nodded warily. "Fair enough. It's just rare to see someone turn things around so drastically. She's full of surprises, that one. The good news is we have the money to buy a steam engine."

Henry agreed quietly, his thoughts lingering on Lena as the conversation moved on to production reports and progress for the new steam engine.

Despite the rumours and whispers, he chose to believe in her integrity. He couldn't bear the thought of her sacrificing her dignity for the sake of the mill, and deep down, he fiercely hoped that the whispered rumours were nothing more than the idle chatter of a busy mill.

CHAPTER 39

$\mathscr{L}$ ibby had watched the dawn light creeping over the horizon, its soft tendrils filtering through the bedroom windows. Lost in her thoughts, she lay there, enveloped in the familiar sighs and snuffles of the room.

A fitful night's sleep had left her grappling with decisions, and she rose early, resolved to take a walk to clear her cluttered mind. Mrs Reid grumbled about the hour as she unlocked the bedroom door, but most of the workers were already up and getting ready for church.

Stepping outside the apprentice house, Libby was greeted by a clear and dry Sunday morning. Remembering what Thea had mentioned about the tranquillity of the Temple Woods, she turned and headed towards the narrow path leading into the forest.

Libby hadn't ventured far along the track when she heard a familiar voice calling out to her. She stopped and looked back, spotting Wilf approaching with his hands full of various items.

"Where are you off to this early?" he inquired as he drew nearer, his shaggy hair and easy smile making it hard to stay cross with him for interrupting her peaceful morning.

"I thought I'd head to the Temple Woods. What's that you've got there?" she asked, gesturing to the long stick he held in his hand.

"It's a fishing pole," he explained, extending the equipment slightly. "I bought it off Nab."

"Why would Nab part with such a thing?" Libby questioned.

Wilf gave a knowing smile but shrugged. "I wasn't going to look a gift horse in the mouth. Care to join me?"

Libby lifted a shoulder, unsure if she would make good company, but she fell into step beside him. They walked in silence for a while, the casual rustle of leaves in the breeze and the early morning birdsong providing the only soundtrack. But the thoughts that had swirled within her throughout the previous night couldn't be contained any longer, and at Wilf's gentle prodding, they tumbled out.

She explained Lena's idea of starting a school at the mill and how Lena wanted her to become a teacher.

Wilf stopped in his tracks, his brows shooting upwards. "What's there to think about, Libby? This is a way out, isn't it? An escape. You're mad not to have given her an answer yet. Why are you waiting? Don't you want a chance at a different life?"

Libby lowered her gaze, a hint of uncertainty in her voice. "Of course," she conceded, "it's a wonderful opportunity." Her voice trailed off.

"What is it?" Wilf probed gently.

"I don't know if I have what it takes," Libby confessed miserably. "It's always taken me a while to pick up new skills, and I'm not a fast reader."

"You're faster than I am," Wilf reminded her, teasing. "Besides, don't these certificates from this fancy college teach you what you need to know?"

She nodded, but her doubts lingered. "I suppose so, but Thea would be the better choice for this. She's bright and clever. I'm none of those..." She was interrupted when he leaned down and kissed her.

Libby's eyes widened in surprise as she pulled away. "What do you think you're doing?"

Wilf grinned down at her unrepentantly, his eyes glinting with mischief. "I'm taking your mind off a decision that you shouldn't even be considering."

Libby shook her head, still bewildered. "How can you say that? It's everything to think about. Miss Pemberton is putting her trust in me. This is her idea to make the place better, to build a legacy, as she says. I don't want to let her down. I don't want to..."

Wilf leaned in again, but this time, his mouth lingered on her—more tender, more deliberate.

It wasn't just an interruption of her racing thoughts; it made her pause and truly look at him. His hair had glints of red in the sunlight, and his brown eyes twinkled as he looked down at her. Her heart began to thud differently.

"Are you going to hit me?" Wilf asked playfully.

Libby's lips curved upwards. It was a teasing remark, and she caught a hint of amusement in his expression as she wrapped her arms around his neck. "Kiss me properly this time," she murmured.

Obliged, Wilf dropped the fishing pole and sack that he carried. The objects clattered to the floor as his arms folded around her back, drawing her closer to him. For that moment, she didn't think about duty or destiny or responsibility. Instead, her world was filled with sensations and kisses and Wilf.

CHAPTER 40

*L*ena watched as Mr Radford stomped across the yard, her accountant climbing into the waiting carriage and slamming the door in temper, disappearing from her line of sight as he leaned back inside the cab. The driver tipped the peak of his cap, his face passive, as if he hadn't just witnessed the most ferocious quarrel.

Lena regretted having the squabble outside her office, but the wretched man had refused to listen to her views or feelings, and she had taken out her bad mood on him. With a resigned sigh, she turned to head back into the office, stopping only when she caught sight of Henry standing in the open doorway of his work shed. Their eyes clashed, and a shiver of awareness trickled along her spine.

Not for the first time, her thoughts meandered to what would have happened if Sally hadn't interrupted their conversation under the oak tree.

Would he have kissed her?

Wouldn't that have changed everything?

She was experienced enough in the attentions of men to know when someone was interested romantically but sitting on the bench next to Henry Wickham that day had felt…different. He made her think differently, challenged her without ridicule; listened to her in a way that meant she trusted him.

"For what it's worth," Henry said, "I think he's right."

Lena rolled her eyes at him. Right now, though, she wasn't in the mood to be challenged. "I've tried every single avenue possible to secure investment. I think that Mr Radford believes I'm not trying, that I'm lying about my efforts in some way."

"That's not how I heard it."

Lena threw her hands in the air, walking towards him. "Why do either of you think that attending this dinner will be any different to what I've tried to do so far? It's a ball, for heaven's sake. Hardly a business meeting. I shall have to attend alone, for starters. "

Henry stepped out through the door into the light, his quiet gaze soothing her somewhat. He was slowly wiping his hands on a rag, then tucked it into a pocket. "Do you want to know what I think?"

Lena sighed. "Not if you're going to tell me that he's right."

Henry's warm chuckle made her own lips twitch in response, which only increased her irritation a little more.

"It's not a laughing matter, really, is it? I'm trying my best. Can't you see that?"

She met him in the doorway, the low embers of the setting sun burnishing his angular face. His dark eyes settled on her, and she wondered why it was that she felt calmer in his presence. The truth of the matter was that she valued his opinion. "Tell me he's wrong."

"He isn't."

With that, Henry turned and made his way back inside his shed, and Lena followed him.

The dusty workshop appeared more organised than when she had last been in it. The looms that had been swapped out for much older ones. The floor was free from discarded pieces, and several lamps illuminated the further corners of the room.

"Of course, he's wrong," Lena cried, flinging her arms wide. "I have no desire to go and speak to a room full of experts when they all believe that a woman has no place at the helm of business. It's bad enough when I am always dismissed in a one-on-one situation. Mr Radford now expects me to sit in a room full of experts and be shot down simultaneously? I refuse to put myself through such an ordeal."

Henry regarded her steadily. "You're making changes. Those changes are having a ripple effect, much like a pebble thrown into a pond. The workers here all appreciate what you're doing. They're telling others, writing to their family and relatives working at other mills in the area. Beyond, even. Those people are asking themselves why their employers aren't implementing all the changes that you are – building a school, shorter working days, recognising work, and offering out materials so that mothers can supplement their families by making clothing. Even paying for doctors to come here when there's an accident.

"Lena… You're changing the industry despite all the obstacles you're facing. Your investor is out there. You will get there. I do not doubt in my mind that you will make a success of this."

Lena gazed at him, the distant rumbling of the water wheel mixing with the cooing doves in the rafters overhead as they roosted for the evening. Her eyes traced his face, impossibly handsome. "No one's ever spoken to me like that before," she whispered.

One side of Henry's mouth hooked up in a smile. "I'm happy to be the first one. I know it's not easy. But you have the strength and determination to make a difference."

Lena's breath hitched in her chest as he moved closer to her. Her mouth parted breathlessly, and she stared up at him, her heart quickening as she gazed into Henry's deep, steady eyes. "Cavendish was a fool for letting you go. I want you to know that I would never have treated you the way he did. He's a fool for not recognising your worth. He's a fool for not believing in you," Henry said, his hand coming up, hovering at first before the back of his knuckles gently grazed her cheek.

Lena's eyes slid closed as emotions crashed over her.

"Look at me," he urged with a whisper.

Her eyes snapped open, her blood pumping with sizzling awareness as he closed the distance between them. His hungry gaze rested on her mouth, tracking the path his thumb made as it swept over her bottom lip. "I know I am not worthy of you, and yet I can't stop myself from thinking about you, Lena. It's not right, I know… but… just once…"

Lena's breath shuddered out, his words sliding over her like warm honey. Her tongue snaked out to moisten her lips. Desire flared in his dark gaze. In that quiet, sunlit workshop, Henry gently cupped the back of her head and slowly, imperceptibly, leaned down to cover her mouth with his.

CHAPTER 41

*L*ena hadn't wanted to come tonight.

But Mr Clark had lent his voice to Mr Radford's and had been persuasive in his argument, about how she needed to curate and repair the business relationships that her father had damaged. Once Henry had given his opinion, she felt as though she'd had no choice but to attend, if only to prove her point that attending these types of events wouldn't work.

Thoughts of Henry filled her mind. It seemed that he filled her every waking moment these days. She felt her cheeks warming. They'd kissed – *just once,* he'd said – and then they'd returned to their normal roles. The day-to-day running of the mill; the repairs and refits needed to make it all work. Yet, each time their eyes had met, she'd been almost lightheaded with anticipation. She'd fallen for a man whom her father would not choose for her. It brought her internal conflict that occupied her mind alongside profit and losses.

The grand dining room of the Manchester Industrial Club hosted a ball every summer. High ceilings adorned with intricate plasterwork, walls lined with rich mahogany panels, and a crystal chandelier that cast a warm, shimmering light over the assembled guests, lent an air of grandeur. Footmen stood sentry in front of sash windows thrown open to the warm evening. The long, polished dining table adorned with fine china and crystal was illuminated by the soft glow of candles in ornate silver holders.

Lena had attended many dinner parties in the past, and their hosts had always seated in favour of precedence.

She recognised two Lords and a viscount with their wives towards the head of the table but surmised that most of the guests here lacked peerage. Instead, they appeared to be seated in order of wealth or influence. The gentleman seated on her left had cut off all conversation as soon as she'd been introduced.

The man on her right seemed engrossed in a conversation with the person sitting on the other side of him, discussing Henry John Temple's election as Prime Minister.

She'd foregone the full black mourning apparel, instead opting for a deep blue satin gown with jet beads at her throat. The truth was that her funds were better off being funnelled into the mill, rather than squandered at the haberdashers. She was confident that her choice of clothing would be the least likely topic this evening, seeing as Thomas and Elizabeth were holding court towards the other end of the table.

Conversation swirled around her; oddments of words that were barbed with Thomas' sneering, intended to sting her. Lena had inadvertently caught him staring at her several times, his presence a thorn in her side that she was doing her best to ignore. The smirk he wore was irksome, as though he was privy to a secret. Elizabeth looked stunning in an emerald-green dress that set off her red hair and golden eyes to perfection. Each time their eyes met; Elizabeth would hold the look in challenge until Lena looked away.

Lena wanted to reassure the other woman that she did not need to be territorial – she had no interest in Thomas Cavendish. Instead, dark eyes and an unsmiling mouth that held her enthralled eddied in her mind's eye.

Looking about the table, she realised that she longed for his support here, amongst the staring and the whispers. Knowing him as she did, she knew that he wouldn't feel comfortable amongst the rule-makers and breakers of industry. Would he have come with her if she'd asked him?

Could she put him through that?

He would have come, she knew, but she wouldn't have asked him in the first place. She wouldn't have wanted to expose him to these supercilious people.

The dinner menu was exquisite, the courses were served with impeccable timing and precision: a delicate consommé to start, followed by roasted quail with vegetables and a raspberry meringue, but she could hardly focus on the food. She was all too aware of the speculation rolling around the table. Rather than strengthening relations and building connections with business owners and financiers, Lena felt more isolated than ever before.

"Miss Pemberton?"

Surprised, Lena's gaze clashed with the vociferous politician-talker, and she tried to recall his name from the earlier introductions.

"What do you think?"

"About what, Mr Berrington?" Relief followed the flash of memory.

"Titus Salt, and his village. There's talk that he's adding in a hospital and an institute for entertainment alongside the houses and alms-houses for his workers." The man had an impeccable posture and an attentive gaze.

Albert had mentioned the village, called Saltaire, to her. Titus Salt was moving several smaller mills to a new site where he was building a larger mill for his business in the wool industry.

"Mr Ripley here tells me that you have made similar entrepreneurial endeavours with your site, continuing on from the efforts of your grandfather. I'm curious as to the fiscal outcomes of the changes you've made so far?"

Lena met his inquiry with a poised nod and a measured smile, aware as the clinking of plates and conversation slowed around her. "We've seen an uptick in profits, modest but meaningful, as efficiency has improved. Reassuringly, accidents have diminished to be almost negligible. Workers aren't as tired, and the safety measures that the engineer has implemented have certainly helped."

"Who is your engineer?"

"Mr Henry Wickham," she replied. Voices silenced around her.

Mr Berrington shifted in his seat. "The same Wickham from Brownshill and Black Marsh mill?"

Lena nodded, recalling the story that Henry had told her about where he'd started. "That's correct."

He leaned back so that his plate could be removed. "You're not concerned about his past?"

Lena's eyes danced around the table, catching the eyes of others who pretended not to be interested. She surmised that many of these men had never stepped foot in their servant quarters, let alone a debtor's prison. "Everyone has a past, Mr Berrington. It's what we do in the present that sets the tone for the future. Mr Wickham has been instrumental in the changes we've made."

Thomas sniggered and aggravation licked through her.

Mr Berrington, perhaps oblivious to the undercurrents, toyed with his dainty glass of port. "That is most commendable. You must support Lord Shaftesbury in the Ten-Hour bill. I worry that the workers will leave mill owners vulnerable by boosting their income with working at two mills, negating any restful leisure time that the Bill is designed to preserve."

Lena's expression remained composed as she replied, "The Ten-Hour Bill has indeed prompted adjustments. However, I have found that offering fair wages and improved working conditions has fostered loyalty. Workers value the stability and safety we provide and seem disinclined to seek supplemental work. My mill manager has instigated several compensating systems, including the opportunity to buy cloth that won't meet exacting industry standards at a lower price. This enables some families to supplement their income that way."

Mr Berrington nodded thoughtfully. "A wise approach."

Mr Akroyd sitting opposite her asked, "With the looming legislative reforms, how do you anticipate they will further impact your practices at the mill?"

"The upcoming changes to the laws are substantial," Lena conceded, conscious that she now held the table. "I welcome them. My aim is not merely to adapt reactively but to anticipate and align our operations with the spirit of progress. Hawks Mill will not only comply with any mandated changes, but we shall also continue to strive to exceed those standards. It is, after all, the welfare of the workers that ultimately sustains the mill's success."

Mr Ripley raised his glass slightly in her direction, a gesture of respect. "Your perspective is refreshing, Miss Pemberton. It is a rare thing to find a business owner who balances the ledger with humanity. I shall be most interested to observe how Hawks Mill navigates the changing tides of industry under your stewardship."

Lena's eyes glinted with determination, her voice firm yet gracious as she responded, "Thank you."

"Industrial tides are indeed changing," Mr Berrington murmured. "I shall watch your trajectory with interest."

After the meal, Lena excused herself, navigating through the maze of corridors to find a moment of solitude. In the powder room, she checked herself in the looking glass. She'd conversed with several other mill owners after her talk with Mr Berrington, and it delighted her to know that these men seemed curious about her. They'd listened to her. Perhaps Henry and Mr Radford had it right, after all. With a small smile on her success, she let herself out of the room, only to collide with Thomas.

"I want a word with the darling of industry," he snarled, expression furious as he caught her by the arm and pulled her deeper into the shadows.

Fear closed off her throat. She struggled in his unyielding grasp, stumbling when he flung her away from him.

His face contorted with anger as he hemmed her into the wall. "How did you do it?"

"Do what?" Lena asked, trying to keep her voice steady.

"Liberty Bank! For twenty years, Hawks Mill has banked with us," he snarled. "You think you're clever, transferring the loan to another investor. Sitting at that table when everyone knows what you're doing to raise funds. At least I now know the cost of climbing into bed with you – a bank loan!"

She held his glare, remaining stubbornly mute, not caring how he'd managed to discover who the new investor was. She was more concerned about getting away from him before he did something terrible to derail her progress here tonight.

He pressed his face towards her. "What will you do when your looks fade? What then, Lena?"

She longed to turn her face away from his fetid breath. "Leave me alone, Thomas."

"After everything my family did for yours, this is the thanks we get?"

She stilled then, fury bursting through her fear. "Thanks? Do you expect my *thanks*? I re-negotiated terms with a new bank because your terms were not favourable. It's business. Nothing more."

"You're no better than a whore at the docks, just with a high-class dress."

She leaned into him; teeth bared. "You disgust me. Your crass insinuations are as unwelcome as your advances. Now get away from me before I scream blue murder."

A sense of dread rolled through her stomach as his face lit up with savagery. For a moment, she expected him to strike her. Instead, he chuckled, his laughter cold and obdurate.

"Murder. How apt that you should choose that word, considering."

A chill crawled along her spine. "What are you talking about?"

"It's all anyone could talk about at the table tonight. The shady past of your engineer. But then, a person in your position cannot be too choosy with who they hire. Of course, no one else will hire him, even after the warm recommendations you've been making for him this evening."

Lena darted out through the gap he'd made, heart thundering as she started to back away from him. She didn't want to think about the time that Henry would be finished at Hawks Mill. "I don't care that Mr Wickham went to debtor's prison."

He stared at her momentarily. The laughter that followed made his eyes glint with malice in the gas lights. "You don't know, do you?"

She spread her hands out, shoulders up. "Just get out whatever snide comment you wish to make and let me be on my way!"

"Oh, my darling, this isn't a comment," Thomas' smile was pure Machiavellian. "I almost want you to carry on obliviously but telling you now means I get to see your reaction to the news first-hand," he pressed his hands together and exhaled happily. "Your precious Mr Wickham is a murderer."

CHAPTER 42

*T*hea's waters broke in the dead of the night.

The pains came on suddenly, and Thea's raw cries echoed throughout the house, including reaching Mrs Reid, who went into a panic. Daisy was quickly dispatched to fetch Agnes Davidson, the woman in the village who was the most experienced in midwifery.

The labour went on, but just when Thea felt she had nothing left to give, a tiny little girl with a mop of black hair came into the world. Lena had arrived just in time to witness the birth. After the baby was cleaned up, Dr Fitch arrived, and at his urging, Thea was transferred delicately to the comfortable chamber in the manor house.

The excitement of the new arrival energised the mill workers, and the shift passed quickly, the dance of weft and thread aligned with good mood and cheer all around.

Due to her disrupted night, Libby ended up working the late shift. As she stepped outside, she was met with the cool evening air, with the dying embers of the sun gilding the treetops and rooftops. She waited for most of the workers to return to the apprentice house when she spotted Wilf in the encroaching dusk.

When their eyes met across the yard, she felt a shiver of anticipation unfurl in her stomach. More often than not, they tried to steal a moment or two every day to be alone. Walking on a Sunday afternoon had become a regular occurrence.

Just as she had guessed, Wilf was kind and sweet, with a good ear for listening as she talked to him about the developments of the school. She was amazed at all the working parts that Miss Pemberton seemed to be dealing with, and a new respect meant that the two women were spending more and more time together as they developed the plans.

Wilf checked that they were alone before his head dipped, and he stole a quick kiss. Laughing, she laid a hand against his chest. "You're pushing your luck, Mr Roberts."

Wilf shot her a wink and dipped his head for one more kiss. "Worth it."

"Did you hear? Thea's had a little girl."

"It's all people have talked about today," he said. "Have you heard how she is?"

Libby shook her head. "I was just debating sneaking off to the manor house now rather than trying to persuade Mrs Reid to let me go after supper. I only want to visit with her just for a few minutes. No doubt the girls will be pestering the old battleaxe for news as we speak."

"Who'd have guessed an apprentice child would be welcomed in an apprentice house," he shook his head. "I'm still not sure how I feel about it all."

"It's not Thea's fault, nor is it the baby's," she tried to reassure him gently. "But the arrival has certainly boosted spirits. That can only be a good thing."

He dipped his head in acknowledgement. "Go now. Mrs Reid can't argue once it's done now, can she?"

Libby chuckled. "Wilf Roberts, there's a little deviant under that thick mop of hair."

"I'll get back to the cottage then and let you get on with your mission. Will I be seeing you on Sunday?"

"At our usual spot," she nodded and turned for the house, making her way under the wisteria arch.

She knocked at the back door of the manor house and walked into the kitchen. Cook had finished for the day, though the aromas of the shared staff meal still lingered as she moved along the long hall and up the narrow back staircase. She called out a few times as she did.

Gwen appeared at the top of the stairs, a broad smile on her face. "Are you here to see Thea?"

"I am," Libby replied. "How is she?"

"About as happy as I've ever seen anybody," Gwen led the way along the back staircase to the next floor up. "Never in my days did I think I'd be taking care of an infant of a millworker in this house."

"I think it's a sign of Miss Pemberton's generosity and benevolence," Libby said quietly as they emerged onto the landing.

The first floor of Hawks Manor was as opulent as the ground floor. Wide hallways had a thin runner of plush carpets down the centre. Wooden floors gleamed on either side in the soft light pouring from the sconces. Gwen turned the corner and made her way to a room at the end of the hall.

She knocked gently before stepping inside. Thea was sitting up in bed, her eyes glowing with contentment. She made a small gasp of happiness as she spotted Libby behind the maid and beckoned her closer, thanking Gwen.

Gingerly, Thea made her way to the edge of the queen-size bed that she'd been occupying.

"Can you believe this? Isn't this room amazing? I keep pinching myself as if I'm in a dream."

The tiny infant lay in a small bassinet by the side of the bed. "Miss Pemberton says I can stay as long as I want, though the doctor assures me I'll be ready for work in a day or two. I don't want to overstay my welcome and take advantage. Is Mrs Reid mad?"

"Not at this moment," Libby said. "I dare say she's glad that she's not having to watch over an extra person. I haven't heard anything from Mr Reid, either. How are you feeling?"

"So tired," Thea admitted. "But yet so alive at the same time." Thea touched her daughter with a fingertip. "She might have been born out of something dark and ugly, but just look at her, Libby. Have you ever seen anything quite so beautiful?"

Libby peered into the bassinet at the round-faced child with her rosebud lips, sleeping soundly. "She's beautiful, Thea. Have you named her yet?"

Thea nodded. "Elena."

Libby looked at her in surprise. "After Miss Pemberton?"

"Yes," Thea said. "She cried when I told her. But without her, none of this would have been possible. I wouldn't have had my daughter if she hadn't made these allowances. She has my never-ending dedication, and I told her as much."

They both gazed down at the sleeping infant, sharing a moment of awe.

Thea sat back; her eyes alight. "But that's not all the good news I've had today. Would you believe it? I'm getting married."

"Pardon?"

Thea laughed at the incredulity in Libby's voice. "I can't believe it myself," she admitted. "I didn't think it was possible. But when he explained his reluctance to propose to me, it all made sense."

Libby stared down at her friend's face and laughed. "Can you make it make sense to me?"

Thea grasped both of Libby's hands. "Did you know that Nab Rose is Jewish? His real name is Abraham Rosenbaum, but he changed his name after his parents died so that he would fit in more with the workers. He's been selling his property so that he has some money to look after Elena and me."

Libby blinked in surprise. " Nab Rose has proposed to you?"

Thea nodded her head, her eyes glistening with unshed tears. "I'm going to be Mrs Thea Rose."

CHAPTER 43

*T*he steam engine's arrival at Hawks Mill was greeted with considerable fanfare, having made its journey on the back of a massive dray, pulled by a strong team of Shire horses.

For two days, in a ballet of man and machine, the imposing cylinder of iron was hoisted into the air by an intricate system of ropes and pulleys. Henry had overseen numerous installations, yet this one felt distinctly personal. It struck him that he was more deeply invested in Hawks Mill than any project before. Perhaps it was Lena's influence, but he found himself caring profoundly, aware of her efforts to secure the mill's future for the workers and herself.

With meticulous care, workers from the vicinity and beyond manoeuvred the engine through the gaping window. The installation of the boiler took an additional half day as it was gently lowered next to the cylinder. A team bustled around it under Henry's vigilant eye, ensuring it was bolted firmly in place, each joint sealed, each connection secure. When the final piece was positioned, a collective sigh of relief echoed through the crowd.

Henry turned to Lena, his smile broad and filled with pride. However, his smile faltered slightly as their eyes met—was it his imagination, or did she seem to distance herself from him deliberately?

In the days that followed, the engine was connected to the mill's network of machinery. Belts and gears were aligned, and steam pathways were checked for any leaks. Albert, Lena, and a cadre of overseers assembled in the engine room as Henry observed the fireman tending to the furnace, ensuring a robust head of steam to drive the engine and power the mill machinery.

As the boiler's fire roared to life, steam built within its iron belly, and with a resounding metallic groan, the engine stirred into action. Triumphantly, amidst the clash of iron and steam, the pistons commenced their rhythmic dance—a flawless symphony of pressure and movement.

"Should the pistons be moving in that fashion?" Albert leaned in close to Henry, raising his voice to be heard over the engine's thunderous roar.

Henry nodded, his hands moving as if conducting an orchestra. "Since I've been here, I've been studying the advancements in modern engines. I've altered the pistons to move vertically, increasing the angle, which allows for greater movement. This means we generate more power per square inch than when they were positioned horizontally as they arrived."

Albert looked suitably impressed, his gaze fixed on the colossal machine and its steady rhythm. Lena stood slightly apart from the group, her complexion glistening with a sheen of perspiration, her expression thoughtful.

Pensive, Henry made his way over to her.

"We'll conduct a few tests over the next days to assess the durability before we fully commission it," he said.

She was distant, her usual warmth not quite reaching her eyes as they scanned the whirring cogs and hissing steam. "I'm sure it will perform admirably under your expertise, Mr Wickham."

Mr Wickham. Not Henry.

"Are you displeased with it?"

She managed a smile and shook her head slightly. "Quite the contrary, I'm grateful."

She excused herself, moving away to speak with Albert. Henry watched her, noting the ease of her laughter when conversing with the mill manager. On reflection, he realised her reticence towards him had been apparent for a few weeks. He cast his mind back, trying to recall when she'd changed.

The kiss?

Had she been distant towards him since then? He wanted to dismiss the thought. After all, she had been fine in the days following it, even when he had expected her to be self-conscious. It seemed his lowly engineer status hadn't put her off, and yet... she was certainly distant with him now.

He quickly looked away as the duo turned towards

him, with Wilf fetching up the rear. "The fireman seems to have it all in hand," Albert announced, voice raised. "We should all get back to work." As the group prepared to leave, feeling the momentous occasion had passed without fanfare, Henry followed Lena, intent on clarity about what was wrong.

"Miss Pemberton?" he called.

She paused; her stance guarded; her expression abstruse as she waited for him to draw near.

"What is it, Mr Wickham?"

"Is everything alright?" he ventured.

She checked that Albert and Wilf were out of earshot and he could not miss the faint trace of mistrust in the smile she summoned. "Why wouldn't it be?" she replied, with a tinge of forced cheerfulness.

For months, he had nurtured the openness between them both. Knowing that she was holding back, hurt him more than he cared to admit. "You seem a little... preoccupied. If you wanted to talk about any issues with the mill...?"

Lena's gaze rippled, a disturbance across the still pond that she'd so carefully curated. "I have Mr Simpson for that," she stated with a finality that suggested the conversation should end there. "If that's all?"

"Is it because I altered the pistons on the steam engine? Having the pistons move vertically makes it more efficient—"

"I have no qualms about your skills, Mr Wickham," she said crisply as if reminding him of his place.

"But you have concerns elsewhere?" He found

himself constrained by the walls she had built around herself, held at a distance she insisted upon. He dropped his voice. "That day, in the shed, if I overstepped a boundary, I apologise. I got caught up in the moment–"

"I have much to do today," she said quickly, her face turning a deep scarlet.

A flash of memory hit him. "Is it Sally? From the day at the fair when she came to fetch me because she means noth–"

He saw a tempest spark within her then, a bitterness sharpening her tone. "Sally is of no consequence. You should know that I no longer concern myself with the trivialities of the heart. I must get on, Mr Wickham."

Henry felt the sting of rejection, the silent plea in his touch to her forearm was met with an arched look from her. He quickly withdrew his hand, aware that he was breaching the line between them, even as he yearned to reclaim the affection she once seemed to hold for him. "I wouldn't wish to cause any discomfort. Please know I'm always here if you need to unburden yourself. My ear is yours."

"Thank you for the offer, but it isn't necessary." Lena's departure was as brisk as her dismissal.

Henry watched her leave, a tangle of unanswered questions weaving through his thoughts like threads on a loom. Regret pulsed through him. Had he tarnished the triumph of the steam engine's installation for her? She had worked tirelessly to reach this point, yet the splendour of their achievement seemed dimmed by her lack of enthusiasm.

As Henry returned to the engine room, he pondered at what point Lena had ceased being just his employer and had become the woman he loved.

CHAPTER 44

"*That's it?*"

Lena drew the piece of paper that Libby had just signed towards her across the desk and smiled. "As of right now, your indenture at Hawks Mill is spent. You are free to leave the mill," she said, collecting a small leather bag and holding it out to Libby. As it dropped into Libby's palm, it clinked with the distinct sound of coins. "This is the money you earned during your overtime. I have a sneaking suspicion that it should've been considerably more seeing how poorly the records were maintained. For that, I can only apologise."

Libby quickly brushed it aside. "I don't think it's right that you should apologise for that, Miss Pemberton. You've been more than kind to me these past few months."

Lena pulled a regretful face. "I hardly feel that makes up for the deficit that many of my apprentices have endured."

"We all know how hard you're working to make these changes. We see it and appreciate it," Libby replied.

Lena sat back in her chair and regarded Libby thoughtfully. "I guess this is the point where you are free to leave here without a backward glance," Lena remarked, her eyes fixed on Libby. "Though you are also invited to stay on here at the mill. Your skills are most valuable as a weaver. Any mill would be glad to have you, I'm certain."

Libby held the small sack of coins in her hand contemplatively. "I'm sorry it's taken me so long to give you an answer about Whitelands," she admitted.

"I'm glad that you've given it some thought, Libby. It shows that you're taking it all very seriously."

"It's just that I... I appreciate everything that you've done, and I don't want to let you down. I don't want to let anyone down. But what if I... What if I can't do it? What if I don't have enough sense to be able to teach people?"

A slow smile spread across Lena's face as she regarded Libby. "I stood in this room not quite a year ago, believing I was going to be married to a hideous man. Two months later, I was standing here with no clue how I was going to run a mill.

"We have no idea what we are capable of unless we try."

Libby gnawed on her bottom lip, twiddling with the leather thong that closed the pouch of coins in her hand.

"I believe in you, Libby. I believe you have the

skills needed to teach the children. Girls these days need to learn more than how to sew and how to dress. To be accomplished ladies, we need to learn how to read and write. To work and make progress in a factory, being able to add up means that a girl can do more than just skin a rabbit and stuff it into a blanket. I've learned just how lucky I was that my father believed in education, though, knowing what I do now, I think that my mother was the one who set me on that path originally," Lena said with conviction.

Libby's gaze lowered for a moment.

"I have contacted Whiteland College and explained the situation. They will be happy for you to start in January. You'll be away for twelve months."

"I'm to leave Hawks, then?"

"It will be temporary. Thea and I have already worked out lesson times, which means that she will be able to fulfil her indenture here as a teacher while taking care of baby Elena. Then, when you're ready, you can return as a fully qualified teacher and begin a whole new career, building a brighter future for yourself."

Butterflies tumbled in Libby's stomach. It felt like a leap into the unknown, but she found herself nodding and accepting the role. She took solace in Lena's happy reaction to this news. "I have some money here for you from Mrs Richmond. She wanted you to be able to afford some new clothes for your new role. You can return your apprentice uniform to Mrs Reid."

Libby took the note made out from a woman she'd

never met. "I don't know what to say. Everyone has been so generous. I keep expecting to wake up from this dream."

Lena smiled warmly. "It's not a dream, Libby. This is happening. You're helping to build a part of my dream, too."

Libby held the other woman's gaze, wondering if she knew the impact that she was having on all her workers' lives. A year ago, it was hard to think about the future. She only thought about getting through each day, one at a time, and seeing out her indenture. Back then, she only wanted a future away from the mill. Now, thanks to Miss Pemberton, she was being gifted with a whole new opportunity as well as a new wardrobe.

"Would it be okay if I stayed at the apprentice's house for a little while longer?" Libby asked.

A line appeared between Lena's brows. "You don't want to find a place of your own?"

Libby shook her head. "I'm not quite ready yet."

"I don't see why not. When you're ready, you are welcome to stay here at the manor house if you like. It will help you to save a little money. No doubt Mr Brown will not like it, but he's got over the shock of having a worker's baby under his roof, so I'm sure he'll get over this. Perhaps when you're back from London you can find a place to rent in the village."

Libby thanked her and turned to leave, but Lena spoke up again, "Before you go, I... There's something I need to ask you."

Tumultuous emotions moved over Lena's face.

"What is it?"

Lena hesitated. "I shouldn't ask you. It's putting you in a difficult situation, and I... "Lena sighed heavily. "There is a pressing question that is preying on my mind."

Libby felt compelled to offer her some reassurance and encouraged her to speak her mind.

Lena took another moment then shook her head and offered her a smile that didn't quite reach her eyes. "It's okay. Forget I said anything. I recommend the seamstress in Overleigh for your new clothing. She's altered and repurposed a few of my old dresses recently, and her skills are to be admired."

Libby thanked her again and left the library, wondering what it was that had the usually calm and unflappable Miss Pemberton so troubled.

CHAPTER 45

The late September sun dissolved into the horizon, the lingering warmth of the day embracing the last of the wedding guests. It had been a day of joy as the entire community came together to witness the wedding of Thea and Nab. Yet, the celebration felt deeper, a kind of unity, with Lena being wholly accepted by those for whom she had stood against tyranny.

Thea had been radiant throughout the day. She wore a simple, plain blue dress that must certainly have been borrowed because, despite alterations, it still hung off her slender frame. The ceremony took place in the quaint little church in the centre of Birchleigh. Wildflowers garnished the pews, scenting the air as the mill workers and their families gathered to witness the union of two of their own.

The village green had come alive with music and laughter after the ceremony. Musicians played cheerful tunes on their fiddles, and couples danced with joyful abandon. Tables groaned under the weight of hearty fare – roast meats, fresh bread, fruit, and vegetables donated from the local gardens – all ensuring that everyone was well-fed.

Lena had never witnessed such a jolly occasion. When she attended weddings in the past, they had been solemn affairs, almost clinical in the process. There wasn't a person present who would doubt the love between Thea and Nab. Their eyes met with happiness, their smiles mirrored each other, and as they danced together, their hearts overflowed with joy. Simple, yes, but it was filled with tenderness and hope.

Lena had thoroughly enjoyed the day. She had discussed many issues, not just about the mill. She felt valued and treasured, and that filled her heart in a way she could never have guessed.

And yet, she still felt as if she were missing something.

She used to dream of finding a husband who would love and cherish her. She'd accepted Thomas as that man, only to be quickly and viciously disillusioned. Indeed, as she had focused her efforts on saving the mill, her dreams had turned to profit and loss.

Henry had been right there alongside her.

He had stirred the yearnings of young Lena once more, making her hopeful for the future, for love, making her dream of finding a good husband who would stand with her.

Thomas's insidious words, cruelly whispered in

the hallway in Manchester, had planted suspicion in her heart, leaving her wary of the man who had helped achieve the concord she'd enjoyed in the village today.

Henry...a murderer?

Had she gotten it so wrong once more? She had fallen for Thomas, and his true nature had become painfully apparent right afterwards. Now, just as she had begun to develop feelings for her engineer, she discovered a hidden side to him as well. Had she once again been led a merry dance by a trickster who, whilst not from the same financial status as Thomas, was still just as devious with concealing his true self?

She'd been kept awake at night, rehashing past conversations with him, seeking a chink in the stories that he'd weaved for her. Her anger welled up, directed at both Thomas and herself.

She'd believed him.

Once again, she felt as if she couldn't trust her judgement.

If she couldn't trust herself, why would investors trust her with their money? Maybe this was the real reason why she'd had so many problems securing investment, and she was simply using her gender as an excuse to mask ineptitude on her part.

She had been avoiding him, of course. She'd felt Henry's questioning gaze resting on her many times. She kept him at arm's distance, wishing that she could penetrate his unreadable gaze as it rested on her.

And wishing that her body wouldn't betray her by reacting whenever he was near.

She'd wanted to know the chapter that he kept hidden but...*this?* Never in her wildest imaginings could she have him pegged as a killer.

She'd declined talks with him – leaving the office once any business talk with him had concluded. She knew that it bothered him, yet he maintained his professionalism with her.

Her feelings were frayed by deceit that had taken root and made it so she couldn't bring herself to confront him. If he admitted to such a heinous crime, where did that leave her?

Could her mill manage without him?

Could she?

More than once, she had gathered up the nerve to ask, yet every time, her courage vanished, and she had kept her mouth closed.

If indeed he was guilty of killing someone, surely, he would have been at the end of a hangman's rope, not languishing in a debtor's prison.

Thea and Nab left the party as dusk settled with much whooping and catcalling from the crowd. She watched them link hands and set off for the tiny cottage that Nab had managed to secure for his family, leaving her feeling a little despondent as she saw the evident love shared with such abandon between the two of them. Not once with Thomas had she ever experienced such adoration.

She had come to regard Henry with higher esteem, seeing him not just as the saviour of the mill but as something more personal. He had been a beacon for her in the chaotic world as she navigated the realm of business. She sought him out now in the crowd, standing head and shoulders above the millworkers around him. Was he truly capable of such a dreadful act? She hoped to believe he wasn't, but this lingering doubt refused to loosen its grip on her thoughts.

A rare smile graced his face as he was deep in conversation with someone out of her line of sight. Her heart clenched at the sight of him, and when the smile deepened, she knew then that her feelings for him ran much deeper than respect; she was in love with him.

Buoyed by several glasses of homemade wine, she set down her cup on a trestle table and began walking toward him. He was a man of accomplishment, of ingenuity, and integrity. She had seen it in every decision he made.

Thomas must have it wrong, perhaps he was just being his usual cruel and spiteful self.

She made her way through the crowd, which seemed to part as she approached him. As she got closer, the crowd split again, and Lena hesitated when she saw who Henry was talking to.

Sally, the young mill worker who had sought him out on the day of the summer fête, laid her hand on his arm as she laughed merrily. Henry bent down closer to catch what she was saying, and hot jealousy speared through Lena as Sally stood up on tiptoes and pressed her lips to his cheek.

Unable to stomach any more, Lena turned on her heel and rushed through the swarm, desperately holding back the tears that stung the back of her eyes.

She was a halfwit, she told herself. He was involved with someone else. A young girl without the cumbersome weight of the Pemberton name hanging on it.

She was a silly, gullible fool in love with a murderer.

CHAPTER 46

"It says nothing more?"

Lena shrugged, waving the letter from Mr Saunders, her salesman, at Albert as if attempting to dislodge further details from the paper. "He says that he wishes to address us all, and he would be arriving this morning at ten."

Albert accepted the cup of tea that Gwen handed him, having taken the seat nearest to the fireplace. "It could be one of two things, I suppose," he murmured, sinking further back into the plush red velvet sofa. "He either has good news for us or he intends to tender his resignation."

Lena's gaze swept over them all, finally resting on Henry, who stood by the large drawing-room window, gazing out across the autumnal grounds. "Has he given any indication of discontent with his position?"

"Not to me," Henry replied, swiftly averting his gaze as Lena's probing eyes lingered. He'd been distant and standoffish with her as much as she had with him, and it made her heart ache in a way she didn't like.

The drawing-room door swung open, and Mr Brown appeared. "Mr Saunders is here to see you, Miss Pemberton."

Mr Saunders burst into the room like a harbinger of change, his face illuminated with gusto as he scanned the assembly. "Good! You're all here."

"At such an ungodly hour on my day off, Saunders," Albert grumbled. "If you've roused me early to announce your departure, I'll be far from pleased."

Saunders instructed Gwen to fill a cup for him, his chuckle resonating warmly. "Quite the opposite, Mr Simpson," he beamed. "I bring tidings most fortuitous, likely to keep you leaping from your bed for months to come."

A hush settled over the room; the significance of his proclamation was palpable.

Lena rose, her pulse quickening. "Does this mean what I think it does?"

Mr Saunders's grin broadened. "The sample cloth we supplied has been lauded by the London manufacturers as the finest in the region. Osband & Sons have commissioned an order." He paused, his gaze drifting over each attendant before returning to Lena. "A considerable one."

Henry leaned in. "How considerable?"

Saunders placed his cup aside and extracted a sheaf of papers from his jacket's inner pocket. "It will indeed test our present output," he began, "but if we fulfil this order, it will go a long way to alleviating the financial burdens of Hawks Mill."

Lena's hand trembled as she reached for the contract. Figures and letters swam before her eyes, and it took a moment to focus. Mr Saunders was correct. An order of this magnitude would undoubtedly resolve many of their issues. They could modernise over a third of the looms, expand the workforce, and consequently increase production. It represented a significant stride towards restoring the mill to its former prominence. "What is this clause here at the end?"

"Oh," Saunders's face clouded slightly. "It seems my assurances were not quite enough to convince them entirely of the mill's operational leadership. Should the mill fail to meet the December thirty-first deadline, a penalty will be enforced."

Lena's breath hitched. "This could obliterate any profit," she observed, noting the clause stipulated a daily penalty.

Henry strode across the room and took the paper from her grasp, his eyes swiftly perusing the contract.

His voice, firm and confident, sliced through her growing alarm. "We are more than capable, Lena. With meticulous planning and dedicated effort, it is achievable."

Lena yearned to embrace the excitement. She had longed for an opportunity for her mill, for someone to invest their trust in her, yet now it all seemed so perilous. Failure would mean forfeiting all that she had laboured for. It would also impact Libby, Wilf, and the other mill workers that she had come to care for. She couldn't bear it if they suffered alongside her because of a wrong decision. She covered her mouth with a hand, her gaze seeking reassurance from Albert.

"Henry and I will ensure everything is in order, you have my word, Miss."

She balled the hand into a fist, reminding herself of how far she'd come, of how much she'd already achieved – and all against the odds. They'd come this far. She had to trust in her team the same way she had every day for the past few months.

"Very well, if you think we can do it."

"This is what you've been working so hard towards, Miss. It's a tall order but it can be done," Albert drained his cup and, with a sigh, rose to his feet. "We need to make a plan. Think it through logically and make a contingency plan, if a loom fails. May as well get a head start on it."

"It's a Sunday, Albert. It can wait until tomorrow."

His foreman's eyes crinkled. "I can't rest after good news like this, Miss. Mr Saunders, let's bring that contract to the office where I can look at it properly with my spectacles. You can fill me in on this meeting." The two men headed for the door when Albert asked, "Henry, are you joining us?"

"I'll be there shortly," Henry said, almost distracted in his reply yet as the door closed, the air in the drawing room changed.

Awareness shivered over her as his dark gaze settled on her, silence descending upon them like a pall as one watched the other. He hadn't moved yet Lena was compelled to take a step back.

His brow flickered in annoyance. "Don't step away from me like that," he said in a low undertone. "I'm not Cavendish."

Her pulse thundered in her ears, and she had to swallow to moisten her suddenly parched throat before she could speak. "I-I know that."

His stare continued, searching her face, and she rubbed her hands to ward off the chill that his gaze induced. She saw him in her mind, kissing the pretty mill worker. She broke the look, turning back to her desk.

"I have a lot to do today, Mr Wickham. Please say what you must and let me get on with my day."

He didn't move.

When she turned to face him, she could feel his annoyance radiating from him. "What's wrong?" she asked.

Henry's frustration bubbled to the surface. "I'd like to ask you the same thing," he retorted. "What have I done to make you act so guarded around me?"

CHAPTER 47

*O*f course, Lena could pretend she didn't understand the implication of his question. For a moment, she contemplated the easy way out, but his eyebrow quirked at her, and she realised he had surmised her tactic.

The air around him seemed to crackle with indignation the longer the silence stretched.

"I shall not leave this room until I receive an explanation," he asserted firmly.

It was her turn to regard him with irritation. "I believe you've forgotten your place, Mr Wickham."

"I am acutely aware of my position here, Miss Pemberton," Henry said tersely, resorting to a more formal name, just as she had. "I had thought by now we had progressed beyond such formalities. I believed we had established a friendship, at the very least."

His words struck her deeply. She had indeed come to think the same and it saddened her to know that Thomas had driven a wedge between them.

She hesitated, knowing that she might not like the truth. But knowing too that she could not carry on this way.

"Lena, please... What has happened? We were... Please, just tell me what's made you change your manner towards me so distinctly?" His soft inquiry affected her more than any heated rebuke might have.

"I attended a business meeting in Manchester before the steam engine arrived," she began, her voice unsteady. "Thomas was there with Elizabeth."

She heard his sharp intake of breath though he remained still.

She continued, unable to look at him. "He seemed quite eager to share a rumour concerning you and your... history."

When he didn't say a word, she risked a glance at him. He'd frozen, his jaw clenched, fists rolled in, and his expression had closed off once more to her. It pained her greatly.

"He didn't give me details, really. Other than the ones he felt were pertinent." She suppressed an urge to go to him. The silence dragged on. "Will you not offer me some explanation?" she pressed.

"My past is beset with rumours, Miss Pemberton. I have no desire to justify or refute each one."

"Henry," she said, extending her hand as if to close the emotional distance that had sprung up between them. "I—"

"Do you believe these rumours?"

She opened her mouth, but words failed her.

Henry took a step away. "Answer me, Miss

Pemberton," his voice was as cold and hard as his coal-dark eyes. "Although your inquiries suggest tell me you've already formed your low opinion."

"I have done no such thing."

"I've heard the whispers about you, too," he said with an edge of resentment. "Rumours about how you've been financing the mill to keep everything afloat."

Lena's face flushed with a mix of anger and mortification. "My finances are none of your concern."

"I chose to disregard the rumours," he spoke over her protests, "trusting instead in the person I've come to know. I defended your honour. Why couldn't you extend me the same courtesy?"

"How dare you speak to me this way?" she spluttered, even as shame crashed over her. "Must I remind you, it's thanks to my efforts that you aren't still rotting in a debtor's prison!"

"That may be true," he conceded sharply. "But let's not pretend you had many choices at the time. You needed an engineer, and I didn't see anyone else beating down your door to work for you. "

"Yes, that's correct," she snapped, furious words tumbling out before she could stop them, "but I thought I was hiring a man of integrity, not a murderer!"

The moment the accusation left her lips, she realised the gravity of her mistake. The words hung heavily in the air, and she saw the hurt they inflicted. His face paled, a mixture of pain and shock overtaking the anger.

He shook out his cap, the movements jerky. "And the truth, at last, is out. At least now I know what you truly think of me, Miss Pemberton."

"Henry –"

"I thought you were different from the high-born snobs I've encountered, but it seems you're just like them – superficial and quick to judge." He looked as though he might add more, but instead, he bowed his head slightly and then settled his cap on his head. "Our contracted agreement was that I would make reparations in the mill and get the looms to a standard where they're efficient, as well as assist in installing the steam engine." He took another step away from her. And again. "You have a new order and now that you have established a good enough reputation here, it means you shouldn't have any trouble finding yourself a new engineer."

"Henry, stop," Lena's heart ached with regret, and she stepped around the desk though he was already at the drawing-room door. "Please, wait."

He paused, his hand on the door handle, looking back at her with that icy gaze. "Thank you for the opportunity. I wish you success with the mill. Good day."

With those final words, he turned and left the room, leaving Lena alone with the crushing silence and the echoes of a conversation that had shattered something precious in her.

CHAPTER 48

*T*he first frost has taken its hard bite of the land, glistening the trees with a crystalline touch. A fire crackled in the hearth, its warmth battling the creeping chill that the winter season had draped over Hawks Manor. Lena sat, ensconced in her favourite armchair, staring out of the tall windows at the world outside. Tree branches shimmered like a landscape borrowed from a fairy tale. But no enchanting tales filled her thoughts; instead, they circled ceaselessly around Henry, leaving her with a heart heavy with unanswered questions.

She hadn't heard from him in days, not since she'd seen watched him vanish in the twilight after he'd emptied his cottage. She chastised herself, trying to justify her distrust. He was, after all, being obstinately evasive about his past, and that alone was reason enough for her to be wary. She tried to convince herself that his silence was his stubbornness. And yet, as she sipped her tea, Lena couldn't shake the conviction that Henry was not capable of a vile crime.

His silence on the matter gnawed at her. If he was not guilty of the crimes, why had he not offered any defence? Was it the mark of a guilty man, or the quiet dignity of the wrongfully accused? A wounded soul guarding his scars?

I defended your honour.

She closed her eyes against the rush of pain that his remembered words brought with them. She knew what others were saying about her and he'd stuck by her when she'd doubted him.

As she pondered, the door creaked open, and Mr Brown entered with his usual impeccable posture.

"Miss Pemberton, you have a visitor," he announced.

For a fleeting moment, hope sprang in Lena's chest, imagining it might be Henry returning to mend their rift.

But as the visitor stepped into the room behind Sergeant Platt, that hope was doused by cold reality. The man was a stranger to her, dressed in a nondescript brown tweed suit that seemed out of place in the grandeur of her family home. His hair, dark and slicked over a balding scalp, lent him a weaselly appearance that she found instantly dislikeable.

"This is Mr Tinsley," Mr Brown began though the error was promptly corrected.

"*Inspector,*" the man interjected with a sharpness that set Lena's nerves on edge. "My name is Inspector Tinsley. I'm from Scotland Yard."

Lena felt a chill that had nothing to do with the frost outside.

Scotland Yard?

Her thoughts raced, every one of them returning to Henry and the dark cloud of his past. She knew then that she had to protect him, regardless of her doubts and fears.

"You're a long way from London, Inspector," she said, her voice betraying none of the anxiety that clawed at her insides.

"Then you'll understand the seriousness of what has brought me this far north, Miss Pemberton," the glowering Inspector replied, his eyes scanning the room with an unsettling thoroughness. "I have a few questions for you."

"Of course," Lena replied, gesturing towards the comfort of the sofa, but the Inspector remained steadfastly on his feet.

"Not here," he clarified with a note of authority that bordered on arrogance. "I must ask you to accompany me to Manchester. We have a station there better suited for this discussion."

"Pardon?" Lena was filled with a growing sense of dread.

The inspector rocked back on his heels, his eyes never leaving hers. "I'm afraid it's quite necessary, Miss Pemberton. Your cooperation is not only appreciated but required."

She followed the inspector into the hallway and waited for Mr Brown to fetch her coat. She felt as if the ground had shifted beneath her feet, her mind reeling, as the reality of the situation began to take shape.

Henry's past was catching up with him, and now it seemed it was entangling her as well.

With a deep breath, she gathered her resolve, preparing to face whatever storm was about to break over Hawks Mill and its inhabitants.

CHAPTER 49

*T*he Stag's Head Tavern was filled to the rafters.

The travelling fair had attracted visitors from far and wide, swelling the dimly lit bar with a cacophony of chatter. The air, thick with pipe smoke and the tang of ale, clung to the patrons like a second skin. The interior was a mix of shadows and light, with oil lamps casting a warm glow on the faces beneath the dark wooden beams that crisscrossed the tobacco-stained ceiling. Stone floors, worn smooth by countless boots over the years, were strewn with straw to combat the winter mud that tracked inside. Long, sturdy tables, etched with the history of many a raucous night, lined the edges of the flagstone floor.

An array of characters occupied these tables, their conversations peppered with calls for ales and the slap of cards against wood.

Young maidens, the roses of the tavern, wove through the throng with practised grace, balancing trays laden with bread and stew on one shoulder while expertly dodging roving hands, their retorts to the regulars as jovial as their banter. Near the hearth, where the fire crackled merrily, patrons gathered for warmth, their faces reddened by the heat, with mill-workers jostling alongside farmers fresh from the fields and travelling salesmen spinning tales as vivid as the fair outside.

In a dimly lit corner sat Henry Wickham, hunched over an untouched pint of dark ale. The boisterous calls and laughter of the tavern faded into the background as he was ensnared in a tempest of thoughts. He was leaving, his new job secured thanks to Lena's initial faith in him, and he was looking forward to a fresh start far away from the town that had become his prison.

Yet he couldn't shake the memory of their confrontation from his mind—the way Lena had looked at him, eyes brimming with accusation, the scared mistrust that had never been there before.

He had started to believe that she was different, that her faith in him had changed his luck. Yet her cutting words to him had revealed the painful truth and he knew now that he had been a fool to think he could escape the ghosts of the past without revealing the whole truth.

He had hoped she was different, true, but in the end, she had proven to be just like those he had always known her type to be.

Though if that statement were true, why did he keep rehashing the conversation in his mind, imagining a different outcome had he handled things with his usual tact, rather than letting his temper prevail?

He was leaving, yet he still felt as if he had unfinished business at Hawks Mill.

Did Lena deserve his explanation?

He had asked her to trust him, but he hadn't allowed her to decide for herself. People would always draw their own conclusions; he had grown weary of explaining himself until he was blue in the face. Even now, cloaked in the comfort of obscurity, Henry felt the weight of unseen gazes, the murmur of unheard whispers. He was leaving it all behind—the mill, the town, and the poignant memories of an unrealised love. Lena's judgment still smarted like a fresh wound, its sting infiltrating his every thought and dream. He had hoped to outrun his past, but it clung to him as persistently as his shadow.

The tavern door creaked open, letting in a gust of cold air along with Mr Saunders, the mill's salesman. Henry's eyes met his and he turned away. He had no desire to engage with someone so closely tied to Lena.

It was time to settle his tab and vanish.

Just as he stood to leave, Saunders slid into the bench opposite him, his tankard thumping onto the scarred wooden table, his indignant gaze confronting Henry's pensive mien.

"I should take you to task, sir."

Henry paused his coin counting to give him a direct stare. "What did you just say?"

"I thought you a man of integrity," Saunders said, after a sip from his tankard, gesturing at Henry with it. "Tell me, Wickham, if you knew what was going to happen, why didn't you warn us?"

A frown deepened on Henry's face. "Warn you about what?"

"It's a crying shame, is what it is," Saunders muttered, seemingly unaware of the tumult behind Henry's stern gaze. "I bent over backwards to secure that order. They said it was the finest cloth they'd ever seen."

"What are you talking about, Saunders?" Henry's voice was a low growl, his patience threadbare.

Saunders sighed, a note of frustration permeating his tone. "The order, Henry. It won't be fulfilled, not with our esteemed Miss Pemberton under arrest. Which means I won't be paid for the hard graft I've put into securing such a deal for her. My question to you is, you must've known something was afoot, given your previous brushes with the law."

Henry slumped back on the bench, a tempest brewing in his mind as he fixed his gaze on the salesman. "Arrested?" The word struck him like a physical blow. "Lena has been arrested?"

The notion seemed implausible. "What for?"

Saunders took another long pull at the tankard. "I expect it's those stories—have you heard? About how she's been financing all the changes at the mill, what with her father leaving them in debt. They must all be true."

A crease formed on Henry's brow, deep and troubled. The image of Lena—so proud, so fiercely resolute—clashed with the vulnerability of her current plight. He had been where she now found herself: powerless, at the whim of others' decisions. After all her efforts for the mill workers, after every obstacle she'd surmounted...

"When did this happen?" Henry demanded.

Saunders gave a despondent shrug. "A few days ago. The mill's at a standstill. My name's mud by now. I promised the manufacturer a prompt and timely delivery, and now... Well, who'll trust me after this?"

Henry barely registered the salesman's lament. His thoughts were with Lena, picturing her confined, perhaps broken, within the bleak walls of a cell. He recalled her words from the day of their first meeting —how her fate might mirror his own should he fail her. His concern for Lena, and the plight of the workers he'd come to call friends, swelled within him.

"What's to become of the mill?"

"Who can say?" Saunders responded with a gesture of resignation. "Word around is she was on the cusp of turning it all around. But she won't be there to oversee any of it. I pity her, I do. I thought she would succeed but... if she's been lifting her skirts for the right price, how can anyone respect a woman like that?"

Unable to help himself, Henry lunged across the table and hauled the spluttering salesman off the bench, his face twisted in anger.

"You watch your mouth!" He roared.

All around him, the conversations fell away, people taking in the spectacle. Henry caught himself; the fear in the other man's eyes, the blatant curiosity of the onlookers. He usually kept himself away from crowds and now he'd drawn attention anyway.

He set the salesman away from him, and Saunders slithered onto the bench.

"I meant no harm," he began, tugging at his collar.

Henry dragged the back of his hand across his mouth, trying to rein in his temper. "Sorry," he muttered. "Are you alright?"

Saunders righted the tankard that had been knocked over in the tussle. "It's fine. I shouldn't have picked a fight with you. I was... I was looking forward to having a success story after so many of the mills have shut down."

"Who shut down the mill? Did Lena? What happened to Albert?"

"The mill hasn't been closed, but the mill workers are refusing to work. With the owner gone, they're worried they won't get paid. Just like me. Who can blame them for downing tools and walking out?"

"They *all* left?"

"Take a good look around, Wickham. More than half of the mill workers from Hawks are in here. They should be at work, yes? How will the order be completed if half the workforce is pouring what's left of their wages down their throats?"

Henry's turbulent gaze travelled around the room. Indeed, he recognised several workers through the murky haze of smoke. A fresh wave of fury bubbled up within him, and he stood abruptly, the bench scraping harshly against the floor. Visions of a distraught Lena invaded his thoughts. They'd all left her at the first hint of trouble, after everything she'd tried to do for them.

Saunders looked up at Henry, startled. "Are you going to fight the whole room?"

Henry paused, conflicted.

I hired a murderer.

He reminded himself that Hawks Mill was no longer his concern. Lena Pemberton had never truly been his to worry about He'd kissed a pretty girl and lost his head over her. And she believed that he was a killer.

Just like Mary.

It was history repeating itself.

He needed to go someplace else and start anew as he'd planned. Leave behind the rumours. He had a new job that was expecting him.

Henry dug into his pocket and tossed a few coins on the table. "There's enough there to replace your ale." Henry dipped for the hessian sack that held his possessions and swung it up over his shoulder.

"Wait – aren't you going to do something?"

"Like what?"

Saunders gestured to the room at large. "They should all be in work. Make them all go back to work to complete that order I fought tooth and nail to get for them!"

Henry shrugged. "There's nothing left here for me. Not at Hawks, certainly not with a Pemberton. I have a job up in the East. Good luck to you."

CHAPTER 50

"First Henry, now Miss Pemberton!" A voice of dissent called out. "What are we supposed to think, Mr Simpson?"

Albert stood on one of the stone blocks in the yard, its surface worn smooth from years of millworkers sitting on it during their breaks. Now, it had become a makeshift platform for him as he tried to rally the crowd of millworkers that had congregated in the yard of Hawks Mill.

News of Lena's arrest had spread like wildfire throughout the community, and Henry's departure had only added to the disarray.

Libby stood among the crowd, feeling the tension pulsating among them all. It seemed like the delicate balance that Lena had managed to maintain had now tipped over the edge into chaos.

"We can't afford to stop now!" Albert implored, his voice booming above the sea of anarchy and uncertainty. "We've come too far to let this order slip through our fingers. Miss Pemberton might be gone, but we can see this through to the end!"

Restlessness rippled through the crowd.

"We won't get paid!"

"The mill is going under."

"Aye! Just like they said it would!"

"Another Pemberton has let us down!"

Libby pulled her shawl closer around her, the brink of collapse that had been threatening them all for so long now seemed very real. She felt close to tears as she looked at the anxious faces all around her.

"I've seen the accounts," Albert tried to explain. "If the order gets fulfilled, you'll get your wages."

"What about what we're owed now, Simpson? I have rent to pay!"

"Everything will turn around!" Albert Simpson patted the air as murmurs of agreement followed, and the atmosphere grew even tenser. "She will be back!"

"She's been arrested! Just as much of a criminal as her father was! We all heard how she was funding the mill, and now she's dragged us all down with her!"

"You'll get your money!" Albert said as the murmurs increased to a crescendo, swallowing up his pleas.

"You're just the foreman, Simpson," Angus Ferguson erupted. "You can't access her money. Are you going to pay us the coin out of your pocket?"

"Henry Wickham saw her for what she was," shouted another, "and that's why he left!"

The crowd exploded at this, and Albert caught Libby's eye, showing his hands helplessly.

Libby, still dressed in her old apprentice uniform, stepped forward. "Listen, everyone," she began. "I understand your frustration, more than most. But we know nothing more than she's been arrested. She will be back."

"She should be back by now," somebody else called out. "We have to take care of our own. Pay our rent. The ones in the cottages are alright, but the rest of us will have a landlord breathing down our necks come Friday!"

Libby moved closer to Albert, having to raise her voice to be heard over the din. "If we abandon the mill, we lose everything that we have all worked so hard for. We can't let her down in her hour of need."

Wilf appeared by her side, and Libby was comforted by the bump of his shoulder against hers as he spoke up, "If we complete this order, we might still have a chance to recover. We can secure our wages that way. Let's all get back to work. We can't give up."

Albert agreed. "They're right, folks. We've come too far to let it slip away. We have a chance to prove ourselves, to show that Hawks Mill is just as good as those at Black Marsh Mill."

Thea, with a slumbering Elena cradled in her arms, lent her voice to theirs. "Think about what this means to our community. Think about how Miss Pemberton has brought us all together for the common good. If we stick together, we can weather this storm."

Discontent rolled through them all, and several of the millworkers began packing up, filing out of the yard, stepping under the arch, and making their way along the cobbled lanes up towards the village.

Libby knew that Henry's departure had shaken their faith, and they viewed Lena's sudden exit as a betrayal.

"I know it's hard," Albert called out to them all in a last-ditch attempt to halt the flow of his workforce. "Let's do right by the mill, and by each other!"

Libby looked around the yard as more people left. Fathers pulled along their wives, and tearful children clung to the skirts of their mothers. Others hesitated, clearly torn between loyalty to the mill and the immediate need for income. Eventually, only a few stalwart workers remained, standing alongside the apprentices.

Albert climbed down from his improvised stage and hobbled over to where Libby was standing with Wilf.

He shook his head, his expression resigned. "Why can't they see sense?"

"Because sense doesn't pay the bills," Nab said calmly. "You can't blame them, Albert. A man won't look at his starving children, knowing that he could've done something to save them. Put yourself in their shoes. Would you have stayed?"

Looms sat idle, silent in the empty workspace. Libby stood in the centre of the mule room floor, her breath forming small puffs in the frigid air. Usually, the

ANNIE SHIELDS

room was stiflingly hot, heated by the roar of the furnaces below them. Now, the uninhabited building echoed with desolation. She could hardly bear the sound of the haunting stillness.

She joined Wilf where he leaned against the grimy window. He had his hands in his pockets, deep in thought. She gazed out across the deserted millyard, her sigh heavy with disappointment.

Wilf put an arm around her shoulders and pulled her close, giving her a reassuring squeeze. Beyond the windows, a few stragglers remained in the yard. Even from this distance, Libby could see the weariness etched on their faces.

Mrs Reid had led the apprentices back into the house rather than having them shiver in the cold winter's air. Albert had retreated to his office.

"It's not enough to run a full shift," he indicated the yard with a dip of his head. "We don't have the manpower to keep the whole mill going."

Libby's eyes filled with tears as she nodded in agreement. "I know, Wilf, but it breaks my heart to see all this slipping away. A chance for all of us to build something when we were so close... it's all gone.

"Not just the mill, but the school too. All those children could've had a chance at something better. Where will they end up now? Back at the poorhouse, that's where," she answered bitterly.

Wilf pressed his lips to her hair, offering her solace. "You can't lose hope. Miss Lena wouldn't want us to give up."

"What else can we do?" She looked up into his

sweet face with a pleading look. "You said it yourself, there isn't enough to fulfil the order. Albert warned us that if we are late, the penalties alone will wipe out any profits."

"We're all cloaked in rumour and supposition. Until we know what's going on, I say we keep going."

Libby wished that she could latch on to a little of his conviction. "Where is Henry?"

"I don't know."

"Why do you think she was arrested?"

His mouth turned downwards. "I don't know that, either."

"Do you think he left because he believed that she was selling herself?"

"If she did what she's saying they did to save us all? Well, I'd say that I understood her reasons. I don't judge her."

"She must have broken a law to be arrested. Henry must have found out."

Wilf lifted a broad shoulder in a shrug. "We don't know that she did break any laws but from what I saw, they got on well. If you'd held my feet to the fire, I would've said that they cared for each other more than a boss and an employee should. I don't know why he left. Albert hasn't said a word about it."

The wintry day outside seemed to mirror the frost that had settled over their hopeful plans. Wind moaned through the creaking wooden beams so that when the door behind them opened, they both jumped.

Albert appeared in the doorway. "There's enough

out there that we can run at least three lines of looms. I've dispatched Angus Ferguson to try and talk some sense into some of the men. I've offered him a bonus for everyone he can bring back. I'm betting that he'll join them in the pub at the Stag's Head though."

"You want to carry on?" Wilf asked.

Albert nodded. "What harm can it do? There's enough in the yard, but I need an overseer. What do you say, Wilf?"

Wilf glanced at Libby and raised an eyebrow in question.

She smiled and gave a small nod.

"That's my boy," Albert grinned and clapped him on the shoulder. The three of them filed out as Albert started to hand out instructions. "I've got young Nab down below. He's a stoker but he knows how to get things started down there. The river has slowed down, so we need the steam to power the ruddy shaft.

"Libby, can you go to the apprentice's house? I'd say they've enjoyed enough of an extra day off, wouldn't you?"

They descended the stone steps into the engine room, and Libby was pleased to see Nab standing in front of the steam engine. His sleeves were pushed back, and black coke marks marred his arms. But it was his aggrieved expression that had Albert asking, "What now?"

Nab rubbed his hands on a filthy rag. "The steam engine won't start. Dead as a doornail."

CHAPTER 51

*L*ena crested the steep hill.

She stood, hands on her hips, to catch her breath. Golden rays of winter sunlight edged over the horizon, the bars striking the clouds. Mists filled the valley below her like a billowing puddle. Only the church spire poked through it, allowing her to gain her bearings.

She'd been tipped out of the police station when it was still dark. The roads had been busier than she'd expected, with wagons hauling coal and the night soil men cheerfully calling out to her as she'd hurried out of the city.

She drew in the crisp morning air, exhaling with a satisfied sigh, knowing she would never again take such a small act for granted.

The police station air had felt tainted with death, permeated with a damp and rotting society. Her father would turn in his grave to know where she had languished for the last few nights. She knew if it wasn't for a certain man speaking up for her, she might very well have spent the rest of her natural life inhaling that dank, contaminated stench. She struck out once more, warmed by the exertion of climbing the hills behind her. Lost in thoughts, she hadn't heard the cart until it was alongside her.

"Miss Pemberton?"

Lena whirled at the voice, shielding her eyes against the bright sunlight. "Sergeant Platt?"

He reined to a stop. "What..." His gaze travelled the road she'd just come along. "You've not walked from the city?"

"It's not that far," Lena said with a smile, happy to see a familiar face. "What brings you out this early?"

"It's my day off," the sergeant explained. "I had planned to visit with my sister. Can I offer you a lift back?"

Lena's brows climbed. "You're facing away from the direction of Birchleigh, Sergeant. And I don't wish to interrupt your plans. I'll be fine."

He shook his head, waving away her objections as he expertly turned the cart in the road. Without much ado, Lena was sitting up alongside him, trotting briskly through the lanes.

"It's not often I get to play the knight in shining armour in my job," he joked. Out of his uniform, Eric Platt looked the epitome of a kindly uncle. His hair had silvered at the temples, and he'd thickened in his waist, but he had a gentle way about him.

"It's very kind of you," Lena said.

"If I'd have known you were going to be released, I

would have sent a constable for you. Can I assume it was all a big misunderstanding?"

Lena could only guess as to what the beastly inspector had insinuated to the sergeant before he'd carted her off. "I'm not out of the woods just yet. It's only thanks to Mr Clark, my solicitor, that I was released this morning. I don't know what strings he pulled but..." She shivered at the recollection of the dire warnings from Inspector Tinsley about not running off. "I'm glad to be away from such a place." She had tried to put the feeling of having a giant blade hanging over her head out of her mind on her walk, but speaking it aloud brought the sensation crashing over her once more.

Impotent rage at the unfairness of it all stole her breath and she blinked against the hot tears that stung her eyes. She was placing all her trust in Mr Clark.

She pulled the edges of her coat around her, chilled now that she was sitting down. Hazy light bathed the countryside but, the shadows cast by trees across the lanes held pockets of cool air, making her shiver.

"Here," Sergeant Platt tugged a heavy woollen blanket out from under his seat.

Lena thanked him and gratefully tucked it around her. The sergeant sat quietly beside her, his eyes fixed on the road ahead, yet she could feel the weight of his curiosity, a palpable thing in the close confines of the cart.

"You know, we have a bit of time to kill before we reach Hawks Manor," he spared her a glance before his eyes returned to the road, the reins steady in his hands. "It's not my place to ask but…"

Lena turned to look at him and realised that his amiable demeanour was but a façade. She could discern the shrewd mind working behind his hazel eyes, and despite everything, she found herself smiling.

"I had presumed you might already be informed of the situation, Sergeant," Lena said, her gaze drifting to the passing landscape, to the fields and farms that were just beginning to stir with the morning's activities. "After all, you are the guardian of the law in our village. You brought the inspector to my house.

"I'm afraid Inspector Tinsley considered me, and I'm quoting him here, 'a country bumpkin', Miss Pemberton. He seems to think I'd struggle to navigate my way out of a privy."

Lena laughed then, a light shake of her head accompanying the sound. "The man is pompously arrogant. I didn't care for him."

Lena's thoughts churned like the wheels of the cart, a tumult of worry and determination. Memories of the unending questions, the barbs, and the unkind comments that the inspector had put to her took the edge off her good mood.

"Then we both agree with that, Miss Pemberton."

The cart creaked and groaned beneath them, the rocking motion a comfort.

"The inspector kept his cards close to his chest." Platt paused before continuing, "He didn't let on why he needed to speak with you. I had no idea he intended to arrest you until I saw the black prisoner carriage in the lane. He claimed he thought I might warn you and that you'd disappear."

Her smile was slight, a mere shadow of its usual warmth. "He said the same to me. It didn't seem to matter that I had a mill to run and people relying on me." The mill, her father's legacy, the workers who depended on her—all of it rested on her shoulders, now heavier than ever. Eyes on the road ahead, she muttered, "Where else would I go?"

The sergeant gave her a side-long look. "Of course, there are rumours. But that's all they are—gossip and speculation."

Unbidden, the image of Henry, his features twisted in disappointment, filled her mind. Her heart couldn't bear to think of him for another moment. "Ah, yes, those rumours. About how I've been funding my mill."

He had the decency to blush, and Lena wished she'd held back with her scornful tone. The cautionary attitude of Inspector Tinsley echoed in her mind. She needed to be careful with what she disclosed about her arrest.

She offered the Sergeant another polite smile. "The truth will be out in due course, Sergeant. For now, my priority is to rescue what remains of my mill, if that's even possible."

His face fell in a grimace. "I spoke with Albert yesterday. He's struggling. News of your detainment has caused many to lose faith in what they see as a sinking ship. Workers are leaving, worrying they won't be paid."

Her worst fears were confirmed by his words and her heart sank. She scrubbed at her gritty eyes, frustration clawing at her.

"Two steps forward," she muttered darkly to herself. Turning to him, she asked, "They've all left?"

The sergeant nodded.

"Then any progress I'd hoped for has been snatched away. I fear this time it might truly be too late."

"This contract that Albert mentioned, that's where you've pinned your hopes?"

"Yes. Hopes, dreams, the entire future of Hawks Mill, to be frank. And once more, I find myself thwarted, thanks to the reckless actions of one individual."

"If you've turned things around once, surely you can do so again, can't you?"

"I only wish it were that simple, Sergeant," she said, her gaze meeting his. "The textile industry is merciless. One must keep pace with the rapid advances in technology or be left behind by those who can afford to purchase more efficient machinery. Fortunately, we had Mr Wickham on our side...for a time, anyway."

Lena was surprised at how steady her voice remained as she spoke his name. During her incarceration, she had ample opportunity to ponder over her interactions with Henry. Recalling their moments together, whether it was by the riverside or working late into the night, and even their kiss, she acknowledged that his reaction to her accusation had stemmed not just from disappointment but from perfidy. She too would have felt wounded had he believed the rumours about her.

"Regrettably," she said huskily, "Mr Wickham has moved on. I doubt we could ever afford the services of another engineer of his calibre. Certainly not now that the London job won't be fulfilled. The penalties alone that come with it will surely put the mill under."

"Mr Wickham did a great deal for Hawks Mill," Sergeant Platt said reflectively. "He's always been headstrong, that one."

Lena's gaze sharpened on the Sergeant. "You've known him a while, then?"

The Sergeant nodded. "Aye, I knew him as a lad and later as a man. His temper often got the best of him, always quick to jump into a fray to defend another. Trouble seemed to be his shadow."

She could easily envision a young Henry, instinctively coming to someone's defence. His loyalty to her had stayed true and whilst hers… bitterness filled her. He was right. She hadn't been loyal to him.

"It was certainly what led him to where he ended up."

It took her a few moments to fully hear what he'd said. She turned suddenly, her heart pumping with interest.

"You know what led to his imprisonment in the debtor's gaol?"

The Sergeant sighed, the sound mingling with the hiss of the cart's wheels on the muddy road. Lena held her breath, awaiting his response. "Henry was always clever, a thinker. He excelled at the mill and in his studies in Manchester. Returning to Black Marsh Mill, he made his family proud by fulfilling his apprenticeship."

"I didn't think he came back locally," she said, recalling the tale of how he'd become an engineer. "He told me that he started off at Black Marsh and trained under an engineer, then after his training, he worked up in Bradford."

"He did for a while. When a job turned up in Overleigh, he came home. He had good reason, mind. He came back for a woman."

Jealousy, hot and fast, spun through her. "A local girl?"

"The family that owned Black Marsh Mill have a daughter."

"Mary Houghton," Lena said quietly, shock tumbling through her.

She'd met the Houghton family twice over the years and knew them only by reputation and for stealing her staff.

"That's right. Seems the girl was rather fond of him, and her father indulged her whenever he could. They'd met when he'd started out working there. They had plans to marry but…"

"But what?"

The sergeant seemed to hesitate, and Lena bit back a growl of frustration when he spoke, "The workers who were there on that day tell a tale of how the family at Black Marsh Mill pushed for shortcuts that

Henry wouldn't abide. It seems they weren't as receptive to change as you have been."

Lena leaned forward, intrigued. "On what day?"

"The day John Bolton died," the sergeant said solemnly.

"Who was he?"

"A veteran millworker, well-versed in the scutching room. Yet the foreman had him reassigned to the engine room that day. The steam engine was ancient, and part of it broke off... poor John didn't stand a chance."

Lena fell silent, the echo of the tragedy paralleling the day young Billy had been hurt.

"Henry was fought endlessly to try and save him. He took the failure of the steam engine as a personal defeat. He took John's death to heart."

"Why?" Lena asked, her voice a faint whisper.

"The piece that failed was one Henry had repaired. It sheared off and struck John in the chest. They said he was gone before he even hit the floor."

Lena recalled the blood staining the workroom floor from Billy's accident, a vivid and grim reminder.

"It wasn't Henry's fault, though," she said softly.

"I'm aware of that. Everyone at Black Marsh Mill knew it, but Henry couldn't forgive himself. He spent the following weeks drowning his sorrows at the Stag's Head. The mill owners dismissed him to avoid an inspection, especially with the turmoil surrounding the Ten Hours Act. They didn't want the scandal."

Distancing themselves from any drama seemed a common tactic among mill owners.

"He's not a murderer," Lena murmured, more to herself than to her companion.

Sergeant Platt gave her a sharp look. "Henry wouldn't harm a fly, let alone a man. He has a temper, yes, but he's not malicious. No," he adjusted his seat huffily. "He most definitely is *not* a murderer. Those bloody rumours have plagued that poor man for years."

Lena closed her eyes and let out a slow breath. She was more like her father, after all.

Oh, Henry, what have I done?

"That I can attest to," Lena affirmed quietly. "I thought Mary married a shipping merchant."

"She did. Her father promptly married her off, as if Henry never existed. And Henry, burdened by guilt over John's death and the subsequent hardship faced by Mrs Bolton and her children, two of whom perished in the following winter, exhausted his savings trying to support them. That's what led him to debtor's prison."

Lena digested the information, remembering the defensively sullen bear of a man she'd found in that cell. "A prison. How dreadful."

"Aye," the sergeant confirmed sadly. "Though knowing young Henry, he likely thought he deserved it. I was pleased as punch when I heard that you'd taken him on. I knew then that you were doing right by local folks. Henry is a good man."

Understanding dawned on Lena—Henry's reluctance to leave the prison, his behaviours, everything made sense now. He was ashamed and believed he was in a place that he deserved. She had shaken the foundation of his self-worth by doubting him again instead of offering her trust. "I fear I've made a terrible mistake, and now it may be too late to amend it."

"Aye, well…" the sergeant twisted his lips. "Albert says Henry's moved on, found work near Newcastle. Dare say he hasn't yet heard about your… troubles."

She thought about the quarrel, about the angry words she'd flung at him. He'd already left for pastures new, she thought. The idea that she wouldn't see him every day hurt her heart.

"Do you know which mill he's gone to?" Lena asked huskily.

"I'm certain Albert will know where; he was the one who had to write a reference for the lad. It's how he knew he'd moved on. He'll have the address for you to write to him, won't he?"

Though she doubted Henry would want to hear from her, Lena nodded. "I'll be sure to get the details from Albert when I return."

As the tall chimney stack of Hawks Mill came into view in the valley below, Lena fell silent. The mill was the heart of her world. The village lay just beyond it where she knew that every eye would be upon her, watching to see what the mistress of Hawks Mill would do next.

Everything she had worked for was at stake. Her arrest had already impacted the business, and she knew that she'd have her work cut out. If Albert remained at the mill, then he was still on her side.

Perhaps not all hope was lost.

She resolved to do her best to ensure the welfare of Libby, Wilf, Thea, and baby Elena. She would write to Henry, seeking his forgiveness. Anything to try and ease this desperate ache for him.

Puffs of smoke rose from the chimneys of village houses as they drove through Birchleigh, and a few early pedestrians raised their hats to the policeman. If they harboured any thoughts about Lena sitting beside him, their faces didn't betray them. Her mind turned to the tasks ahead.

As they turned into the mill's driveway, Lena tilted her head. "Sergeant, do you hear...?"

"Your millwheel is running," the sergeant observed simultaneously.

"I thought I was imagining it," Lena said, not waiting for the carriage to stop completely before she tossed back the blanket and quickly clambered down.

Her mind whirled with possibilities of which workers might have remained. Even a small crew would be better than nothing. Albert must have persuaded some to stay.

She hurried through the side door, racing up the stairs, a bubble of hope growing within her. She burst into the mule room and her face broke into a smile.

To her utter astonishment, she was greeted not by a handful of workers, but by a full workforce. She hailed her overseer.

With his cloth cap in hand, Wilf broke away from the crowd. "Welcome back, Miss Pemberton."

"Wilf?" Lena gushed happily, her eyes travelling around the sea of faces before her, all bent in concentration.

Looms rumbled, belts thundered overhead, carriages rolled, weft and thread tumbled. It was music to her ears.

"Thank you, Wilf. It's very nice to be back. I'd heard a distressing rumour that... I had been abandoned."

Wilf grinned, giving her a wink. "I won't lie, Miss Lena. It was touch and go for a while. But then the voice of reason brought everyone back to their senses."

"The voice of reason? Who?"

Wilf nodded towards a corner. Lena's gaze followed, her heart skipping a beat as she recognised the familiar figure standing there, his darkly intense gaze fixed on her.

HENRY.

CHAPTER 52

 *wo nights before...*

HENRY STEPPED out of The Stag's Head and into the frigid air, fallen leaves crunching under his boots as he struck out along the moist cobbled roads. Vestiges of his temper after grabbing at Mr Saunders burned at the edges of his conscience. The streets of Birchleigh were packed with late-night revellers from the winter fair. In the distance, he could hear the musical metallic plinking, the joyful shouts of laughter burning his already-sore temper. He shouldn't have grabbed at the salesman like that. Many of the workers in there remembered him from Black Marsh mill. Some of them might even have been there the day that John died. He knew then that his visceral reaction to Lena's harsh words the other day wasn't because she hadn't believed him, but because he'd forgotten.

He's forgotten when it felt like to live a life out of the shadows of the past.

He'd forgotten what it was like to enjoy people – their lives, their company. He'd begun to build a life for him, to find friends again.

He'd forgotten John.

After what he'd done, he didn't deserve to forget.

He hunkered down into his jacket, ducking into the icy winds, making his way toward his lodgings when he heard his name being called. He ignored it, lengthening his stride, not wanting to deal with whatever fight was heading his way. He needed to leave here.

Away from memories of home. Of Mary. Of Lena.

"Henry! Henry Wickham!"

Henry spun, fists balled, glowering. "What?"

Instead of one of the mill workers, it was Simon Skepper who stumbled back in, hands up defensively. "It's just me! Sorry, I didn't mean to startle you."

Henry checked around them, nodding briefly. Folks just hurrying home, minding their own business. He tamped down on his aggravation. "What do you want, Skepper?"

The man was slender, his skin soft and pale from years of working in his father's pawn shop. His cheeks were rosy, and he weaved on his feet, the after-effects of spending too long in the Stag's Head.

"I tried to catch you before you left the Stag,"

Simon tugged at his collar to ward off the lazy winds that barrelled along the road.

"I didn't hear you," Henry muttered.

"Do you know how I can get hold of Miss Pemberton? I have been trying to get hold of her in the past week. I heard about her...troubles which explains why she's not replied to my letters, but I have some good news for her."

Henry frowned. "Lena has business with you?"

"Why, yes, but..."

"Is she buying or selling?"

Simon blinked blearily at him, and Henry could see the confusion swimming in his face. "I'm not sure I should discuss those details with you. I just need to get a message to–"

Henry advanced on him, using his considerable breadth advantage to crowd him back a few steps. "What's the message? I'll make sure she gets it," he growled when the young man gawked at him.

"I finally managed to find a buyer for her grandmother's exquisite sapphire set that she brought in. It's the last of the lot and –"

Suddenly, he knew how Lena had been sourcing the extra funds for her mill. Before Simon Skepper had finished speaking to him, Henry was already straight-arming his way back in through the door of The Stag's Head.

CHAPTER 53

*S*he stared across the space, unsure if he was a figment of her tired mind. But he broke the look, returning to his work. The sounds of the mule room returned, and she had to scramble to keep up with what Wilf was saying to her.

"...engine wasn't working. We'd all just about given up hope of getting things turned around when we heard it. Couldn't believe my eyes when I went to the door of the engine room but there he was, walking across the yard, with a stream of workers walking in behind him. He'd made them all see sense, about how you were behind us all, and that we'd be hard-pressed to find an employer like you elsewhere.

He got the engine back up and running, as quick as you like, and away we went," Wilf nodded, eyes glowing. "Full complement of workers, and with Henry's new looms, we're catching up on the lost time. Albert reckons we're on track to make that deadline. Shall I go fetch Mr Simpson for you?"

Lena looked at Henry again, and was hit with a wave of regret, longing, remorse, gratitude…. Love. She owed him everything. Murmuring an excuse to Wilf, she wound her way through the workers, intent on him. She ground to a halt a few feet away. As though drawn by a thread, he turned to her. His eyes raked her face, searching. Just being near him smoothed away her rough edges, borne out of being tossed about by circumstances beyond her control in the last few days. He set down the rag, his mouth moving but she didn't hear what he said. She simply looked at him.

He was here. *Still here.*

He frowned and she shook her head. Understanding, he steered her through the door at the back of the mule room, leading to the stairs that accessed other floors. She walked down them, heart thundering, his footsteps following behind her. Sergeant Platt's cart still sat in the yard, though he was nowhere to be seen. Henry took her elbow and led her around the side of the building. Towards the shed, she realised, her skin zinging where his fingers still held her.

He opened the door, urged her through, and pulled it to behind him, cocooning them in the dusty interior that was warmer than the crisp morning.

Her entire body hummed as his dark gaze blazed down at her.

"Are you hurt?" He asked, not a vestige of emotion showing on his face.

She shook her head, unable to speak past the lump in her throat.

Of all the things she expected him to say, considering their last words had been spoken in anger, his concern for her welfare touched her deeply. The turmoil of the past few days, losing her freedom, and facing constant questioning had taken its toll, and she burst into tears. Even when Henry wrapped his arms around her, her sobs didn't subside. She'd been as strong as she could for as long as she could but right now, in the privacy of his dusty workshop, she felt broken.

The loss of her father, the worry, and the many sleepless nights standing at the edge of losing everything... the knowledge that she wasn't yet free from the ghosts of the past swamped her emotions. Henry held her as she cried, gently rubbing her back.

Until she was spent. Still, she stood in his caress, resting against him. His cheek rubbed her crown, his lips lightly grazing the side of her temple. She drew back, meeting his gaze before he could conceal his feelings.

She studied him in the dim light. "They said you'd left."

"I did," he admitted gruffly, his arms still around her. "At least, I..."

"Say what you were going to say," she prompted when he hesitated.

"Simon Skepper," he said. "He asked me to give you a message." Lena tried to move away but he held her in place, dark eyes searching her face. "He said he's finally managed to sell the last of your grandmother's and mother's jewels. He said there were lots of things you took to him."

Months of keeping secrets, sneaking about, and making deals that were away from the scrutiny of the men involved in the business slid away from her, and she slowly exhaled. She felt bound to explain herself.

"My father had died. Thomas had walked away. He was only with me because of the mill. Hawks was on the brink of ruin, and he wanted me to give it up, and to sign ownership over to Cavendish bank. I... I often went into my father's bedroom. I would spend my evenings sitting on his bed and... it helped me feel closer to him.

"Of course, there was no fire lit in there. One night it was particularly chilly, and I opened the old chest at the foot of his bed to find a blanket. I pulled out a blanket and heard something knock against the inside."

She remembered now how she'd reached into the chest and found the bundle, neatly tied with a piece of string. She'd unwrapped a wooden jewellery box with an intricately carved lid. She had been swamped with memories of her father showing it to her, of those happier times in her childhood.

"I'd not seen the box for years – until that day, I'd forgotten all about it. When I opened it, I found jewellery that had belonged to my mother, to my grandmother."

Emeralds as big as a baby's fist, loose diamonds in a pouch, pieces of gold... exquisite pieces that belonged to a time before Lena was born.

She wiped her tears away with the back of her hand and sniffed. "I don't know why my father kept them...perhaps he'd forgotten about them, too, or perhaps he was saving them. I know that he was determined that I would marry Thomas, even when I refused.

"I wasn't sure if it was my father guiding me that night. Or indeed, my mother steering me, showing me a way out of the situation. Of course, Alistair and Thomas Cavendish believed the mill had no assets left, so I had to do everything in secret. If they had known about the jewellery, they might have seized it to pay against the loan. All I knew was that I did not need such beautiful things when I was facing bankruptcy.

"I began by taking one piece of jewellery to at least pay the house staff and the mill workers. The gemstone meant that I could settle the outstanding accounts with the local suppliers, too – the butchers and the like. I sold another to buy the materials needed for repairs when you arrived.

"It was wrong of me to deceive them the Cavendish's that way I did. After all, they were owed the money but... I didn't want them to take away the only chance I had left to try and save the mill, to help my workers. I travelled into Manchester, to Liverpool, even to Birmingham – wherever I could sell the jewellery anonymously so that nothing would get back to Thomas."

"You did what you had to do, even at great personal cost because that jewellery was all that remained of your mother," he said, offering a sympathetic smile.

"Mr Brown has provided me with several memories of my mother that have shown me I'm much more like her than I ever thought," She reached into the neckline of her dress and drew out a gold locket. "I did keep this though. I couldn't quite bring myself to part with it."

"Why didn't you tell me that that was how you were funding everything until the investors came on board?"

Lena pondered the question, idly twirling the gold chain. "I wasn't sure whom I could trust. Every day, there was something new to deal with. Mr Dower and then Mr Blackwood, more bills, changes... Thomas is a devious man. He has already shown me just how far-reaching his connections in the textile industry are. I kept everything a secret because it was easier. The only person who knew was Mr Clark, who'd found out by accident, but thank goodness he did."

"Why 'thank goodness'?"

Lena hesitated as the dire warnings of the Inspector rang out in her mind. Henry tilted his head, catching the tear that rolled down her cheek with his thumb.

"I suppose you'll find out eventually," she whispered, her face wrinkling in sadness. "It is thanks to Mr Clark that I'm standing here before you."

Henry's eyes held hers. "Lena...why were you arrested?"

CHAPTER 54

"*B*ecause of Thomas."

Henry's eyes flashed ominously. "What did he do to you?"

"Nothing," she said quickly, "at least, nothing directly to me but… it's complicated."

"I'm not going anywhere," Henry told her gently.

Lena wasn't sure where to begin, so she started at the beginning. "Thomas has always been resentful of the control his father held over him. Alistair is a bully, that's certain, and he didn't care much for his son's opinions on many things. Our fathers were the ones to arrange a marriage between the both of us and, at first, Thomas was as charming as could be.

"Some time ago, unbeknownst to anyone – Inspector Tinsley was vague on dates – Thomas hatched a daring plan to escape out from under the shadows of his father's prosperous bank. Using his knowledge of the bank's operations, he meticulously forged a series of loan documents, creating the illusion of legitimate transactions. These fabricated papers were carefully designed to allow him to siphon large sums of money from the bank's coffers. He had even convinced trusted bank employees to unwittingly participate in his scheme, forging signatures and facilitating the illicit transfers.

He wanted to buy Hawk's Mill so that he would have a legitimate business to sink the money into, in case his forgeries were discovered. It was why he kept coming back to persuade me to sell. He was in the process of purchasing a silver mine in America, a business far away from the prying eyes of his father's business empire when a bank employee queried a missing date for a banker's note with Alistair. It was what alerted Alistair to his son's misdeeds.

"By then, it was too late. I dare say Thomas didn't anticipate that this web of lies he's entangled everyone in would lead to the ultimate destruction of his family. Cavendish Bank is about to fold. Thomas is in Newgate prison in London. Inspector Tinsley was convinced I was involved because of the rumours that I'd been securing money secretly from somewhere."

She swallowed then, hot tears burning the backs of her eyes once more. "It took Mr Clark a few days to get the proof required to prove that I'd funded the mill legitimately. He presented the evidence to that wretched Inspector. I don't think he believed me, but he couldn't refute what the documents proved.

"I was released in the dark. I think he expected me to sit around and wait for daylight but I…" she shook her head. "I couldn't bear to sit in that police station a moment longer. I left when it was dark and walked back, meeting Sergeant Platt who brought me home."

"You walked home from the city? Lena, anything could have happened to you!"

"It didn't."

"So, it's over, then?"

Instead of relief, Lena only felt frustration. She shrugged. "I don't know. I hope that it is but the way my luck has been of late, who knows? In the meantime, I have to keep pushing on. Thanks to you, Hawks at least has a chance of making that end-of-year deadline," her voice grew husky with unshed tears once more. "I don't know how to thank you, Henry. After everything I said to you... I have gone over and over things in my mind. Things I said, certainly things I had no right in saying to you... I'm sorry I ever doubted you."

His mouth gave a slight twist. "You deserved to know the truth, Lena. If I had told you from the start, Cavendish's words wouldn't have made you doubt me. You see–"

"I know about John Bolton, Henry."

Pain, real and fresh, moved over his expression and this time, it was she who offered him comfort by laying a hand on his arm.

"I know about the accident. About Mary and their family turning their back on you and not standing by you. I know that you put yourself into debt to try and help John's widow," she turned his face to look at her, "I know that you still blame yourself even though it was an accident – a terrible, awful accident."

"I fitted the part," Henry said bitterly. "What if I missed something?"

"John shouldn't have been in the engine room that day. He was a scutcher. That wasn't your fault. It was Mr Houghton's fault."

Henry lowered his forehead to rest against hers, his breath fanning her cheeks. "Thank you for saying that."

"You're a good man, Henry. You've saved many more lives by the work you're doing here. I couldn't have done any of what I've achieved here without your guidance."

He held her gaze, his mouth a whisper away from hers. "That's not true. The workers here, they believe in you. They follow you because they believe in your vision."

"They came back to work because of you, not me," she stated wryly.

A smile propped up the edge of his mouth. "I simply reminded them which side their bread was buttered." He paused for effect. "I believe in you."

"And now another mill will benefit from your experience," she teased him.

He framed her face between his hands, thumbs gently grazing her cheeks, those fathomless dark eyes searching hers openly. "Just say the word and I'll stay."

"I know you'll stay if I ask you, but there's a piece of you inside that wants to honour the agreement you've already made with the manager over there."

He laughed low in his throat. "You know me so

well, Lena. I have committed to the mill there for a three-month term."

"Then go, Henry," she whispered, all the while knowing that she would miss him dreadfully, but that she needed to let him go. "If you wish to rebuild your reputation, you can't do that by letting people down. Then, once your contract has been fulfilled, you're welcome to come back here."

"Try and stop me," he murmured, before closing the distance between them and sweeping her up into a tender kiss that made her heart sing with possibilities.

EPILOGUE

*F*at snowflakes gently tumbled outside the doors of the new village hall in Birchleigh. Although she had initially dreamed of holding Wilf and Libby's wedding celebration at Hawks Manor House, Lena had to come to terms with the fact that the grand house simply couldn't accommodate the growing number of people who wished to share in this joyous occasion.

Lena sat on a bench, away from the draughty doors, holding a slumbering baby Elena, while her parents enjoyed a rare moment alone. Observing the pleasure on their faces, Lena wondered if she might lose her teacher again soon, especially with another baby on the way.

Surrounded by happy couples, her thoughts inevitably turned to Henry. His latest letter had explained the delay in his return, with apologies for the inconvenience. She had spent her evening poring over each letter, tracing the elegant flow of his prose as if that could bridge the miles between them.

He'd left not long after her entanglement with that dreadful Inspector Tinsley, once he was certain that the steam engine was behaving itself once more. The newspapers were still filled with screaming headlines about the collapse of the Cavendish Bank. She'd avoided reading them, having had just a brief taster of life behind bars. Thomas's devious acts had brought about the end of his father's business, and he'd lost his liberty in the process. He would hate being trapped inside a prison, and it was enough for her to know that he would never bother her again.

She'd said as much in her regular letters to Henry. He'd transformed the efficiency of the looms in Bradford, just as he had at Hawks Mill. Still, she'd missed his presence terribly. On the bright side, Henry's absence from the mill had allowed Nab to continue the valuable training that Henry had started with him, preparing him to potentially become an engineer one day.

Since the mill's salvation, following the successful completion of the London order, news of Lena's achievements had spread like wildfire throughout the textile industry. More work flowed into Hawks Mill, and Lena's reputation as a capable and visionary mill owner resonated across the land. Thanks to her efforts in improving working conditions, influential figures were reaching out to her for input into their own enterprises.

Lena eagerly anticipated sharing that morning's

good news. Titus Salt, a giant in the textile industry, had written to her expressing interest in a meeting to discuss the improvements she had made at Hawks Mill. The meeting filled her with excitement, knowing she could exchange knowledge with a man who'd already integrated a hospital and a school into his working village, a venture requiring substantial finance but filled her with possibilities for her workers' well-being.

Her gaze travelled around the room, taking in the various workers who were relaxed and enjoying the celebration. Libby looked radiant in her elegant lilac dress, adding to the overall joy of this special day. The young woman was getting ready to leave for Whiteland College to start her teaching course. She finally seemed excited rather than nervous about the prospect of leaving Birchleigh. Lena couldn't wait to see her face later when she showed them both the cottage that she'd renovated for them on the edge of Pemberton lands.

She knew the second he'd walked into the hall – felt it as a shiver from awareness rather than the cold air that followed him in. She turned, slowly, and watched him dust the snow from his hair, the half-smile in place as mill workers flowed around him to welcome him in.

Lena tried not to hurry, wanting to savour the moment a little longer. She passed Elena to Bess Ferguson and stood. She took her time to enjoy simply looking at him.

Broad shoulders, wild black curls and those eyes,

assessing the room even as he was speaking with others and shaking their hands.

When his gaze landed on her, she felt the fluttering in the pit of her stomach.

Henry.

She'd crossed the room without having to make her body move – she drifted over the floor and allowed him to lead her through the doors, out into the flurries. She didn't feel the cold, but he draped his coat over her shoulders when he turned to face her.

His warmth, his scent, enveloped her. "You're here."

He swept a glossy curl back from her cheek, and she turned into the caress. "I'm sorry I'm late."

She burrowed her face into his hand. "I haven't missed you, at all," she murmured with a smile.

A dark brow quirked, and he gave her curl a playful tug. "I don't believe you."

"Good," she angled her head to look at him coyly, "because it was a lie."

He pulled the edges of his coat around her, the snowflakes in his hair, settling on his shoulders. "I need to ask you something. I'd planned an elaborate speech about all the reasons it's a good idea, but I don't want you to freeze to death whilst you wait for me to explain."

She allowed him to fuss her, renewing his features in her mind once more. "I'm too giddy to be cold."

His hands stilled at the edges of the jacket collar, and he caught her chin between his thumb and forefinger. "I love you, Lena Pemberton."

Her heart leapt with joy at the simple and honest statement. "I love you, too."

"I want to come back to Hawks Mill, not as your engineer, but as your husband. I have nothing to offer you, but I will work to make you happy every day until I fall down dead in a heap."

He paused, lowering down on one knee. "Will you marry me?" He held out a ring to her. One that she recognised.

A startled gasp slipped past her open lips. "My grandmother's sapphire."

He nodded. "I arranged with Simon to buy it back from the person who bought it out of the pawn shop. Do you mind that it's not new?"

"It's perfect," she whispered thickly, her happy tears mingling with the snowflakes. "So very perfect, Henry. Yes, I will marry you, though I'd rather you not work yourself into the ground simply to keep me content."

He laughed, low down in his throat, as he stood and slipped the ring onto the hand she held out. Having the stunning cornflower blue stone winking back at her felt complete. It felt right.

"I won't give up work," she said.

"I would never dream of asking you to. At least, not yet," he added. "I would like children if we can. If we don't, that is fine, too. I think we make a pretty good team as it is."

She sniffed, turning the ring in the snowy air. It twinkled back at her. "A team," she echoed him. "I like the sound of that."

Wordlessly, he drew her towards him, his arms cradling her to him, his eyes burning as he lowered his mouth to hers. Gently, fervently, greedily, he kissed her with all the promise of a shared future that would see them through the trials and triumphs of life.

ABOUT THE AUTHOR

Annie Shields lives in Shropshire with her husband and two daughters.

When she doesn't have her nose in a book, you'll find her exploring old buildings and following historical trails, dragging her ever-patient husband along with his trusty map.

If you would like to be amongst the first to hear when she releases a new book and free books by similar authors, you can join her mailing list HERE

As a thank you, you will receive a **FREE** copy of her eBook The Barefoot Workhouse Orphan - the prequel to the book, In The Shadows of the Workhouse where we meet William Finnegan and Connie for the first time.

Your details won't be passed along to anyone else and you can unsubscribe at any time.

ALSO BY ANNIE SHIELDS

The Dockland Darling

In the haunting aftermath of her father's sudden death, Ella Tomlinson finds herself at the mercy of her cruel stepmother, Clara.

Desperate to escape a forced marriage, Ella seeks refuge with her estranged uncle in his lively tavern, hidden in the heart of London's bustling Docklands. Here, she is plunged into a dangerous world filled with sailors, boatmen, and shadowy traders.

Seth Milford, driven by duty to marry well and strengthen his father's shipping empire, has long avoided the insipid women his mother presents to him. But when he meets Ella, his world is turned upside down.

Relentlessly pursued by Clara, who is determined to silence Ella and bury her secret forever, Ella is faced with a choice between love and truth. But she knows that revealing her past would devastate Seth.

Torn between his love for Ella and his unwavering loyalty to his father, Seth faces a heart-wrenching decision.

Yet, even the dockyard darling knows she cannot gamble with Seth's heart or risk his company's future as her dangerous past looms ever closer.

In the Shadows of the Workhouse

In the heart of Brookford workhouse, darkness festers.

Portia Summerhill, the spirited new schoolmistress, arrives full of hope, eager to bring light into the lives of the forsaken souls trapped within its walls. Yet, as she delves deeper, a chilling truth emerges from the shadows.

Maisie Milne, a brave orphan on the brink of a new life outside the workhouse, whispers haunting tales of unspeakable deeds.

With time running out and Maisie's future hanging in the balance, Portia is drawn into a race against time, determined to unveil the harrowing secrets lurking behind closed doors. Will they unravel the truth before the clock chimes its final hour?

Step into a tale of dark mysteries and secrets lurking in the shadows of the workhouse.

Printed in Great Britain
by Amazon